YOU'VE GOT TO CONQUER THE PAST
BEFORE YOU CAN CONQUER THE FUTURE....

## Praise for the Novels
### of Patti Callahan Henry

### *When Light Breaks*

"Not just a beautifully written story, but an important one as well. It's about all the things that make us worthy as human beings—integrity, honesty, and living the life you are meant to live. And perhaps most important, it shows us what brings genuine happiness . . . a triumph!"
—Dorothea Benton Frank, *New York Times* bestselling author of *Full of Grace*

"A passionate, unforgettable novel of self-discovery, regret, and the illuminating power of love. Patti Callahan Henry's writing is as lush and magical as the Lowcountry she loves. Once caught in the emotional currents of her story, you'll not be released until the last, satisfying page."
—Mary Alice Monroe, *New York Times* bestselling author of *Sweetgrass*

"Henry writes movingly about love and family. . . . She has been compared to Pat Conroy and Anne Rivers Siddons, and she proves once again that she belongs in their distinguished company." —*The Island Packet* (SC)

"Henry is showing us that while those happy families may be utterly similar, they are also a gift—to everyone." —*Atlanta Woman* magazine

"Known for her lyrical writing in *Losing the Moon* and *Where the River Runs*, Henry doesn't disappoint in this beautiful novel of discovery and self-acceptance, a romance with universal appeal." —*Booklist* (starred review)

*continued . . .*

"Even for those readers—most, I would imagine—who don't have some epic, tragic, teenage first love, the ideas still resonate . . . a quick, enjoyable read [that] stays with you afterward, as you wonder if there are hints of your own heart worth a listen." —*The Herald-Sun* (NC)

"A compelling tale . . . part romance, part self-discovery, completely entertaining. Compared to major Southern writers, Patti Callahan Henry holds her own." —*Topsail Magazine*

"A fascinating character study." —The Best Reviews

"We fall in love with [Henry's] characters and her words as she enfolds us in a story that stays with us long after we've turned the last page." —*Southern Lady*

### Where the River Runs

"Brilliant. Powerful. Magical. Do not miss this book." —Haywood Smith, *New York Times* bestselling author of *The Red Hats Ride Again*

"Books about the journey to self-realization often make us contemplate our own lives and choices. You travel with the character through joy, heartache, and redemption, and when it's over, you have laughed and cried. This book proves no exception. . . . Descriptive language, paired with heartfelt characters, accentuates the story, which is peppered with Lowcountry culture and customs. . . . After reading this tale, cherishing family and home becomes the reader's own mantra." —*Southern Living*

"Quietly reflective and softly compelling, this tale of a Lowcountry woman's reblossoming will touch your heart and make you wonder about long-forgotten possibilities waiting to be rediscovered in your own family and soul." —*Charleston Post and Courier* (SC)

"A melodious, encouraging tale that upholds memories, friendship, and family." —*Atlanta Woman* magazine

"*Where the River Runs* is an expression of love between author and story. Readers will instantly fall for Patti Callahan Henry's unique voice and lyrical writing style in this satisfying story of a secret revealed." —*Topsail Magazine*

"A poignant tale . . . Fans of Anne Rivers Siddons will want to read Patti Callahan Henry's deep character study." —The Best Reviews

"As in Henry's debut, *Losing the Moon,* and this beautifully written story, the sheer lyricism of the author's voice transports the reader. Fans of such books as Mary Alice Monroe's *Skyward,* also about the Gullah, and Patricia Gaffney's *Flight Lessons* will add this book to their list of favorites." —*Booklist*

"This poignant story of a woman reclaiming her life touched me in a way a book hasn't in quite a long time. The powerful message is translated through Meridy's eyes and has an added impact being written in the first person. . . . With exceptional storytelling skills, newcomer Patti Callahan Henry conveys pure, potent emotions sure to reach out to every reader."
—The Romance Reader's Connection

"Well crafted . . . *Where the River Runs* is the perfect pick for an easygoing sunny day on a Lowcountry beach—and a good substitute for chocolate."
—*The Beaufort Gazette* (SC)

### Losing the Moon

"Henry's beautifully written debut romance is meant to be savored, with its poetic descriptions and settings deftly mirroring the emotions of the characters. Readers who enjoy the lyrical voices of Patricia Gaffney and Mary Alice Monroe will also be drawn to this talented newcomer."
—*Booklist* (starred review)

"Patti Callahan Henry joins the ranks of Anne Rivers Siddons and Pat Conroy with this debut novel. *Losing the Moon* is lyrical, sensual, and as delicate as a seashell. Lovely and poignant."
—Deborah Smith, *New York Times* bestselling author of *Charming Grace*

"I loved *Losing the Moon*! Patti Callahan Henry's engaging story and compelling characters captured my heart from page one, and stayed with me long after the final, satisfying conclusion. Don't miss this wonderful book."
—Haywood Smith

"A dazzling example of the new style of fiction writing to come out of the South. Chosen as the first book in the Margaret Mitchell House and Museum's Emerging Writers' program, Henry has been hailed as being included first in the ranks of important Southern writers such as Pat Conroy and Anne Rivers Siddons. If this debut novel is any indication of what we can expect from Patti Callahan Henry, we can look forward to many years of reading enjoyment to come." —*The Wichita Falls Times Record News*

# THE TIDES

Patti Callahan Henry

NAL Accent
Published by New American Library, a division of
Penguin Group (USA) Inc., 375 Hudson Street,
New York, New York 10014, USA
Penguin Group (Canada), 90 Eglinton Avenue East, Suite 700, Toronto,
Ontario M4P 2Y3, Canada (a division of Pearson Penguin Canada Inc.)
Penguin Books Ltd., 80 Strand, London WC2R 0RL, England
Penguin Ireland, 25 St. Stephen's Green, Dublin 2,
Ireland (a division of Penguin Books Ltd.)
Penguin Group (Australia), 250 Camberwell Road, Camberwell, Victoria 3124,
Australia (a division of Pearson Australia Group Pty. Ltd.)
Penguin Books India Pvt. Ltd., 11 Community Centre, Panchsheel Park,
New Delhi - 110 017, India
Penguin Group (NZ), 67 Apollo Road, Rosedale, North Shore,
Auckland 1311, New Zealand (a division of Pearson New Zealand Ltd.)
Penguin Books (South Africa) (Pty.) Ltd., 24 Sturdee Avenue,
Rosebank, Johannesburg 2196, South Africa

Penguin Books Ltd., Registered Offices:
80 Strand, London WC2R 0RL, England

First published by NAL Accent, an imprint of New American Library,
a division of Penguin Group (USA) Inc.

First Printing, June 2007
10  9  8  7  6  5  4  3

REGISTERED TRADEMARK—MARCA REGISTRADA

LIBRARY OF CONGRESS CATALOGING-IN-PUBLICATION DATA:
Henry, Patti Callahan.
Between the tides/Patti Callahan Henry.
p. cm.
ISBN: 978-0-451-22114-8
1. College teachers—Fiction. 2. Fathers and daughters—Fiction. 3. Family secrets—Fiction. 4.
South Carolina—Fiction. 5. Self-realization—Fiction. I. Title.
PS3608.E578B48 2997
813'.6—dc22                    2006034220

Set in Adobe Garamond
Designed by Spring Hoteling

Printed in the United States of America

… *W*ith deep love to Pat Henry, as from the very beginning of this story.

# ACKNOWLEDGMENTS

This, my fourth novel, is a new version of the first full-length manuscript I wrote six years ago. So my gratitude for this finished novel spreads across many years and people too numerous to mention. To those who first read my work and believed in it, to those who helped me mold the story, who taught me about structure and character development, who listened to me attempt to work out the tangles of the story line and my own heart in the early days of writing—I am deeply grateful.

To those who have helped me shape this present version, I also offer my profound thanks: Sally Pisarchick, PhD, for the three questions that helped direct Catherine's metaphorical future; John Searby, Director of Basketball Operations at Auburn University (War Eagle!), for information on basketball recruiting and the NCAA rules and regulations (if any mistakes have been made, they are mine alone); Jack Riggs, a talented author and teacher with a beautiful heart who offered his knowledge about college literature programs and professorships. To my long-suffering agent, Kimberly Whalen—wow, we finally finished *Between the Tides* and I couldn't have done it without you. To Katherine McComis, who has been there to help in so many ways since the first day I decided to write. To Mary Alice Monroe for making sure I never, ever forget why I write.

To everyone at New American Library who has supported my work throughout these past four novels. To Ellen Edwards, for her sharp sword of editing. To Kara Welsh, Claire Zion, Leslie Gelbman, Molly Boyle, Carolyn Birbiglia, and all those unknown others behind the scenes whom I never meet—I am honored to be published by such an amazing group of people. And, of course, I am beyond grateful to the sales force at NAL for the time and effort they put into selling my work; to the art department for the creativity and attention to detail given to my covers.

Every time I write a novel, I want to use pages and pages to list all my friends, writing buddies, booksellers, reviewers, and fans who have made this such an adventure-filled journey. So please know I adore every single one of you.

My family—close and extended—has watched this novel from the first hidden pages to this finished novel, and they have never lost faith in the story or in me. I would not have been able to finish this novel without them. I love all of you.

*"Whereof what is past is prologue . . . "*
—WILLIAM SHAKESPEARE

### The World Is Green Again

Low limbs of the live oak twist
like overlapping black rivers
across the sky. It is easy
to feel lost in the maze
of their convoluted journey,

but there are small birds
we cannot see, singing
in the silvery sun—
nests balanced on the tips
of branches like bowls of light.

An osprey looks down from a nest
of twigs and Spanish Moss.
The broad crown of the oak
is thick with green leaves rippling
in waves. Sometimes, hovering

over water, searching the surface
for fish, he remembers this tree—
the absolute permanence,
considers its great weight
and all the lives intertwining.

He exists as a mass of feathers,
talons, and bone—a dark winged
fishhawk weaving a life from air.
Loyal to this place and patient,
he trusts the hours that pass

through wind and cold bursts of rain.
Like the live oak, like this place
he inhabits with his whole heart,
he waits until the days lengthen,
and the whole world is green again.

—Marjory Wentworth

# PROLOGUE

$\mathcal{B}$efore that summer of my twelfth year, we always jumped from the end of the dock, rather than enter the river from the shore's safe edge. God help us, maybe that was why Sam went in that day. Maybe after watching us so many times, he too jumped when the sunlight fell in sharp edges onto the moss-encrusted grass, the tide flowed in, and the day whispered good-bye.

His mother's voice ripped through the evening, tearing it in half. "Where's Sam?"

I looked up at Ellie standing at the river's edge, the picnic basket at her feet, the lavender-azure rays of a sunset surrounding her like a blessing.

"He's hiding in the hole of that oak tree," I answered, pointed to the fallen tree. "Boyd scared him."

Ellie walked toward the tree and I felt it then: what had haunted me all summer, followed me, wakened me with sweat; what I had labeled expectation or youth or even love now had a name—pure, immeasurable fear.

Ellie bent over the tree and called two-year-old Sam's name, and then she stood and screamed his name. She did not turn to me for help. She never fully turned her face or her voice or her all-encompassing love toward me again. She screamed Sam's name with a mother's primal terror, which brought her husband, Jim, and my parents running to the river.

I screamed too, but not Sam's name, just a sound of such total animalistic fear that Sam's brother, thirteen-year-old Boyd, clapped his hand over my mouth. "Stop, Cappy. Stop. We'll find him. Let's find him . . . *now*." Then Boyd hollered Sam's name in a cracked and wounded voice I had never heard from him before. This, and this alone, let me know my fear was alive for a reason, a solid and unequivocal reason—Sam was gone.

The voices overlapped. I couldn't identify which adult spoke each phrase, and I could not, in any way, answer.

"Sam. Sam. Who was watching Sam?"

"Did you put on his life jacket yet?"

"Do you have Sam?"

"I was packing the picnic."

"Cappy had him."

"Cappy had him?"

"No, Boyd had him."

"Yes, Cappy."

"Cap, where is he? Where is he?"

"Is he hiding behind the old oak?"

"Shit, quit arguing, find him."

"Find him. . . ." Ellie's voice rent time and space into the before and after of Sam. "Find him."

Nothing, no answer. But not silence either, just the clamor of screeching seagulls, arguing blue jays, croaking frogs, peeping cicadas, slapping waves—sounds of nature as harsh against Sam's silence as the mangled screech of metal against metal.

I turned to Boyd, who stared at me with his mouth open, as if unformed words were trapped in the same place as Sam's breath. I looked up to the top of the dead oak tree, to the screeching osprey in her nest; she stared down at me with her yellow eyes, then covered her babies with her wings.

I ran sobbing with the violent realization of Sam's death. My childhood was destroyed, never to be repaired, never sewn into a whole piece. It was my fault. Nothing good could ever come to me again.

# ONE

*"I had always felt life first as a story. . . ."*
—G. K. Chesterton

I knew I looked like a complete fool, standing on the front step of the porch in drawstring pajama bottoms and a tank top, watching Thurman drive away in the gritty light of predawn. My unruly hair fell out of a tangled ponytail while a strap slipped off my shoulder. The taillights of his car moved down the street like two open eyes staring at me, and I hoped, in vain, that I'd see the brake lights, that he'd stop, turn around, and remember it was my birthday, that he'd throw his arms around me and say with a laugh, "Oh, Catherine, how could I have forgotten it was your thirtieth birthday?" I would hug him back, kiss him and run my hand up his neck and through his blond hair before he left again.

But, of course, he didn't return to me; he was late for

his trip to Alabama. In our four years together, this was the first time he'd ever forgotten my birthday. I saw this fact as a bad omen even as I told myself it was probably nothing more, or less, than the result of forgetfulness, fatigue, and preoccupation.

I sat and watched the streaks of morning come over the South Carolina mountain peaks in a stretching, yawning awakening. I closed my eyes and grasped like a child for that elusive but palpable sense of possibility I remembered from childhood birthday mornings.

I'd once believed that each new year brought me closer to becoming one of the beautiful and brave characters in the novels piled around my bedroom. *This,* I would think when I was young, *will be the year I'll be as curious as Lucy in* Narnia, *as courageous as Scout in* Mockingbird, *or as cunning as Nancy Drew.*

In that fateful summer of my twelfth year, however, I discovered that such story-time fantasies were not and never would be mine. No Atticus would rush to my rescue; no clue in the old clock would fix my family; Aslan would not save me from my sin. For some people sudden realizations in life come in one breath of their own, but mine had come in a breath not taken by another.

Now, at thirty, I'd found all I needed in the sweet, real world of Cedar Valley, where I lived—the mountain peaks forming a torn-edged horizon, like a castle's crenellated walls, protecting me within a bowl of neatly laid out streets lined with well-established homes and mature trees. I never climbed to the top of the surrounding hills to enjoy the distant vistas other people talked about after hiking up the mountainsides. I was content in my leafy bower.

I hadn't left Cedar Valley—except for family vacations to Disney World or the Florida beaches to visit Dad's parents in Sarasota—since I'd moved here eighteen years ago. Even those few times I had traveled with my parents, I didn't feel completely right until we returned. Away from home, it seemed as though every encounter and experience held more import, more chance for pain, than it did when I was inside my safe valley home.

I sat on my front steps, breathed in the green-rich air of another year and thought how I might spend that particular birthday. My boyfriend, Thurman, the head basketball coach for Southern University, was off on a recruiting trip, but right then I missed Dad more than Thurman.

Dad, a man of books who lived, moved, and had his being in the themes and metaphors of novels, who believed that all of life was a story, had been gone for nine months. Just thinking about him with a book in one hand and a huge grin on his white-bearded face made me smile.

He had been the English department chair, and taught one freshman class on Southern literature. He'd passed away from a heart attack while teaching his class the literary nuances of Faulkner's *The Sound and the Fury*. In the middle of his attempt to make the students understand that Faulkner's words conveyed many meanings, he grabbed his chest. His students thought he was acting, being dramatic about an asinine comment just made by a boy in the back row.

Even when he fell to the floor, they were still laughing.

I was certain this was exactly, and I mean exactly, how Daddy would've wanted to go: teaching, laughing, standing in front of the classroom wearing his tweed jacket with the patches on the elbows, holding a piece of chalk in one hand, a book in the other, his junior professor, Forrest Anderson, at his side.

Soon I discovered I was wrong about this, and then that I was wrong about so many other things too. But at that moment, the thought of him dying in his element, with the man he'd mentored for ten years, was a comfort to me.

After Dad was gone, I discovered that as an only child I inherited his house in this valley of South Carolina, in which I now lived, and all his earthly belongings, including our beloved dog, Murphy. I was also heir to his last request, handwritten in a letter attached to his will: to scatter his ashes in the Seaboro River. I had still not completed this task. There I sat, on my birthday, and thought, with stomach-turning regret, how I had not fulfilled his last request of me. Yet since I was a child and we lived on the shores of the South Carolina Lowcountry, he had always been the one to make my birthday special: a pink ribbon on the magnolia tree in the front yard, a cake with so much icing you couldn't find the cake inside, a present hidden in boxes inside boxes until I found the small gift at the bottom. Even when Mother was alive, she believed that this sort of indulgence spoiled a child. Of course she did, but she tolerated it for Dad's sake.

I hadn't scattered Dad's ashes not because I didn't love him and respect his wishes, but because I couldn't imagine returning to the place I still mourned, a place where my childhood lived as its own entity without my permission, and more important, a place I had forced my family to leave. I didn't know why Dad would want to send me back there.

I rubbed my eyes, stood, and stretched to face another day at the Athletic Office at Southern University, where I worked in the media-relations department. "Happy birthday to me," I said to the ripening chestnut tree in the front yard, not yet knowing that the gifts I would receive that day would make me agree to return, reluctantly and to protect sacred secrets, to the grief-breathing place of childhood, to the Seaboro River.

When I returned from work at day's end, the cedar-shake house was unlocked, which meant I'd left it unsecured when I'd hurried off to the office—late. Buried in work that day, I hadn't made it home to walk Murphy, and she'd been in the fenced backyard all day, going in and out her dog door looking for me, I was sure. I entered the house and inhaled the familiar scents of home: some combination of toast, warm blankets, and the autumn smell of crisp leaves that permeated the wood even in summer.

This was the house Dad and Mother had bought when we moved here eighteen years ago, the home I'd shared with them until I went to college at SU. When Dad had died, I'd returned to live in the home without my parents, and yet I still slept in my old bedroom at the top of the stairs: a room with the pink-and-white checked bathroom and the four-poster bed transported from the coast.

Murphy bounded around the corner from the living room and buried her nose in my held-out hand. "Hey, best dog in the whole world," I said, and rubbed her behind the ears. "Want to go for a walk? Huh?"

Murphy was fourteen years old, but no one had told her that. Her face was white, her auburn fur curled and coarse. Dad and I had bought her together for my sixteenth birthday, and here she was celebrating my thirtieth with me. I clipped on her leash and opened the back screen door, which slammed behind me when I tripped over the back welcome mat. The air was cooler that evening than it had been, and I imagined I could hear summer saying, *Not yet, not yet . . . just a few more days.*

Dad's neighbors, Mr. and Mrs. Hancock, waved to me from their front porch when I passed. "Who is that?" Mr. Hancock asked in the loud voice of the hard of hearing, leaned forward in his rocking chair and squinted at me when I waved back.

"You know, dear." Mrs. Hancock's voice quavered on the still evening air. "That's Grayson Leary's daughter. She moved back into the family house—you know, she dates that coach."

I laughed when Murphy and I rounded the corner. Yes, the beloved professor's daughter, the basketball coach's girlfriend—always defined by my relationship to others.

I glanced up at the top of the peaks in the west where the sun dropped behind Cedar Falls: a fir- and rhododendron-covered summit that towered over the campus. Once, the mountains had overlooked the decrepit shacks of cotton mill workers and their children. Now they stared down at the steeples and slanted roofs of three colleges and a university, quaint bed-and-breakfasts, and brick-lined streets with coffee shops and bookstores.

Southern University had been founded in 1852, and, in one way or another, my life had been stitched into this institution—from Dad's professorship, to Mother's fundraising, to my own college degree, and now my job at the Athletic Office.

The end of the school year usually meant a reprieve from busier days, but our basketball program was under investigation by the NCAA for recruiting violations. We were being accused of breaking NCAA rules in recruiting basketball players. Almost all my work that past month had been focused on reassuring the press and boosters that these accusations were false, just a means of taking down Southern

University's basketball program, which was beginning to rival the powerhouse of the University of North Carolina. So it felt good to be on my feet moving down the sidewalk rather than at my desk dealing with the constant influx of mail and phone calls.

I returned home and entered the kitchen to a ringing phone. I unclipped Murphy's leash and ran for it, found Thurman on the line.

"Hey, baby," he said, drawing out *baby* like a multisyllable word. Then he sang "Happy Birthday to You." I leaned against the kitchen wall and let him finish the entire song, knowing it would be the only time I would hear it that day.

"That was off-key," I said when he was done.

"Thank you, my sweet." He laughed, and I heard the hum of a radio in the background.

"Where are you?" I asked.

"Driving out to Darius's house in Nowhere, Alabama. I've tried to call you all day."

"I was swamped—you forgot until you got there, didn't you?"

"Forgot what?"

My answer was silence; let him figure it out for himself.

"No, I did *not* forget your birthday . . . I just was so damn late this morning I forgot to say anything."

"Hmmm . . ." I said.

"Really. Go to the front hallway table."

"What?" I walked toward the hall with the portable

phone. A small velvet box rested on the scarred trestle table. "When did you put this here?" I asked as I took the box back to the kitchen and sat at the table.

He laughed. "Open the box, Catherine."

I did, and took in a deep breath. Nestled in black velvet was a circle of diamonds hanging from a silver chain as fine as spun silk. "It's beautiful."

"It's an everlasting circle. It's supposed to represent love that never ends."

"I love it, Thurman. Thank you."

"I promise that the next diamond will be in a small circle that fits on a finger."

"I've heard that before," I said, touched my empty ring finger. Thurman had been promising our engagement for months—and I'd been the one to change the subject, move to another topic of our conversation. He was being so sweet now that I felt as if I needed to brush my hand through the air, clean it of all the muddy thoughts I'd had about his leaving that morning.

"Darling," he said, "I have to go now. I'll call you tomorrow. Cross your fingers that I can finally talk Darius into coming to Southern instead of Alabama."

"Thurman, I don't understand why you're there, really. I mean, he already committed to Alabama, school starts in three months, and you know you're being watched like a hawk by the NCAA."

"I have to bag this player. I'm not giving up until the

uniform is on and the first game has started. And you can tell the NCAA to get off my freaking back; I ain't doing nothing wrong. I have one more visit in my 'official visits'—no rules broken here."

"Good luck," I said, and hung up.

I plucked the necklace from the box and clasped it around my neck. The circle fell on my breastbone with a pleasing weight—a reminder of his love. He couldn't help it that he had to be out of town on my birthday; it was his job.

I grabbed the watering can from below the kitchen sink and headed toward Dad's office, where I still kept his many varieties of ivy. A bulletin board over the entire brick wall was covered with literary quotes on small, ripped pieces of paper. Even though this was now my house, I hadn't been able to touch or move a single scrap of paper; it felt invasive and final to move anything Dad had tacked onto the board.

I had never been able to see any pattern to Dad's collection of quotes. Maybe, I had once thought, he divided them up by author or subject. Shakespeare, Graham Greene, Hemingway, Faulkner, C. S. Lewis, e.e. cummings . . . the authors went on and on, but they weren't in any order I could see.

I shook my head and said out loud, "Dad, you were crazy."

A laugh, low and loud, came from behind me. I jumped forward; water splattered across my shirt. I spun to face Forrest Anderson and his crooked smile.

Now, there were certain men who made me uncomfortable because they didn't know me, but Forrest made me uncomfortable because he did know me—well. We had gone to college together and even dated for a few months in our sophomore year. But, breakup or not, there was no getting Forrest Anderson out of my life.

He had been Dad's teaching assistant in the years after college; then, after gaining his master's degree elsewhere, he'd returned to Southern, where Dad had overseen Forrest's doctoral dissertation on some obscure facet of Faulkner's novels. The faculty board had hired Forrest as a junior professor with ABD—"all but dissertation"—and he soon became known as a boy wonder around the English department. He was rumored to be the one who would eventually take over Dad's job. The two men had spent as much time together as Dad and I had, and to my mind Forrest had become much too accustomed to walking into my house unannounced.

He had a wild mass of brown curls, a wide stance, and a comfortable way with laughter. I consistently avoided straight contact with his brown eyes because I knew his look carried a hint of "could have been, but definitely was not meant to be" feeling. Looking Forrest in the eye and lingering there was about as close to cheating on Thurman Whittaker as I'd ever come.

"Forrest, you scared the hell out of me. What are you doing here? Don't you know how to knock?" I set the watering can on the slate floor. "You cannot walk in here like that anymore."

"Happy birthday," he said.

Of course Forrest remembered; Dad would be so pleased. "Thanks," I said.

"Aren't you gonna ask me how I know?"

Now, that was what infuriated me about him—he knew exactly what I wanted to ask, but hadn't. "No," I said.

He laughed. "Okay, you stubborn old friend."

I scrunched up my face. "You haven't answered me: What are you doing here?"

He laughed again. "I knocked four times. I'm here on a birthday mission," he said, and sat in Dad's desk chair, spun around to face me.

"Oh?"

"Yep," he said, then yanked a wrapped package from the briefcase I hadn't seen him set on the floor. The box was the size of a book, wrapped in plain brown paper with a bright pink organza ribbon twisted into a huge bow.

"Wow," I said, took a step toward him.

He grinned. "You like the wrapping."

"My dad," I said. "He used to put a ribbon just like that on the tree outside our house when I was a little girl."

"I know; he told me. That's why I did it."

I pushed Forrest's feet off the desk. "Why'd he tell you that?"

He shook his head. "Because *you* are all he ever talked about, Cappy Leary."

I picked up the present. "Don't call me that." I twisted

the ribbon in my hand, but stared at his mouth, not his eyes. "You didn't have to get me anything, you know."

"I know, but I thought with this being the first birthday without your dad . . . I don't know. . . ." He shrugged and dropped his hands in his lap. "Just wanted to get you something special."

My name was scrawled across the bottom of the wrapping paper. CAP it said in three capital letters, like a monogram.

"Open it, Cappy," he said in such a soft voice it made me want to cry.

"That is not my name," I said. I'd told Forrest this so many times—*not* to call me the nickname my dad had called me. No one could—it was my name from childhood.

"Okay, okay, just open it."

"Fine," I said. "You do know you make me crazy."

"Yes," he said. "I do."

I moved to the screened-in porch and sat on the large wicker rocking chair—an heirloom from Grandma that had sat on porches from Cedar Valley to Seaboro and back to Cedar Valley again.

Forrest's footsteps came behind me, but I didn't turn to him. I unrolled the ribbon and placed it on my lap, then peeled the tape off the wrapping to see an old edition of *To Kill a Mockingbird*. The cloth-and-cardboard cover was brown, with a leafy tree slanted across the center, the title in stark black letters above the tree. A black-and-white portrait of Harper Lee behind tall grass filled the back cover. My heart rolled around inside my chest like it was dancing: a wild childhood dance.

I placed my hand over my mouth. "Oh, Forrest."

He shrugged. "Your dad told me it was your favorite book when you were young."

I closed my eyes so I wouldn't cry in front of him. "You shouldn't have done this." I opened the cover and stared at the words, *First edition, Book Club, 1960.* I ran my finger over the date, over the yellow-edged pages, and then I did look at him. "I know how much first editions cost . . . this is crazy."

"I knew this would be a hard birthday for you." He touched the book. "Harper Lee's photo on the back was taken by Truman Capote."

All I could do was nod. Forrest sat on the wicker couch next to me. "Your dad would love for you to read it again, I'm sure."

"I'm sure," I said, and irritation instead of gratefulness rose like smoke inside me. I knew that my lack of interest in reading, and my desire to avoid discussing the subject, had hurt Dad, confused him over the years. Forrest did not need to remind me. But how was I to explain to Dad or Forrest that reading only made me want another life—a richer one, a deeper one, and that sometimes, just sometimes not wanting is better than wanting and not having?

"What are you doing for the rest of your birthday weekend?" Forrest asked, leaned back against the brown-checked cushions.

"Nothing, really. Thurman is out of town, and I didn't make plans with any of our friends. . . ." Now it was my turn to shrug.

"How about going to Seaboro with me—take a trip to the beach, finally scatter those ashes?"

I took in a breath. *Slow, now, Catherine, steady.* "What did you just say?"

"Did I say something wrong?"

"How do you know about the ashes?"

"I spent more time with your dad than anyone. We talked. We were best friends. When he told me about his weekend trips to Seaboro, I asked him why, and the only thing he told me was that it was a place he loved so much, it was where he wanted to have his ashes scattered. Of course, he didn't realize it would be so soon before . . ." His voice trailed off into that place I knew well—that place where you had to say the words *he died.*

"Dad didn't go back to Seaboro," I said. "Not for at least eighteen years." An unnamed emotion that resembled fear moved inside my chest.

Forrest glanced around the screened-in porch as if someone else were there. "Yes, he did." He paused, then leaned even closer to me. "A couple times a year."

The ground slipped from below my feet, the room spun

in concentric circles, my heart rose to the base of my throat. "What?"

"You didn't know that?" His voice faded like I had mufflers over my ears.

I shook my head in quick, small movements. Forrest grabbed my hand, but I yanked it from him. "No, that's not right. He just talked about Seaboro. He didn't go back. Not ever."

"Yes, he did."

I hated the certainty in Forrest's voice; I hated that he mentioned Seaboro as if he knew what had happened there; I hated the thought of this man knowing more about my dad than I did.

"Are you sure?"

Forrest nodded.

I stood and paced the room.

"Are you okay?" he asked.

"Do you know why he went back?"

"I was going to ask you. You see, I'm writing a memorial essay about your dad for the SU literary magazine. In this article I am using the top five classic novels he taught and showing how each one changed at least one life. I've gathered five life stories—one for each novel. The only thing I'm missing is some of his past history—you know, the years before he moved here. I was hoping you could tell me a little bit about Seaboro, about your life with him in the Lowcountry."

I wanted to scream the word *no*, over and over, but again I just shook my head.

"Are you sure you're okay? I didn't mean to startle you or anything. I just wanted to give you a birthday present and ask you if . . ." He stopped, touched my elbow.

"Ask me what?" My voice came raw, as if I'd been crying. My hands gripped *To Kill a Mockingbird* so tightly I felt ridges in the cover art.

"If I could come with you to scatter his ashes in Seaboro. I don't think you've done it yet. I thought . . . well, thought maybe this would be a good weekend to do it, what with a three-day holiday and all."

"I am *not* going," I said, choosing anger over fear.

He shrugged. "Okay. Well, then, I think I'll go down there by myself. I was hoping you'd go with me, but I just need to get a feel of the town before I wrap up this article."

"You didn't ask me if you could write an article about my dad. Isn't that something you should ask me?" My voice rose higher.

Forrest turned away. "Grayson was not only my mentor, but also my best friend. I don't need permission to write about that." He glanced over his shoulder. "Happy birthday." The door slammed behind him in a staccato sound as he left me alone with my book, my thoughts, and a thousand questions. Why would my dad return to Seaboro and never tell me, yet tell Forrest?

I kicked the side of the rocking chair. If Forrest went to

Seaboro and started asking questions, started researching our family, he would find out more than the facts of Dad's life. He would discover the facts of *my* life. However, if I went with him, I could scatter Dad's ashes and provide Forrest with only the specifics and incidents I wanted him to know.

I ran out the side door of the porch to the driveway, waved my arms at Forrest as he backed his beat-up pickup truck out of the driveway. He stopped, but didn't get out. I walked to the driver's-side window. "I'll go with you," I said with streaky electric shots of panic running inside me.

He lifted his eyebrows. "Really?"

I nodded.

He put the truck in park, turned it off, and jumped out. "I've been wrestling with telling you something for a while, and I think now might be a good time."

"What is that supposed to mean?" I asked.

Forrest leaned against his truck, and I stood in front of him with my arms crossed, my feet spread wide. The air hummed with the possibility of what he might say. I already knew that his words were a "before and after" moment— before Forrest said this, after Forrest said this; before Sam disappeared, after Sam disappeared; before Dad died, after Dad died.

Forrest stared up at the sky. "I want to do this right— give your dad's words justice and integrity."

"Forrest, either tell me what you're talking about or leave."

"Okay, here goes." He took a long, deep breath and then stared at me. He reached out his hand, and I thought he might touch my cheek or the blunt-cut edges of my hair, but his hand wavered and then dropped. Every once in a while this happened: I remembered his gentleness, the way he touched me without demanding anything in return. I looked away.

"About ten months ago, your dad and I attended a conference where we were each asked to answer three questions. We spent hours, well into the night, debating them."

"Only you and Dad could talk about questions until the wee hours of the morning."

"Just listen."

"I'm trying, but where are we going with this?"

"Well, your dad worked through those questions and finally answered them for himself. It seemed real important to him at the time, and I know he was going to write you a letter for your thirtieth birthday in which he asked the questions of you too."

"But he didn't make it to my thirtieth, did he?"

Forrest shook his head. "That's what I've been wrestling with—whether to tell you or not, because he didn't get to do it himself—but I do know he wanted to."

"Go ahead."

"Well, he said he was going to write you a letter for this birthday because it was *medias res* for you. You know—the literary term for 'in the middle of things'—a good place to start a story."

"This is about starting a good story?"

"No, I believe this is about *your* story."

I exhaled. "I am not a story. I know how you and Dad saw everything through your epic-novel glasses, but not me."

"Just let me finish."

I sighed and, wrapping my arms tightly around myself, nodded.

"Okay, here are the three questions. One: What do you want to be doing when you die? Two: If you die today, what will you regret not having done? And three: What do you want your tombstone to say?" Forrest nodded as though his head were the dot on a question mark.

There was a long pause. When Forrest didn't speak again, I loosened my hands to lift them. "That's it? You two spent hours and hours discussing that?"

"Yes."

"Okay, I give. What were his answers?"

"First, he said he wanted to die writing his lesson plans."

A sob crawled up the inside of my chest, but I pushed it down. "Well, I guess he almost got his wish—he died teaching his lesson, not writing it. This is incredibly morbid, Forrest."

"Second, he said his one regret was that he had torn

pages from your childhood story and hadn't yet returned them to you."

"For God's sake, what does that mean?" I shoved the open driver's-side door shut.

Forrest glanced at the truck, then shook his head. "He said he would give you back those pages for your birthday this year. He always had a flair for the dramatic, you know?"

"I'm assuming these are metaphorical pages?" I dug my fingernails into my palms.

"He didn't tell me."

"Last question. What did he want on his tombstone?"

"He said he didn't want a tombstone, just his ashes scattered in the Seaboro River."

"Oh," I said. "That's how you knew. . . ."

"Yes."

*In medias res,* missing pages, tombstones, and Seaboro— none of these odd pieces of the conversation were coming together to make a single picture. I rubbed my forehead against an oncoming headache. "Do you have any idea what this birthday letter was going to say?"

"Only the three questions and something about your childhood that you didn't know. That's all he told me."

I took a step closer to Forrest, squinted at him. "And you swear to God you have no idea what these 'pages' are?"

He held up his right hand. "I swear. That seemed incredibly private, and I didn't probe."

I turned away from him, deciding. "I'll call and make

reservations at a bed-and-breakfast in Seaboro. Be here by nine a.m. One day, Forrest. One day. I'll show you around, fulfill Dad's wishes with the ashes, and we'll come home by Sunday. Okay?"

He nodded. "Yes, ma'am."

"You"—I tapped his chest—"are infuriating."

"I know." He smiled and climbed back in his truck, waved out the window while he backed from the driveway.

His truck was halfway down the street when his brake lights flashed. For the briefest second I thought he would return, but he'd only paused at a stop sign. I thought how Thurman must have driven straight through it that morning.

The questions Forrest had left with me poked like needles, one after the other, while I made small circles with my finger around the new diamonds on my neck, and thought of a quote that was *not* on Dad's bulletin board. *What goes around comes around.*

I was going back to Seaboro. I should have known my past would return to me no matter how much I had tried to avoid it, shove it away and lock it up. The stunning part was not that I would have to face my past sin, or that I must now do it with Forrest Anderson. What came hardest was that it was my dad who was asking me to do so.

# Two

*"He felt the loyalty we feel to unhappiness—*
*the sense that is where we really belong."*
—GRAHAM GREENE,
*The Heart of the Matter*

*T*he air in Cedar Valley was charged with a desperate hur-
riedness that morning while I waited for Forrest to pick me
up; I shifted from foot to foot because he was fifteen minutes
late. I clipped a leash on Murphy so I could drop her off at
the animal clinic on the way out of town. They would spoil
her rotten with treats and walks and playtime. They adored
her there.

I didn't know whom to blame for this trip—Forrest or
Dad, who had never asked me to return to Seaboro while
he was alive, yet now it was his request that sent me there. I

ran my fingers around Murphy's neck and into the tangled knots behind her ear. "I wish you could come, girl, but you remember the last time you sneaked in somewhere?"

Dad and Mother were moving me into dorm ten at Southern University, where I'd been assigned to a roommate named Marietta. I was sure she would be a terrible debutante Southern belle, but she ended up becoming one of my best friends. Mother was wearing a blue silk dress with pearls around her neck, and a charm bracelet that dangled as we walked up the stairs, a sound I always associated with her entrance into any room.

Dad had Murphy on a leash, and sneaked her through the back dorm door that was open for moving day. Dad knew, as Mother hadn't, that even though I didn't show it, I was nervous about moving out. For all my bravado and declarations of independence, I needed an extra boost of family—namely, Murphy—and Dad understood that.

Mother and I stood facing the empty space—a cinderblock room with two single metal beds, two gray metal desks, and two scarred wooden bedside tables. Mother lifted her hand to her mouth; her bracelet jangled. "Oh, Catherine. Maybe you should just live at home?"

"Mother, I can make this home. I can. Plus I'm only two minutes away." I rolled my eyes at her, but for once I actually agreed with her: Maybe I should live at home.

Then Dad came into the room; Murphy jumped on me and I dropped to the floor to hug her. Dad laughed, spread his hands. "Wow, look at this fantastic room. You are going to have the best time; your life will change here."

Mother and Dad looked at each other when he spoke. I knew what he was doing—trying to make this easier on me, and telling Mother to do the same. Mother placed a large smile on her face. "Okay, let's unpack and decorate, make it cozy."

Murphy barked, and almost instantly a woman with a scowl and khaki pants buckled too high on her waist came into the room. "It is clearly posted that there are no dogs allowed. Are you Ms. Leary or Ms. Collins?" she asked.

"I'm Ms. Leary." I bit my lower lip.

"You have now started the year with one demerit mark. When you get three, you lose privileges." The woman turned and left the room.

I glanced at Mother and grimaced. "Must be the dorm mother," I said.

Mother smiled. "Well, Catherine, looks like you will be grounded as often here as you were at home."

Dad hugged me long and hard. "I'll leave you and Mother to do the decorating—I'll get Murphy out of here so you don't get expelled before school even starts."

I nodded but didn't speak.

This memory of Dad, how he always tried to make good of everything, how he knew the little things—like bringing the dog—that would soften the harder edges of a situation, made me smile. I twirled the car keys around my forefinger, then sat on the edge of my overnight bag. The three questions had been probing inside me all night while I slept. It was as if these questions knew that I had no answer for any of them.

I heard Forrest's truck before I saw it round the corner and pull into the driveway. He jumped out of the driver's side. "Sorry," he said, tipped his baseball cap at me. "I know I'm late . . . there was construction on Main."

I stood, held out my hand with the keys. "We're taking my car. I am not driving five hours in your pickup truck with my bag tumbling around in the back and only the most remote chance it will still be there when we arrive."

He smiled. "Whatever you say, boss."

"Very funny," I said, and walked toward my car; I had expected more of a fight, but I tossed my bag in the trunk, walked around to the driver's side, and whistled for Murphy to jump into the backseat.

I'd called Thurman four times the night before to tell him where I was going and why, but had been unable to reach him on his cell phone. Hopefully that meant things were going well with the recruit he was chasing down. Meanwhile, I had to get into a car with Forrest Anderson, tell him all about Dad, scatter the ashes, get home. Simple enough, right?

Forrest threw his duffel bag in the back, climbed into the passenger seat, and smiled at me. "Okay, let's go."

"I've got to drop Murphy off."

Forrest reached behind him to pat my dog. "Can't we bring her? She's the best."

"I know . . . but I don't think the inn takes dogs," I said, then stuck the key in the ignition, started the car. I turned the radio up to avoid the naked emotions running through me.

After we dropped Murphy at the animal clinic, Forrest switched the station to talk radio; I flicked his hand off the knob and turned it back to country. "Driver," I said, "is always in charge of the radio."

"Great," he said, reached to the hand lever to drop his seat to recline, closed his eyes.

"You just gonna leave me to drive while you sleep?" I pulled out of the animal clinic parking lot onto the road.

He opened one eye, stared at me sideways. "Unless you feel like talking."

"Not so much," I said. "Not right now."

"Okay then." He closed his eyes.

I turned the radio up louder and left the mountains with a sense of a protective shell being peeled off.

The road unwound while I flipped radio stations and pretended I was going somewhere else, anywhere else. I'd always prided myself on not wasting a lot of time remembering childhood in the sick-sweet way I heard others talk of theirs. The cotton-candy way in which they seemed to have fluffed their childhood into nothing but sugar and the sweet taste of youth. They remembered their childhood in such detail, in logical and chronological order. On and on their memories went until adulthood.

But for me pulling up childhood memories led me down paths I no longer walked—paths of carpeted pine needles, thick marshes, and cloying black mud at the edge of oyster beds. It was a path that crossed rivers and forests. My memories of childhood mainly consisted of sensory impressions, a specific smell, song, or picture: the musk of decaying marsh, oysters on the bonfire, a boat on an open sea, a dock over the river, sogged earth, or the cloying smell of mildew and salt. They were fractured, blurred memories of nonsequential moments in time. The specifics and order were hidden beneath the years and layered silt of adolescence, college, and adulthood.

The land of Seaboro, South Carolina, was always wet to me; the river, sea, rain, and humid air soaked me to the core. I'd been cushioned in their amniotic fluid, protected in the embryo of my youth. Until Ellie's baby, Sam, was lost in the waters in a shift of tide that changed everything: who I was, what I became, where I lived. For he didn't just die; he drowned. In my river. In my childhood. And the worst horror: It was my fault.

Then my family moved.

If what Forrest said was true—if Dad had been going back to visit without telling me—then I would now return his ashes to a place he had continued to love. But this is what I didn't understand, what I asked as I watched Forrest sleep next to me, as the landscape whipped past the car windows: *Why?*

This was not the question I would ask Forrest, who was sleeping as unself-consciously as if he were home. I would tell him only how the place felt in the better days, how Dad loved the river and sea. This was all Forrest needed to know for his article, and it was all I would explain to him—how the air always carried a portent of expectation, how the water's bounty consistently reminded us how lucky we were to live there. And if I hurried and talked about the beauty of the Lowcountry, maybe he wouldn't ask any more questions.

I glanced over at Forrest's sleeping face, all squished on the side of the seat, and a slight tug of regret pulled under my chest. In an instant, I remembered this same childlike face when I'd broken up with him, told him that it just wasn't going to work out between us.

We had been dating for six months and were at a poetry reading at the coffeehouse downtown. The night was a snapshot I still had in my mind: the brick walls, the dim-lit room, the slanted microphone in the corner, the bearded poet who read from a wrinkled piece of paper. The air had been filled with the sweet smell of coffee, patchouli, and close human contact as the room was full, every folding chair and couch occupied.

The poet had read something—a line I couldn't even recall the next day, much less years later—that caused my heart to rise in my chest, made me feel expansive and expectant. It was a familiar, but far-distant feeling. I'd sat back in my seat and enjoyed the emotion, smiled at Forrest and probed my gut to remember when I'd felt that way before. And then it came to me in a tidal wave—running with Boyd at the edge of a river when I was supposed to be watching his brother, Sam.

My teeth slammed down on one another; my heart shut. Forrest smiled back at me, pushed a strand of hair off my face, and the joyful feeling threatened to return. He ran his hand up my back and along my neck. I shivered. When we returned to my dorm, I told him that it just wasn't going to work out between us. At all.

When he pushed for a reason, I wasn't able to give him one, unable to find the words to explain that the feeling I'd had with him that night was a dangerous feeling, one inevitably followed by disaster and changed lives.

When he left me that night, he looked over his shoulder and his profile wavered in the lamplight's glare. He looked like a boy, hurt and resigned, his eyes at half-mast. "When and if you want to talk about it, when you want to figure out why you would ruin a good thing . . . I'll be here."

"I'm sorry," I said.

He never brought it up again, never pursued me or asked me out. His relationship with Dad had already begun and it continued. At first I ignored him whenever he came around or when Dad brought him home, but eventually I realized that he wasn't pushing any kind of relationship with me, and I relaxed, glad to have him there without the demands of love, commitment, or long talks about the future.

Now I realized I'd missed his presence at dinner with Dad, his laughter and his keen insights into people and events. This was nice—being friends without the implications of dating.

I poked Forrest. "Wake up," I said.

He rubbed his face with an open palm. "Are we there?" he said, and flipped the seat up.

"We're only about an hour away," I said.

"You tired?" he asked. "Sorry I passed out like that. I was up till three this morning grading papers. Want me to drive for a while?"

"No, thanks," I said. "Just thought you might want to start looking at the scenery if you'd really like to know where Dad came from—if that's really why you're here."

He turned away without grabbing at the "let's bicker" bait. He stared out the window. "A lot of farmland here," he said.

"Yep, this is the Piedmont—flat farmland on the way to the Lowcountry, where there is more water than land."

He nodded. "When did he move down there?"

"Right after he and Mother married," I said, and turned off the radio. These were things I could talk about. "I was born there."

Forrest rolled the window halfway down. "I wonder why

he left the mountains." The wind took his words to the green and cotton-rich sloping fields.

I shrugged. "I never asked why he left Cedar Valley. He just said he and Mother had always wanted to live by the water."

"Then," he said, and turned to me, "why did he come back?"

I was amazed that this question was being asked already— I had wanted to explain about the tides, rivers, shrimp boils, and small-town trivia before he asked me the one question, the only question, that mattered.

"He was asked to join the English department at Southern—and he'd get to teach his favorite class, Southern Literature. All in his hometown—why wouldn't he come back?"

"I heard he'd been asked numerous times before and always said no; then he suddenly changed his mind."

I stared out the windshield and tried not to grit my teeth. "Who knows any man's reasons?"

"It doesn't make sense—and whenever something doesn't make sense it means some part of the story is missing." Wind from his lowered window tossed his hair; dust, which might be small pieces of cotton from the field, fluttered into the car, landed on his curls.

"Forrest," I said, pointed to myself, "one more time—I am not a story."

"All of life is a story," he said.

"Don't quote *my* dad to *me*."

He leaned against the passenger-side door and stared at me hard, as if he were trying to see through me. "He taught me that—I wasn't trying to quote him to you, Cappy. Relax."

"What else did he teach you?" I asked. "To call me Cappy? That life is some sort of epic journey? Don't be thinking you can tell me anything about him I don't know."

"Well, you can tell me things about him *I* don't know."

"Doesn't sound like it," I said.

"He wouldn't talk about his time in Seaboro—you can tell me about that. You can tell me about the past. 'What is past is prologue.' "

"Shakespeare," I said.

"I'm impressed." He held his hand out the window and pushed his palm against the wind. "Is there one word you would use to describe the dad you grew up with?"

Reaching deep for this word took me to places I didn't want to visit or define. I shrugged. "No, not one word."

"Come on, just one."

"Content," I said, let the shiver of the one emotion I understood I had taken away from my dad run over me.

"Oh." Forrest tapped the dashboard. "Doesn't make sense. You know?"

"No, I don't know."

"If he was . . . content, why'd he leave?"

I bit my lower lip, pointed out the windshield. "We're almost there." We crossed the first bridge onto the string of islands. The landscape rolled by like a carpet of sweet-grass and marshland all the way to Seaboro. The perimeter of water and maritime forest that was once my playground moved past us in blurred green and brown waves, melding into a sage memory.

I told Forrest, "We'll cross about six bridges to get to our little town." I told him the history of rice, indigo, and cotton. He listened, but didn't comment. I reached into my purse for directions to the Seaboro Bed-and-Breakfast and discovered I didn't need them: I remembered every turn, every corner, and even the back road that wound behind Bay Street.

"We're here," he said, as we passed a weathered wooden sign declaring, WELCOME TO SEABORO. The letters were carved into the wood, then painted a dark green. He pulled out a notebook from a briefcase at his feet and scribbled on the pages.

"What are you writing?" I asked.

"What this feels like—all this sea and marsh surrounding us, like we can walk on water."

I smiled. "That is a nice way to say it . . . really nice."

The car went the speed limit down the main road into town, and I became an observer, detached and distant, as though the town before us were on a movie screen. I pointed. "That's Morgan's Grocery, where your purchases will probably still be rung up on an old cash register next to the *Farmer's Almanac* display."

Forrest laughed, wrote in his book again. There were new stores on the main street now: a bookstore, a jewelry boutique, and an art gallery. I took a deep breath and continued to talk about the town—which was much easier than talking about Dad. "Seaboro has had five flags flown over its waters: Spain, France, Scotland, the United States, and, of course, the Confederate South. I remember when the downtown square would have a mixture of locals, quail hunters, fishermen, Gullah, and even a fighter pilot who had ambled over from the Beaufort marine base, all at the same time.

"If I take a left there"—I pointed—"on Palmetto Drive, we'll eventually arrive where the old lighthouse burned down during a graduation party, when the bonfire got out of control. That event ruined our chances of partying there when we reached high school age. As seventh graders, we were more concerned about the future prospects for beach parties than the fact that someone had died that night."

"Tragic small-town history, huh?" He wrote in his notebook again.

"You going to write down everything I say?" There was a bite to my words that I hadn't anticipated.

"Okay, I'm going to put that off to crankiness from the long drive and ignore it."

I sighed. "Sorry." The word felt familiar on my tongue, because I knew I said it more than most.

After the main road cut through town, it wound under a canopy of live oaks and Spanish moss so dense that the shadows became long and the road was lit by the sifting light rather than the full sun. We passed low-lying horse fences that, to the right and left, bordered the proud homes of the cotton and rice settlements of the past. The plantation owners had erected these homes with sweeping views of the river, and now the vast lawns and ancient trees whispered to me to look, to remember.

Forrest spoke softly next to me, as if he knew he'd disturbed some ghosts. "Wow, this is beautiful."

"I know," I said, rolled down my own window.

He scrunched up his nose. "What is that . . . smell?"

"Ancient earth . . . pluff mud, live and decaying sea life, all mixed together."

Forrest continued to take notes.

"The last time I was on this road I was in a wood-paneled station wagon while Mother, Dad, and I followed a moving van to Cedar Valley."

"You haven't been back since the day you moved?" He closed his notebook.

The sorrow I'd felt eighteen years ago while driving down this road lodged itself into an old niche below my breast. I fought against this irrational grief, believing I'd long since outgrown this particular pain the same way I'd outgrown my pink tutu with the red roses glued to the tulle.

"No, I haven't been back," I said.

"I thought maybe you'd come with your dad."

"Forrest—I didn't know he ever came here. Okay?"

He nodded. "Don't you want to know why he was coming?"

I stopped the car, pulled to the side of the road, and glared at Forrest. "Listen, if Dad wanted me to know why he came, or even that he did come, he would've told me. He must not have wanted me to know—it was his business."

"Or maybe he just didn't have a chance to tell you."

"What is that supposed to mean?"

"It's not like he knew he was going to die. We all think we have time to say what we want to say. There he was, less than a year ago, telling me how he wanted to return missing pages of your childhood to you."

My insides quivered as if the earth shook, as if the car vibrated with Forrest's words. I looked away from him, then pulled the car back onto the potholed road. "I am here to toss his ashes, tell you a little bit about the town and what Dad loved about it—then go home. Get it?"

"Of course. You could never stand to come too close to anything . . . or anyone. Keep your distance, right? From the truth, from people." His voice was lower, rougher.

I bit my lower lip to stop the caustic words I felt rising, made a U-turn, and veered back onto the road. This was the first time Forrest had ever said anything like that, challenged me on my distance from him.

"What are you doing?" he asked.

"Taking you to the B & B where we have reservations. I will do this thing by myself. Dad asked *me* to toss his ashes.

Not you and me together. In fact, I don't think he asked you to come here and write about his past either."

"No, he didn't," Forrest said, "but I believe he would like that I am."

"Well, then, that is where our opinions differ."

"Of course they do," he said, stared out the window and turned his back to me. I thought he was through talking to me, but when I drove up to the B & B he got out, stood at the side of my car with his duffel bag thrown over his shoulder, then leaned into the window. "Cappy, I am not here to piss you off. I am here because I loved your dad."

"You're here for your article, and don't call me Cappy," I said, and drove off while his hand was still on the windowsill.

With anger as my companion, I drove toward the river to finally and completely fulfill Dad's wishes. Who did Forrest think he was? An expert on Dad? My family? Me?

How could anyone write accurately and absolutely about a family if they weren't part of it? I was in the middle of it, literally, and I wasn't sure I could even begin to summarize or categorize the past or the present of the Leary family. Dad had mystery in his eyes, in his decisions. Mother was an enigma I hadn't—to that day—been able to find one word to define.

I had considered her calculating to the extreme—always knowing whom to invite to the dinner party, what street to live on, whose name to drop, what outfit to wear. Then one afternoon, in my senior year in college, I had come home to grab my winter coat to take back to the dorm and found my assumptions and my one-word definition shattered.

I'd run in the front door, even left it open in the rush of the quick "get in, get out" philosophy I had when Mother was home. I didn't need her asking about my grades, or whom I was dating, or why so-and-so saw me at the coffee shop with such and such. I opened the back hall closet and grabbed the gray-and-white checked wool coat, threw it over my arm, and headed back out the door—safe.

Until I heard what sounded like someone talking in Dad's study. I stopped. Surely it wasn't Mother talking to herself. Was Grandma visiting? Did Mother have a friend over?

I took a few steps toward the back of the house and poked my head around the corner of Dad's room that led to the screened-in porch. Mother sat on the couch in a pair of jeans (I didn't know she owned a pair) and one of Dad's flannel shirts. Pictures, boxes, and scrapbooks were scattered across the glass-topped wicker coffee table. The photos were sorted into piles, the rectangular boxes labeled and lined up like dominoes end to end and side to side. The scrapbook lay open, and Mother held a picture in one hand, a glue stick in the other.

My mind raced in opposite directions trying to make sense of this scene: Mother sorting photos, Mother in a pair of jeans without makeup, Mother speaking to faded photos.

I felt I needed to tilt my head in order to right the world, correct the image in front of me. I took two steps back when she heard me and looked up.

She wiped her face in a rapid gesture, using the back of her hand. "Catherine," she said.

"Hey, Mother. I came to get my winter coat. They're expecting frost over the weekend."

"Yes, I know," she said. "I was going to call and tell you that a front was moving in. . . ." Her voice became quieter with each word, until the last word trailed off into the still air.

"Old pictures?" I asked, gestured toward the table.

She nodded. "Yes, I thought I should finally get them organized—at least by years."

I dropped my coat on the rocking chair and walked toward the couch, sat down next to her one cushion over. I bent my left leg underneath me and turned to face her. "Can I see some of them?"

She held out the yellowed picture in her right hand, and I took it by the edges. The image was black and white, a baby girl wearing a frilly dress that could have been any light color, with only a bit of hair and a small curl on top of her head. She sat on a blanket in sand, yet one couldn't see the water, as the picture had been taken while standing up and looking down at the baby. This child looked up at the camera and smiled a large, toothless grin.

"Me?" I asked, recognizing the omnipresent curl, which

appeared in every one of my childhood photos until I was two years old.

"Yes," Mother said. "On the beach in Seaboro. You were one year old."

I lifted a pile of photos off the coffee table and flipped through them in rapid succession, saw myself in varying poses with different people from age one to about twelve years old. Then abruptly there were no more photos, as if that were where life ended.

I laughed and looked at Mother. "Did you stop taking pictures when I hit puberty?"

She smiled. "No, those are in that pile over there."

"Oh," I said, but didn't reach for the second pile.

There was a small moment, tiny enough to slip through the hole in the screen door, to ask her why she divided my years into before and after twelve years old . . . and then it was gone before I found the words.

Mother stood, clapped her hands together. "Well, well. The afternoon has just slipped away from me. I'll finish this later—I must go get ready for Mildred's Botanical Society meeting." She kissed my cheek. "I'll see you Sunday afternoon for dinner, yes?"

I nodded while I held the photo of myself at one year old on the beach, a circle of glue still on the back side. "Can I take this?" I asked.

"Sure." She gestured toward the table. "As you can see, I have plenty to sort through and organize."

Mother walked away, and I called after her. She looked over her shoulder. "Yes?"

There was something I wanted to say, or ask, I wasn't sure what, but all that came out was, "Thanks."

"No problem. See you Sunday."

Then she was gone, and so was the moment and any questions I would ever have asked about the division of before and after my twelfth year. What also disappeared was my one-word definition of my mother, or any definition that made sense. A year later I was told she had rapidly progressing and incurable ovarian cancer. Two years later I stood at her grave site and wondered if she had ever finished the scrapbook.

These were the moments in my family that Forrest would never understand. He would not be able to define my dad's life or his time in Seaboro with an introductory paragraph or two in a literary article. I slammed my hand down on the steering wheel and took a sharp left onto Seaboro Run, where I knew the dirt road would take me to a path that led to the river, to a public-access dock five or six lots down from Ellie's house, away from the osprey nest that had overlooked the place where I lost Sam.

# THREE

> " 'Begin at the beginning,' the King said gravely,
> 'and go on till you come to the end: then stop.' "
> —LEWIS CARROLL,
> *Alice's Adventures in Wonderland*

Alone in the car, I rolled down the driver's-side window as I reached the end of the forked land leading to the slice of river where Ellie Loughlin once lived with her husband, Jim, and her sons, Boyd and Sam. One tine of the fork stretched to the marsh side of the river, the other tine to a strip of land reaching into the sound, almost all the way to a barrier island. It was as if the land almost succeeded in caressing the island, then curled back in on itself to create a river basin where the Loughlin home still stood, or at least I assumed it did.

I had never cared about or understood all the fuss over our best friends' Seaboro-drenched family name. Mother had wished she could answer the question, "Who are your people?" in the same way Jim and Ellie Loughlin answered: "Oh, from here, of course, so far back we're not even sure when they came." Mother had once hoped our name would carry the same weight as the Loughlins' in this small town, and I believe she mourned this loss as much as she did moving away. I suspected it was why she never came back to visit before she died five years ago. For her, visiting would be like pulling out old photographs of a passed loved one and not only weeping for their loss, but also grieving that the faded photo couldn't capture their essence, bring them back to touch.

But this was only a guess on my part, as my parents never discussed the move after it happened. Not once. And now I would have to discuss it with Forrest.

A sage-blue thread of water came into view: the river. A low thrumming began in my stomach and moved outward to the tips of my hands, my feet, between my legs. I recognized this vibration—fear. I would do this for Dad—scatter the ashes, then go home, lay my head on Thurman's shoulder, and exhale.

I parked the car at the edge of the road, stared at a barn with a red door in front of me—the last place I had slept in Seaboro. I shivered and shoved the memory away, which was about as effective as trying to push smoke out of the air.

Now I knew why Mother never returned. It was difficult to avoid memories in another setting, but nearly impossible when you were standing on the ground where the events had occurred.

Why would Dad ask me to do this? Clearly he'd gone overboard with his theory that life was an epic journey; now he was subjecting his daughter to it.

These betraying thoughts about Dad made me nauseous. He must, just must have had good reasons.

I took a long, deep breath and stepped out of the car. I wondered if Ellie still lived a few lots up from here with the osprey nest next to her dock, if Alice and Mack McPherson still owned the house behind me. But these were dull wonderings that merely allowed me to avoid the sight of the water, the life-taking water, thoughts that protected me from the outside world like thick cotton padding.

Crushed under my feet, the pine needles released an aroma so sweet I felt the sting of tears. I took the urn containing Dad's ashes from the backseat and walked toward the public-access path that I knew led between the barn and Alice's old house down to the town dock. Surely Alice was gone now, yet I hadn't even said good-bye to her before I moved. Regret rose.

I turned toward the old path, now overgrown; the magnolia tree was larger, the hemlock taller and wider, the palmettos shedding and craggy. I didn't know why I'd thought that everything here would be frozen in time, that just because I left this place it would stay as it was. It must be some type of self-centered adolescent belief that life continues only when we are inside it. Unfortunately I had taken this belief with me, so I was stunned by the changes that indicated the passage of time. Large swaths of time.

I stepped around the old cedar tree where my best friend, Piper, had whittled our names and *BFF*—for Best Friends Forever—with Boyd's pocketknife. I circled the tree, but couldn't find the carvings, then walked down the path alongside of the barn and allowed only the immediate feelings to intrude into my thoughts: the brush of a palm frond, the soft earth under my feet, the wet heat pressing down on top of my head.

The dock came into faded view like an old watercolor, ancient and wind-whipped. It looked as if not one board had been replaced in the eighteen years I'd been gone. After pressing on each board for safety, I walked to the far end over the water and sat on the edge of the dock, feet dangling over the tumultuous moving tide. A numbness spread over me, and I was grateful for its gift.

I ran my finger over the top of the iron urn, around the lid. The river moved so fast I knew it was a retreating tide. The next day the tide would flow out about an hour later than right then. Fragments of oyster shell mounds rose from the water like round-backed dolphins. I thought how oyster season had closed in mid-April. These facts of tide and season returned to me, although I hadn't thought of them in years.

The summer I left Seaboro was the season my hips loosened, as though rubber bands had been attached to my bones; the cartilage softened, and I moved in a tempting walk that felt good to me. Seaboro had been mud-thick with humidity and the sultry atmosphere of change. I had felt transformation approaching my life in my swinging walk, in the sweat behind my neck and knees, in the damp sheets that woke me in the middle of the night, heavy as winter wool. Later I realized that the expectation was merely the knowledge of leaving that rested in me unaware.

My Seaboro home had been situated in the hub of the town, as if it were dropped in the middle of a puff of cotton. Or at least, that was how I liked to think of it. We were protected in the center, but Mother hated that we weren't on the water—like the Loughlin family. She was obsessed with water-view homes, and I overheard at least a dozen fights between my parents about moving to the river. But we never did.

I also didn't care that "our people" weren't from Seaboro, but from the base of the South Carolina mountains, where both sets of my grandparents lived, where they'd lived since their Presbyterian Scots-Irish ancestors called "hillbillies" had first arrived. These were the basic facts I understood, but my life was centered on the river, with its changing tides.

My mother, Margaret, had met my father, Grayson, in high school, where they'd vowed together to leave the university-dominated town and build a life by the sea. I,

solely, had ruined their plans when I'd forced them to abandon the life they'd dreamed of and planned for, caused them
to return to the white-columned university and mountain-
based small town. I soothed myself with the thought that
they could have chosen another sea, another coast, but they
had not; they had chosen to return to their origins.

When Dad was working on his thesis for his doctor-
ate degree, he was recruited to run the English division for
all the high schools in Setter County, where Seaboro was
located. He agreed to the job if he could teach at least one
class at the local high school and live in Seaboro; the county
had agreed.

I was born exactly—my mother always used the word
*exactly*—nine months after they moved here. During my
birth, Mother tore so badly as to almost die, and the doc-
tors removed any chance of her bearing more children. After
hearing this from her, I forever understood that I was more
than the sum of my parts, more than the green eyes and curly
hair, more than a petite stature and polite manners. I was
also the child who had ripped the womb from my very own
mother. I understood that I must live up to my own potential, but also the potential of all the children I had deprived
Mother of having: I must make up for them too.

Knowing you have to do something and then doing it
are two completely different things. I had never figured out
how to be everything and more for Mother, or anyone else,
for that matter. This sin of mine and our return to the moun-

tains were all she could ever tolerate from me, and although she was never cruel to me during my teen years in Cedar Valley, her turning away was as painful as outright cruelty.

I was lost in these remembrances when the dock shifted to the left; I grabbed onto the moss-slippery edge as a strawberry-blond-haired woman settled down beside me. I scooted over, covered the urn. "Excuse me," I said.

The woman laughed, and then a giggle bubbled up from somewhere inside me, where I'd thought I'd stopped giggling: Piper—my childhood best friend. I knew her immediately with a quick roll of my heart. Years unwound. . . .

She threw her arms around me and I grasped the urn tighter.

"Oh, Lordy, it is you, Cappy." Her voice shook.

I was too stunned to hug her back, but she didn't seem to notice.

She released me, wiped tears from her eyes. "I can't believe you're here." She touched the side of my face, as if she needed proof I was real. "God, how I've missed you."

I would have grabbed Piper's hand, but I was afraid to let go of the urn, frightened that it would fall into the river. "It is really good to see you too," I said. "Wow, this is crazy— look at you here."

She laughed. "No, look at you here."

Piper was still cute in that sun-kissed way she had had eighteen years ago. Her hair was longer, flowing down her back in streaked waves. I realized she looked younger than I did, in her dress and style more than in her physical appearance. "You look great," I said.

"Thanks, and of course so do you. Oh, Cappy, how are you? Where do you live? What do you do? How many kids do you have? And . . . why are you here, on the end of this dock holding that vase?"

"Whoa," I said, "which question first?"

"I'm nosy—so the vase first."

"It's an urn."

She pushed her curls from her face. "Who?" she whispered.

"Dad."

She bit her lower lip. "I should've known he would be the only one who would bring you back."

Something round and whole surrounded Piper in unspoken words. "Say it." I touched her arm.

She bit her lower lip. "Say what?"

"Whatever it is that you didn't just say."

Her cat eyes went wide and full, her pupils large enough to almost fill the green. "I knew your dad was the only one who would ever make you come back. I saw him last year, at the courthouse, and asked him why you weren't with him. He told me he would bring you someday. I didn't know that he meant . . ." She turned away, then back to touch the urn. "I didn't know he meant like this. . . ."

"You saw him?" I took in a breath, glanced backward as if he might be watching. If Dad was capable of returning to this memory-soaked place without my knowledge, it seemed just as likely that he could still be alive. "What was he . . . doing when you saw him?"

"It was just for a minute. He was in the art exhibit room at the courthouse, and I was a chaperone for my son's field trip, so I didn't get to talk to him except for a minute."

"The art exhibit." A sense of unreality wrapped me in prickly heat. What was this? Some type of alternate universe Dad had lived in while I went about my daily business at the base of the mountains?

She nodded.

"Did you ever see him down here?" I patted the dock.

"At the river? No. I only saw him that once . . . why?"

"This is where he wants me to . . . toss his ashes."

"Oh," she said, and covered her mouth with her hand.

"He wants to stay right here . . . right here." I glanced around the river, back toward the road and empty lawns, and remembered the first of the three questions Forrest had asked me the night before: *What do you want to be doing when you die?* And yet I didn't think of my own answer, or even Dad's answer. There at the edge of the dock, I thought of Sam and his howling, empty, wordless answer.

My throat swelled, and I turned to the solid, real world of Piper. "How did you know I was here?" I asked. "This is so . . . weird that you just showed up."

"Well, it's not that weird." Piper waved toward the house behind us. "Alice saw you from her window and called me."

"Alice?"

"Yep . . ."

"What is she now, a hundred years old?"

"Something like that. But she knew who you were right away."

"Oh, God, I forgot what it was like to live here. I can't believe she knew who I was."

"She saw you almost every day of your whole life . . . until you moved."

"I guess so." I groaned. "I just wanted to get in, get out without anyone seeing me."

Piper twisted her hair behind her. "How long are you staying in town?"

"I have reservations at the B & B for just tonight. I'll leave tomorrow."

"Give yourself a couple days, old friend."

I shook my head when a cacophony of boy voices roiled across the lawn, hollering in that visceral way of children running at full blast—all day. For a brief second I thought it might be Boyd or Sam—Ellie's boys. Of course, I knew that couldn't be true, and maybe I had lost my mind and there was no noise at all.

Then the boys tumbled over the grass like puppies—three of them so entangled and boisterous that I released a laugh.

"Mama," the oldest-looking child yelled, pushed away a smaller one who was trying to cover his mouth. "Zach broke one of those little white glass girls that sits on Ms. Alice's table. It went everywhere—like a gazillion pieces of broken stuff on her floors. Ooh . . . she's so mad I thought she was gonna keel over right there—"

Piper held up her hand. The boys froze; words ceased. We stood and walked to the boys on the grassy area at the end of the dock. I placed the urn in a safe nest of pinestraw against an oak tree.

"Joe, Tyler, and Zach Barber," Piper said. "Stop now. Return to the car and wait for me. You will probably be grounded for at least the rest of your pitiful lives. Now go."

"Yes, ma'am," the littlest one said, then leaned in to mutter, in the way that young children do when they don't really know how to whisper, "Who is that pretty lady with the vase?"

Piper released an exasperated sigh and looked at me. "Do you have boys?"

"No . . . but yours are adorable." I bent down to the kids. "Hi, I'm Catherine Leary," I said to them.

"She was my best friend when I was your age." Piper tapped the oldest on the head.

"Oh," they all said in offbeat voices.

The middle child—a towhead with large olive eyes—squealed, lifted a turtle from the ground. "Mom . . . look, a turtle."

All three boys gathered in a semicircle to touch the shell.

"Put it down, Zach."

"Hey, Mom," said the oldest—Joe, I thought. "Did you know turtles can breathe out of their butts?"

Explosive laughter emanated from all three boys, and Piper groaned. "Go. To. The. Car," she said.

The oldest held up his hand as though he wanted to be called on in a classroom. "Mom, can I please go check on the osprey nest while the idiots go to the car?"

Piper flicked him lightly on the head. "Do not call your brothers names . . . and yes, go check, and I'll pick you up at the end of the road."

They all ran while the youngest ineffectually punched the oldest, who then grabbed the little one's head and said, "You know what? Your head has an amazing resemblance to your butt."

Piper dropped her head into her hands. "I'm sorry."

"No need," I said. "I just learned something new about turtles." I waved toward the bend in the river. "Is there really *still* an osprey nest up there?"

She squinted, then opened her eyes wide. "That's right. It was there when you were here. Well . . . yes, it's still there, or was there. I guess these particular ospreys have been returning to the nest for twenty years or so, but a while ago, the tree finally fell down. The mama bird was circling for weeks, so Joe started a project at school, raised enough money to erect a platform for a new nest."

I looked off to the horizon where river, land, and sky

blurred into a fuzzy line. "I remember . . . they return to nest every year, and if even a little bit, a small piece of the nest remains, they'll stay. God, why do I remember these weird factoids?"

Piper laughed. "Well, I guess there was enough of her home left when the tree fell that she hasn't given up on staying, so Joe is determined to hurry and get that platform up before she changes her mind and leaves. He's recruited every man in town to help erect the thing tomorrow." She placed her palm over her heart. "As crazy as he is, I'm proud of him. He's been obsessed with making sure that now that the bird has returned, she'll get her home back. I swear he's gonna be a vet."

"Good kid." I rubbed my neck.

Piper touched my arm. "Listen, I have to apologize to Ms. Alice and get these boys home. Can I stop by and see you tonight at the B & B?" She pouted, then added, "Please?"

I meant to say no, I really did, but I said yes when I looked into her eyes. Then I asked, "Is Ellie still there?" I waved toward the end of the land. "In the same house?"

She nodded. "Yes, but you do know . . . she has Alzheimer's, right?"

"God, no. I didn't know that."

"It started a couple of years ago. One time I found her sitting on Morgan's Grocery's front steps with a bag of food, and she had no idea where she was. It's gotten a lot worse the past year. She has a live-in, and Boyd comes to visit a lot . . . but it's really sad. Everyone loves her so much."

"I know," I said, and it was truer than anything I'd heard in a long time: Everyone loved Ellie.

# FOUR

*"There is always one moment in childhood*
*when the door opens and lets the future in."*
—GRAHAM GREENE,
*The Power and the Glory*

*I* wanted to prove I was no longer a gawky child who stumbled with untamed mouth and curls, but when I drove up the palmetto-lined driveway to Ellie's house, even I wasn't sure it was true. As much as I wanted to toss Dad's ashes and leave, I also felt betrayed by what Forrest and then Piper had told me about Dad having returned to this place. Now I had to know why he'd been coming. I felt he owed me an explanation before I fulfilled his wish. Ellie Loughlin would know.

She was a woman I didn't want to share with Forrest; he

didn't need to meet her, ask her questions, and probe into the darker corners of what had once been a light-filled room. Ellie was the one person in my life who had made me believe I was truly and utterly loved.

Mother had loved me, but much was expected in return. Ellie Loughlin . . . God, she gave love with all of herself: no conditions, no limits. As her wild house and garden spread down to the river, so her heart reached mine. Boyd and Sam were her sons, but I was her girl. Ellie was the one who started calling me Cappy, her version of how one-year-old Sam said my name.

I had hated my full name: Catherine Carrington Leary, a formal name that had been my grandmother's; a name that, to me, had a grating sound of heritage and blood that were misplaced in me, because I was nothing like my mother.

The Loughlin house on the edge of the river was just a short bike ride from our home in the village center. Two homes: one family. I was never sure when the family friendship started—it was there since memory began for me. Somehow I knew that Ellie and Dad had met when she taught a painting class in the high school where Dad taught creative writing. Then Dad had met Jim, her husband, and they had instantly bonded over the fine art of fishing and crabbing in the narrow creeks behind Seaboro.

I also knew without being told that Daddy's gift of teaching and writing were highly valued, but that Mother's family money was what paid for the nicer things in our home.

Ellie's sons became the boys Daddy never had, his gentle manner and sense of humor filling a vacuum left when Jim traveled frequently for his job as the highway inspector for the state of South Carolina. Dad reveled in the mysteries of coastal life with Boyd as if Dad had always lived in Seaboro: fishing and also hunting in the deep forests where I believed Gullah spirits roamed at night and were apt to steal my very soul. I didn't begrudge Boyd these moments with my precious dad because that was when I had Ellie to myself as Sam napped or slept on the wide beach.

I valued times alone with Ellie more than I did the treasure Blackbeard was purported to have hidden on these islands. She told me that my green eyes were like raindrop circles reflecting a calm sea. I loved that idea that my eyes, my body were formed of the water, that the fluid motions of my body on the horses from Seaboro's stables, running against the wind, or my swimming against the tide, diving for the bottom of the river, were one with all that surrounded me. My eyes were proof of this; even my curly chestnut hair was like the kelp strewn on the beach after a storm, Ellie once told me. This image of myself was much more appealing than the one of my baby self ripping open my mother's womb.

Ellie and Mother were the antithesis of each other, and yet somehow together they made one complete mom for me. My own mother religiously adhered to the Southern etiquette handed down to her from generations of genteel women in white linen dresses who lived in the manicured homes of Cedar Valley. Mother believed I desperately needed to learn the ways and means of achieving the precarious balance between being a Southern girl, and a full-fledged woman. Ellie, who was actually from this sea world, loved nature and all that God tossed around us. Woven from the smooth ropes of the two women's individuality was a solid hammock of security in which I swayed through childhood.

Even our two houses conveyed the Leary and Loughlin differences. To the dismay of the town's elite, Ellie and Jim had decided to sell the family's antebellum home handed down for at least five generations. That some Yankees bought it for a vacation place furthered the town's outrage. Instead, soon after I was born, the Loughlins built a log house under Ellie's loving eye. She handpicked each log, window, door, and accessory. Pine from the cleared land was used for the floors and walls. The shingles were salvaged from Seaboro's cottage library, which had been torn down to make way for the new and improved library with its many pillars.

Our Leary house was a landmark building that stood as a showpiece of the Old South, while the Loughlins' rustic home seemed to have sprung from the land itself, at one with its surrounding marsh, sea, and sky.

On the first day of my last summer in Seaboro, the owl's call woke me early and I couldn't return to my damp sleep. The house had the absolute stillness of when Mother and Dad were still asleep and before our cook, Clara, came to roll the morning biscuits. I realized Ellie would be up—she was always up early—so I rolled from bed and slipped on the cutoff jeans and pink tube top I wore all that summer, then dropped a Nancy Drew book into my bike basket—I was never without a book, just in case there were empty moments to slip into a life that wasn't mine.

I knew the way to Ellie's house with my eyes closed. I need only be alert for a startled deer or a lazy toad. I'd heard the latter would give me warts if I squashed it beneath my flip-flops. My hair flew in curls that I had no need to tame. I grabbed my rusting pink banana-seat bike from the side shed and pedaled as fast as I could through the back alleys and over the dirt roads. The river was at ebb tide, and I saw the faint blur of the shrimp boats as the men cast their nets into the sound before I cut through the rice bog and over the footbridge to Ellie's stretch of packed crushed-shell road.

Her house was still and waiting. My breath alone seemed loud enough to awaken everyone; I had never known her house to be so mute. This could only mean something was wrong. I cut through the kitchen, trying to calm my breathing in the misplaced quiet. I should have known that the morning silence foreshadowed our ominous change but in reality I saw omens only in hindsight.

Ellie sat in her sunroom study, a room that defined her, one I never entered without permission. Pictures and cards were pinned to the wooden walls in no apparent order. Some were framed, others just tacked to the wood with pushpins.

A desk lamp with a faded-ochre chintz shade clashed with the bright floral chair in which Ellie sat. Her books, everywhere her books: on the shelves, floors, stacked on chairs. Only she knew the cataloging.

Her back was to me as she leaned over her pine desk with a thick black book of scribbled pages. She was writing, and her shoulders and back quivered in a stuttered movement. I understood something was wrong, but was unable to define what. I whispered her name as I released the breath I didn't realize I held. "Ellie . . ."

When she turned to me with tears on her face that she did not wipe away, I couldn't speak. Ellie—of beauty, joy, and love—had tears, which meant that I—of sheer gauze and little substance—would surely have more tears than I could imagine. I couldn't move; I couldn't breathe. I swore I heard the slight ripping of my own heart.

Then Ellie held her arms out to me and comfort poured in. I buried my head in her long blond hair, and took deep breaths to inhale the lavender soap she always bought in Savannah.

"What's wrong, Ellie?" I whispered. I knew it must be terrible, so I closed my eyes and waited; I would be brave.

"Oh, Cappy, dear. Nothing is wrong. Sometimes my heart is so full that it comes out . . . on paper and in tears." Her laugh was soft, like rain falling. "I promise, I'm fine." She laid her cheek against mine, and I realized that my own tears mixed with hers. She moved her face so we were forehead to forehead. "Look at me; I'm perfectly fine. It's just the morning that brings me to tears sometimes." Ellie let go and wiped my face; she smiled.

I nodded, but was silent.

"Have you eaten breakfast? You're up so early," she said.

"I woke up and couldn't go back to sleep . . . I thought you'd be up."

"Let's go in the kitchen and wait for the lazy boys. I'll cook us some pancakes and we can watch the rest of the morning arrive. Me and you on the first day of summer vacation."

So we sat on her back porch and ate pancakes with too much syrup—just the way we liked them—and the waters of my life once again sloshed over and soothed me. I was Ellie's and she was mine. We talked of the heart and all it could hold, and watched morning come in waves over the salt marshes.

I went home that night and watched Mother perform her nightly ritual with cleansing lotions, creams, and tangled hairnets, which tamed the Carrington curls on her head. She sat at her antique vanity, a cherry-wood original that I was to never touch "until you are twenty-one years old." Silver brushes, bottles, mirrors, and fragile accoutrements of beauty lined the lace-covered surface. I had used some of Mother's perfume once, and when she went to get ready for bed that night, she'd known that the bottle had been touched, moved. I was made to understand, "in no uncertain terms, young lady," that I was never to touch her things again. I didn't want to anyway—the perfume had smelled like Grandmother's bedroom.

"Mother," I said, "do you ever cry, you know . . . just because your heart is too full?" I had to know if this was something all women did, like getting your period or watching coarse hair appear on translucent skin.

Mother looked at me sideways as she rubbed thick white cream into her face with circular motions. "No, Catherine. No. Now why would I do that? Sure, I cry when something sad happens. But I don't understand exactly what you're asking." She finished her nightly offerings to the gods of youth and turned to me. "Catherine, look around you. Look at your life, your family, and your home. What in God's name could there possibly be to cry about? It would be an insult to Him, to what He has given us, to cry about it. We should rejoice and say thank you and be appreciative for what we have when so many have so little."

For an instant I saw the beatings of Mother's heart, and I wondered how it sent blood to body and limb when its small, though perfectly formed chambers had room for so little. I went to bed and prayed for a bigger heart than my mother had, and then, as I drifted into the soaked sleep of that summer, begged forgiveness for making such a terrible request.

All these years later, I sat in the car in Ellie's driveway and listened for a note, maybe even a full song of my memories of her to return. I couldn't seem to move toward the front porch because in some deep place I wanted to keep only the good memories, not tarnish those sterling pictures with reality. The car's air conditioner spit lukewarm air out of the vents, and sweat dripped down my back. I climbed out of the car and walked up to Ellie's front porch, then stood there as if I were taking inventory: yes, the porch boards were still painted white; yes, the roof was painted haint blue, casting an oceanic hue over the rockers and wicker tables. Yes, the shutter on the right side hung slightly crooked. All this was so familiar that I expected to look down and see my pink flip-flops with the plastic daisies pasted on the toe straps, or hear Boyd holler across the yard to hurry up or we'd miss the tide.

Would I recognize Ellie when all I knew of her was what I remembered as a child, an essence of what I could only then call *pretty*? I knew as an adult it would have been better to say elegant. Back then, she rarely wore makeup, and she floated more than moved. I knew these were childhood memories, faded at the edges, cracked on the interior, but they were what I had of Ellie.

Jim had died several years after we moved, in a boating accident. That was all I was ever told, and only in a brief mention before bed one night during my junior year in high school.

I shook my head, lifted my hand to knock on the front door, but before my hand reached wood, a woman opened it. She was taller than me by at least a foot; her hair swirled around her head in the quintessential once-a-week hairdo that always reminded me of meringue on top of key lime pie. She started, and then smiled at me. There was a large smudge of red lipstick across her front teeth.

"Well, hello, there," she said. "You scared the wee devil out of me."

"Sorry," I said, attempted to stand taller. "I've come to see Ellie Loughlin. Is she here?"

The woman squinted at me. "You look awfully familiar, dear. Do I know you?"

I shrugged, but before I could speak she said, "Oh, my. Oh, my, my. You are Catherine Leary."

I nodded.

She placed her hands on either side of her face and shook her head back and forth. "How wonderful to have you back in town. Ellie will be so thrilled to see you." Then her mouth dropped into a frown. "That is"—she leaned closer to me—"if she recognizes you. She has some . . . days that are better than others."

I nodded again; I hadn't said a word, and this woman was still talking to me.

"We all take turns bringing her dinner—tonight was my turn. You see, they've shut off her oven and stove; she thinks they're broken. We're so afraid she'll burn the place down. Now she has a live-in, but . . ." The woman stopped. "I'm babbling, aren't I?" She threw her hands above her head.

"No." I laughed. "Thanks for the warning. Is she . . . awake?"

"Yes, her nurse is in there with her . . . just go in. I hope . . . I mean, I really hope she recognizes you. It will make her heart so happy to see you. You know, she talks about you sometimes."

I did not want to know what Ellie said about me in her fogged state; maybe something about finding Sam, or running faster, or . . .

At my silence, the woman touched her hair. "Well, then, good luck, Catherine."

"Yes, ma'am." I smiled, slipped with ease into the role of the cute, sweet daughter of Margaret and Grayson Leary.

"I'm sorry about your father. I read about it in the local paper months ago. I actually meant to send you a note. . . ." She smiled, patted my arm as if I were still a child.

"Oh, well, thank you." I looked away, stumbled over my words while my heart pounded against my chest so hard I thought she could see it through my pale blue linen shirt.

She stared at me for a moment longer than was comfortable. "Well, it sure is sweet of you to come. Ellie loved you so."

The woman tottered off in her high heels to a car parked under a magnolia tree. Who was she? The old librarian, a neighbor, my second-grade teacher? My arms and legs felt separate from me, and I watched as if I weren't part of the scene. It was a technique I had been using my entire life—

talking and functioning without ever noticing the whole picture, just the particulars: the smudge of lipstick, how many steps to the front door, what color dress someone was wearing.

The woman had left the door ajar, and I entered the house, called in a soft voice, "Hello . . . hello?"

A young blonde in medical scrubs came around the corner. Her hair was pulled into a ponytail, and she held a dirty plate in one hand and a glass of what looked like the remains of milk in the other.

"Hi, I'm Catherine Leary," I said. "I've come to visit Ellie—I'm an old family friend."

She nodded toward the living room. "She's in there by the fireplace. She just finished eating . . . she might be asleep. You can check."

I stepped with quiet care toward the large room that I knew held a brick fireplace massive enough to crawl into. It was a room that had once encompassed everything I loved about this house and about Ellie: masses of artwork, windows open to nature, several rustic game tables. I closed my eyes. I wanted this room to be the same, and I prepared myself for a great change in Ellie.

I stepped into the room and a quiver began below my breast. It was similar to the room I remembered; it smelled the same. The chairs and couches had been moved around, a few added, a few gone, but the essence remained.

A lounge chair stretched beside the fireplace, its back to

me so all I saw were two tiny slippered feet dangling from the end. I peeked around the chair to see a small woman with silver-gray hair pulled off her face, her eyes closed, soft puffs of air coming from her lips. Ellie was as delicate as I remembered, her features relaxed in sleep.

I backed toward the front stairwell, grasped the end of the banister, and ran my hand across the finial that had been added after the house was built. I remembered when Ellie had found one she loved in a junk shop in Charleston, the butter yellow paint peeling to reveal a pale green finish beneath, neither color matching the stained oak banister.

The living room spread across the rear of the house and led into Ellie's small sunroom. The mismatched, large, and comfortable furniture sprawled about the room in random patterns. Flowered chairs cuddled up next to gingham couches. Sheer curtains hung to the floor. Ellie had never seen a reason to cover the windows with anything more, blocking the view of her fields to the left. She had said the view was better than any oil painting or framed artwork. The light shifting, colors changing, and wildlife revealing itself could not be improved upon by any brushstroke. She was perpetually admiring God's handiwork and telling us to notice it too.

The brick fireplace dominated the room; Sam had been small enough to walk into it without touching the top of his head. Solid and wide, the hearth held wood in the winter and often, in the spring and summer, a plant or flower arrangement. There was no TV to demand our attention. I remembered only checkers, cards, books, kids, and Ellie.

I walked to the end of the room, touching the furniture. The wide plank floors, iron nails embedded in the edges, had grown darker. Worn patches showed the paler shade they had been. Small, randomly placed rugs covered the areas of highest traffic.

I walked to the threshold of Ellie's sunroom. A few of the pictures were different, but otherwise the room was unchanged, and I entered with a slight nag of betrayal: I had *not* asked permission. I picked up a tarnished silver frame containing a picture of Boyd and me at the top of the old live oak that had stood behind the house. Forbidden to climb the branches, as the tree was too old and might crack under our weight, we had dared each other until neither could stand it. We climbed to its highest point before Ellie came out and took this picture, right before grounding us for a week.

I lifted an ornate wooden picture frame and took a sharp breath. Dad held a one-year-old Sam above his head. A slim blue river traced a line behind their bodies. Dad seemed unaware of his photo being taken, and his eyes were locked with Sam's. Dad's wavy, sun-streaked hair flashed against the camera lens, leaving a round star of light between their faces. I looked away, as if the picture were an intimate photo of a man and woman in an embrace. I placed it exactly where I'd found it.

I walked back into the living room and glanced at the

various artwork scattered around the room in mismatched frames and done in many mediums.

"Ellie?" I stepped around the lounge chair.

She looked up, and it required everything in me not to drop to my knees and release the words I'd long since stored in a place I wasn't even sure I could find. I'd once composed long speeches and apologies, agonizing words of regret that I'd never said or sent to her.

She stared at me with watery blue eyes. She wore a white terry-cloth robe, and her face was soft with wrinkles that had been only hinted at when I knew her. "May I help you?" she said, touched the edge of her collar, pulled at a loose thread.

I sat on the chair next to her, grasped one of her hands. She pulled away from me.

The nurse came up behind me. "Sometimes she knows people, but today has been a bad day. Don't take it personally."

I wanted to tell this nurse that Ellie had probably forgotten me long before the Alzheimer's, long before this day, made a conscious, concerted effort to forget.

I nodded at the nurse, but turned back to Ellie. If I allowed it, my heart would break right there, in Ellie's living room, in front of the fireplace. It'd break and I would never be able to find the pieces to put it back together.

I would do only what I'd come to do. "Ellie, it's me, Catherine Leary. I've come to say hello. . . ."

She stared at me, then brought her hand up to cover

her mouth. I'd wanted to ask if Dad had been there, but her face stopped all my questions. She sat still like that for a long moment, and I prepared to stand and leave. This was a foolish idea—a bad idea about to get worse. Then I saw her hand shake, and the movement grew until it spread down her arm.

"Cappy?" Her voice came from behind her hand, and only I would know what she had just said, so quiet, so distorted was the word. But I'd heard her say my name so many times I would've known it muffled or clear.

"Yes," I whispered.

"Does your mother know you've come early for the oyster roast? She hates when you come without telling her. And I haven't even told her I invited the Mercer family. Oh, will you go get the green beans from the kitchen? We can break them outside while the boys . . ."

I closed my eyes. She knew me, but in her mind I was eleven years old and early for the oyster roast in their backyard. I couldn't possibly ask if Dad had been to visit in present time.

I was ill prepared for this; I didn't know what one was supposed to do with confused patients—did you ground them in reality or go along with them? I glanced around for the nurse, but she was gone.

"Ellie . . . I'm grown now. Mother is gone. . . ."

She rubbed her face, pulled her robe tighter against her chest. "Of course. Of course." Then she reached for my hands. "Forgive me; an old lady gets confused. By the way, have you seen Sam? I think he went upstairs to get his kite."

"What?"

"Sam, have you seen him?"

Cold air forced its way into my chest, through my bloodstream. I couldn't move or speak. I stared at Ellie and it started to happen—my heart was breaking. I couldn't stop it—and it maimed like sharp glass.

Then I ran.

It was all I knew to do.

I passed the nurse in the hall; I thought I even bumped into her as I bounced through the front door and to my car in a desperate need to escape the present. If only I could return to that oyster roast with Ellie. It was the fall of my eleventh year on the dock behind Ellie and Jim's house.

Ellie had set the picnic table in her broad backyard with bright blue mismatched dishes, Mason jars full of wildflowers and honeysuckle. I plucked the honeysuckle from the vases to suck the sweet juice from the stems; Mother hollered at me not to touch the centerpieces. Paper lanterns hung from the live oak trees and flickered in the evening like fireflies.

I'd noticed there were eleven place settings and only seven of us. I asked Ellie why, and she told me that when she'd been at the fish market buying the oysters, she'd invited the Mercer family, who had been counting out their pennies to pay for some fresh vegetables. I liked the Mercer boys—they were loud and funny—but just as I was about to say this, Mother's smile straightened into a thin line, and she turned away. I knew the look: disapproval.

Dad, Jim, and Mr. Mercer set up the metal sheet on top of the fire pit to roast the oysters, the sweet smell of burning wood and roasting shellfish filled the backyard. Ellie sat on a red wooden chair breaking off the ends of the green beans and throwing them into a bowl; she laughed with Mrs. Mercer, who showed Ellie how to fix a hole in a shrimp cast net. Mr. Mercer crafted handmade cast nets—a business that had become almost obsolete. Boyd, the Mercer boys, and I cast fishing lines off the dock and made bets about who would catch the biggest fish first. Sam slept at Ellie's feet in a baby chair.

Mother was inside the Loughlin house. When I strained my neck, I could see her shadow crossing the kitchen window.

Soon Ellie dropped the green beans into the bowl without finishing them, and wound her hands in the net with Mrs. Mercer, walked out onto the dock. Mr. Mercer demonstrated a trick he knew for throwing the perfect, round cast net into the river to catch shrimp and baitfish.

Boyd was the first one to attempt the new wrist twist Mr. Mercer taught us. The mesh flew through the air with the small metal weights at the edge, then boomeranged backward, hit Boyd in the gut, and wrapped around his legs. Boyd hollered, backed away from the net, tripped and fell into the river, leaving the net, and the rest of us on the dock laughing so hard I had to sit down.

When Boyd came up he shook his head so that water flew all over me; then he dared me to try to do better than him. My cast ended up in an odd bent oval shape, but I did pull up a handful of baitfish, which Boyd grabbed and tossed in a bucket for further fishing. Then he punched me in the arm. "Beginner's luck," he said.

"No, just talent." I handed the net to Ellie.

She held up her hands. "No. I'll ruin the beautiful handiwork."

"Come on," Mrs. Mercer said. "Try it. Rob makes a perfectly balanced net; it's easy."

Smoke from the oyster roast blew over the dock with a quick breeze, and we all glanced at Dad and Jim. Jim hollered, "Go ahead, darling. Try it."

Ellie shrugged her shoulders, her hair blew in the breeze across her face, and she slipped her sunglasses to the top of her head, grabbed the net, and talked herself through Mr. Mercer's instructions until the final throw. When she cast the round net over the water we all watched in awe as it formed a circle of glistening water drops over the river, hovered, then dropped into the water in one concentric splash.

"Oh, oh . . ." she hollered. "Now what?"

Mr. Mercer ran to her side, yanked the cords, and pulled the net up with her. "Jim," he hollered over his shoulder, "your wife just caught enough crab and shrimp to feed the masses."

Jim and Dad ran onto the dock and we all jumped,

hollered, and scooped up the shrimp and menhaden that Ellie dropped out of the net and onto the dock. We threw the shrimp into a cooler of ice at the end of the dock and tried to return the baitfish to the water. Blue crabs skittered across the dock as Boyd tried to catch them and throw them into the cooler, but one escaped his grasp and ran sideways as they do, straight for my bare feet. I did a little jig to keep the claws from finding my toes, but I failed. This particular blue crab grabbed onto the pinkie toe of my right foot and pinched for his life.

I hopped around on my good foot, screaming in pain and not knowing how to get the crab off. I made it to the grass, where Ellie sat me down, then pried the crab from my foot and threw it in the cooler. "Thanks for catching the biggest one, Cappy. It's all yours for dinner," she said, knowing crab was my favorite.

I picked my foot up in the air, totally sure my pinkie toe was gone and in the cooler with the crab. But my toe remained unharmed except for a pinch mark below the joint. I looked at Ellie and wanted to cry, but laughter came instead. And there we were, all ten of us, laughing with shrimp, crab, and fish floundering on the dock when Mother came out onto the lawn and stood with her hands on her hips. "What is going on?"

"Oh, Mother," I said. "You should've seen it. Ellie threw the net in a perfect cast and caught a billion shrimp and crab."

Mother walked toward us, leaned over the cooler, then squinted at me. I leaned forward and stared inside the cooler at approximately ten shrimp and two crabs. "Well," I said, "it seemed like more."

And the laughter came again, with smoke rising from the metal sheet of frying oysters, with the sweet smell of honeysuckle in the warmth of the setting sun.

Mother shook her head.

"Where were you?" Mrs. Mercer asked Mother. "You missed it: Boyd fell in, and Cappy threw a great cast."

Mother stared at Mrs. Mercer for an uncomfortable moment, then spoke in measured words. "There was a potato salad to prepare, iced tea to make, a pie that needed to come out of the oven."

Mrs. Mercer smiled. "Can I help at all?"

"No," Mother said. "It's all done now." And she turned and walked back toward the house.

Later that evening, on the drive home, I sat in the backseat and listened to Mother and Dad's hushed, hurried conversation in the front seat. I don't remember what the exact words were, but the thrust was how Mother always did all the work while everyone else had fun, and Dad emphasized that no one wanted or needed a fancy potato salad or peach pie, that everyone was perfectly happy with sliced tomatoes and fresh peaches, that Mother didn't have to turn everything into a production. The warm, humid air turned frigid inside the car from more than just the humming air conditioner, and I leaned back on the seat and smiled as I thought how I wanted to fly above the water just like that net thrown from Ellie's hands.

I needed a large dose of present time, of my real life. Back inside my car, I grabbed the cell phone to call Thurman. His voice mail picked up, and I left another message to please call me.

I was at the graveyard entrance before I knew I'd driven there, before I understood where I had gone and why. I drove down an unmarked gravel road ending at a cemetery used for those Mother called "the real Seaboro": those who were from here, had long ago settled, were threads in the town's sturdy netting, from Gullah islanders to slave descendants to the founders of the town.

An iron fence skirted the yard and twisted down to the edge of the maritime forest, weeping its black paint for the dead. Fresh flowers and plastic ones, faded to clear, rested on tombstones littered with moss and pine needles. Small trinkets also scattered over the stones attested to the local Gullah tradition.

I walked toward the forked oak where I knew the Lough-lin family plot was located. The ground had a familiar cushiony feel.

Thick moss draped in sheets off the tree branches offered a serenity to Sam's final resting place. There were two marble stones, simple and small, with the etched dates for Jim and Sam. I could barely glance at the markings on the smaller grave: proof of a life lived in a small span of time, a life that still earned a dash between the dates.

It was only after I fell to the ground that I realized I'd carried Dad's urn out to the graveyard. And, for the first time, I wanted to cry for all that was lost—Dad, Mother, Sam, innocence—but I could not. When I reached for the feeling that would allow me to weep, I found only a hollowed-out place inside me that I had spent years emptying of any memory or emotion. What I had wished for myself at twelve years old—that I would not feel the pain of loss again—had finally come true.

# FIVE

*"Nature and books belong to the eyes that see them."*
—RALPH WALDO EMERSON

Seaboro Bed and Breakfast occupied a corner lot in front of the protected sand dunes. A square white sign leaning too far to the left was missing the E from the word *Bed,* and had a shrimp boat painted on the lower left. Prissy flowers spilled from planters and window boxes on the white clapboard house. A fishnet curtain hung on the front porthole window.

I grabbed my overnight bag from the trunk of the car and walked up the cobblestone walkway. Behind a pine desk situated in the middle of the large foyer stood a pencil-thin woman with her hair so tightly wrapped in a chignon that her eyes were pulled back. She punched something onto a keyboard. I made a small noise in the back of my throat before she looked up.

She nodded at me with a single movement of her head, like a puppet. "Hello, I'm Mrs. Hamilton; my husband and I own this B & B. May I help you?" Her gaze wandered down to my beige skirt, and then her eyes slanted sideways, as if she'd seen a spider or some repulsive detail.

I glanced down and saw graveyard mud smeared across the hemline. "Yes, I have a room reservation," I said, waved a scrap of paper on which I'd written the confirmation number.

She held out her hand, then read the paper as if it were of the utmost importance, furrowed her brow, made clicking noises with her tongue. "My, my. We thought you weren't coming until tomorrow."

I grabbed the paper from her hand, pointed to the dates. "This says my reservation starts tonight."

"I saw that," she said. "But that is not what is in my computer. Now, of course we have a room. You'll just have to wait a few minutes for me to get it ready."

She rang a little bell on the desk, beckoning forward a young woman in a white outfit who took tiny, fast steps into the foyer.

Mrs. Hamilton looked at me. "You may wait in the library if you'd like. You can leave your bag here." She looked away from me to the young woman. "Will you please show Ms. Leary into the library before you prepare her room?"

"Yes, ma'am," the girl said, and made a motion for me to follow her.

I tapped the front desk. "Has Forrest Anderson checked into his room?"

The woman nodded. "Yes, hours ago."

"So his room was ready?" I lifted my eyebrows.

She nodded. I made a groaning noise in the back of my throat and followed the young woman down the hall.

The dark-paneled library-turned-bar drew me in with a magnetic force. Books that looked as if they hadn't been touched in years wallpapered the room. A pang of sorrow stung me—surely the authors intended for their work to be more than decoration. I thought of all those books of my youth tattered and wet in my bicycle basket, piled haphazardly on my bedside table. These books were immaculate, but unloved. I turned to the bar: A framed sign declared that the bar was carved from a massive piece of oak cut from a tree in the back of the property after it had supported its last drape of Spanish moss. This remnant of tree now held the drinks and pretzels of travelers. A traveler—that's what I'd become. In Seaboro I'd never slept anywhere but in my own house, at Ellie's, or, in the last days, Alice's barn.

I sat down on a bar stool and rubbed at my face, which I could see in dim light in the warped back mirror, where there were shelves of crystal decanters lined up like neat soldiers. A martini would be good if a bartender made an appearance. I stood and walked to the book-lined wall, and ran my hands over the spines.

"Would you like something to eat or drink while you wait, ma'am?"

I startled, dropped a book, and turned to see a mirage of *The Old Man and the Sea*—a man who so closely resembled a sketch from a schoolbook about Ernest Hemingway that I was certain it was more intentional than coincidental. He had to be Mr. Hamilton, the proprietor. He'd aged as anyone would over eighteen years, his face as cragged and salt-aged as the bark of the cedar tree on the front walkway. I assumed that his shrimp boat was now as old and rusty as he was, and I wondered if he and his boat still provided all the shrimp for the annual boil on Charles Island. But I didn't ask—he might remember me if I started making small talk.

I leaned over, picked up the book, and placed it back on the shelf. "Yes, I'd like a vodka martini straight up, please. Three olives."

His bushy white eyebrows drew together in concern. "You sure you don't want anything to eat? We have a kitchen; my wife could make you a sandwich, some soup?"

"No, really, I'm good."

"Are you sure?"

"Okay, then throw in an extra olive." I smiled instead of explaining that I wasn't hungry, that the thick air of memory had so filled me, that I couldn't absorb any more than just being there afforded.

I turned away from Mr. Hamilton and slid into an old leather chair, which was worn to silk in places. I tipped off my shoes and curled my legs beneath me. I flipped open a book and hid behind its cover. Doubts about fulfilling Dad's wish consumed me. Since the moment I had left the mountain valley, I'd felt as though I'd been hooked to an oxygen tank with only two days' worth of air in it. I had to hurry, hurry, hurry and scatter his ashes, while at the same time I needed to breathe slowly and steadily so I wouldn't use up all the oxygen.

I leaned back in the chair when Mr. Hamilton appeared with my martini. I thanked him, and he informed me that my room was almost ready and the drink was on the house.

Across the room hung a collection of nautical sketches inside metal frames made from scraps of tin ceiling tiles. I rose and went closer, stared at four separate shrimp boats shown at various times of the day. There wasn't a signature on the bottom, but I recognized them as Ellie Loughlin's handiwork. I shivered as though someone had just turned the air conditioner on full blast.

I touched one of the sketches—a shrimp boat with the name *Blind Faith* painted on the side. Was this the real name of the boat, or one Ellie had made up, which would be just like her to do?

In those summer days she had taught me how to sketch to capture all the nature and joy around us, how the word *art* was inside the word *heart,* how including the details added to the big picture. She had given me large black sketchbooks, sharpened charcoal and pastels, and somehow magically known when each book was full, handing me another and saying, "Keep noticing the details, Cappy." And I did notice the details that summer: so many details, too many details. They came fast and furious: bird, dolphin, sunset, and landscape took on sharp, clearly delineated features. I painted the osprey nest behind Ellie's home from multiple angles, fascinated with the babies inside, with how the mother left and returned to the exact same nest with the same mate every single year.

When my heart couldn't hold all I felt, I rode horses along the edges of the river, faster than Eve, my horse trainer, deemed safe. Horseback riding at the town stables was an integral part of my lady-in-Seaboro training. I pretended only to tolerate it along with etiquette, piano, and dance lessons, but I loved the horses, loved Eve, and was concerned that if Mother knew how much I loved them, she would take them away from me. So I stalked off to the stables, feigning disinterest even as my heart lifted at the sight of the pasture.

I also ran to my neighbors, Alice and Mack, escaped to Alice's flowers and herbs, her wise and eccentric advice. Mack had a workshop in the barn where he constructed my dollhouse furniture and taught Boyd how to carve wood, educated him about the curve of the live oak branch that had once been valued for use as the hull of ships.

I sketched every tree and tabby ruin and shrimp boat I saw, felt their form take shape under my hand. I filled the hours I wasn't with my friends or Ellie by drawing and painting my surroundings. I didn't have the words to describe what I was seeing and feeling, but no one had to teach me how to draw—it just came naturally.

I set my sketches in glossy plastic frames, on which I spent my entire allowance at the five and dime. I wouldn't dare dent the plaster walls of our house with a nail or tack, so I lined the pictures up against the dresser and desk in my room. Mother actually had a carpenter hang the family's "official" artwork, so as not to ruin the walls of our fortress, as if the plaster itself mustn't be dented just as the lives of my parents mustn't be: It must all remain smooth, clean, unmarred.

One evening before one of Mother's dinner parties, I lay on my bed reading *Alice in Wonderland* as the dense and pungent scent of jasmine worked its way over my windowsill, and I made up a story about how my one true love would find me on a twilight evening. Sweat trickled between my budding breasts as I contemplated going to my parents' room, where the window air conditioner could make my teeth chatter if I turned the knob all the way to C. But Mother entered the room before I could get up; she began to gather my framed sketches into a pile.

I sat motionless on the antique coverlet of my four-poster rice bed. If I spoke or questioned my mother's actions, the pictures might be gone for good. Mother turned to me, rested her chin atop the rectangular pile of cheap frames. I knew that, out of respect, she must speak first.

"Darling, pull down your coverlet before you lie or sit on the bed. Your great-grandmother quilted that and we wouldn't want it to be ruined . . . body oils, you know."

I sat up and neatly folded the quilt into a square, as I'd been taught, and laid it on the end of the bed; my hands and tongue were slow with wondering what Mother intended to do with my art.

She twisted her chignon-adorned head to the left and right. "You cleaned your room quite well, honey. We will be having a tour of the house during the dinner party tonight, so I am going to put these pictures in your closet until the party is over. You may put them back where you wish afterward."

There was no question in her voice, no need for a response. "Yes, ma'am," I said.

Mother laid them in a neat pile on the whitewashed shelf of my organized closet, closed the door with the glass knob and turned back to me. I was incapable of comment. Clearly Mother was embarrassed by my art, did not want her friends to see the pictures. My own mother wasn't proud of me; I was good enough only in the things Mother contributed to me: my looks, my room, my clothes, my manners.

Then Mother reached up and pulled a green silk dress with an ivory satin collar from the top rod of the closet and laid it on the bed. "You know, it's not that I don't like the pictures. They are oh, so precious, and you are learning to draw so well, but when people tour the house they are looking at the antiques and furnishings." She kissed the top of my head. "This dress will be perfect for dinner tonight."

"Yes, ma'am."

Mother smiled at me. That "you understand, don't you?" smile. The one that made me agree for fear of disapproval. I wanted to say that I did not agree with anything: that the dress itched my neck and made my green eyes look the pukey color of pea soup. But I smiled and nodded. Later I would run to Ellie's house. Through the years, I had learned to keep disapproval at bay, but I satisfied my heart the moment I heard the door on Ellie's back porch door scrape across the entranceway.

"Mother," I said, "do I have to stay for the whole party? Can't I go to the Loughlins' tonight? No one will notice, and you'll be so busy."

Mother rubbed her forehead, as if I tested the end of her patience. "I don't understand why you want to run over to that house full of boys when there is a nice dinner party here tonight. Camilla is coming; her mom is serving at the party. You'll have someone to play with."

"Oooh gross, Mom. I don't like Camilla. She's strange, she hates me, and she's always lurking around Boyd."

"That is no way for a little lady to speak of a friend. We do not talk about whom we do or do not like. It is not polite."

I wanted to tell her I was not in any way a little lady, but all I said was, "Please?"

"Oh, Catherine . . . yes, yes. After you say hello to every-one, you may run over to Ellie's. Please remember to take off the dress: I'm sure you'll get something on it with those boys. Have Mr. Jim walk you home by nine thirty p.m. sharp."

It was a compromise that we had reached before: the expected in exchange for the wanted. It was a good bargain for me. After smiling and handing out puff pastries filled with shrimp to the social elite, I would spend the evening in the Loughlins' loud, raucous kitchen.

Summer came to an abrupt and heinous halt two days later, and I never did pull those framed sketches out of the closet.

I took a long sip of the martini Mr. Hamilton had brought me and wondered where those sketches were now, the boats and trees and ospreys and horses I'd set to paper. And I realized I didn't have anyone to ask—not one person would know. The best I could do was search the attic.

Despair threatened, like fingers running along my arm ready to grab me. Where was Forrest? But when I turned away from the shrimp boats I faced Piper, staring at me with an odd look on her face. She had a hand over her mouth and her eyes were at half-mast, as though she had just woken up.

"What's wrong?" I asked.

"You looked so . . . lost and sad." Piper moved toward me, hugged me. "I didn't want to interrupt you. . . ."

I pointed to the sketches. "Aren't those beautiful?"

Piper nodded. "Yes, they are." She touched my cheek. "I'm so glad you're here. I was so afraid that by the time I fed everyone . . . and put the kids to bed, that you'd be gone."

I held up both hands. "Nope, still here."

She pointed at my dirty skirt. "What happened?"

I attempted to rub at the moss and mud, but merely smeared it more. "I went to the graveyard," I said.

"Oh, are you okay?"

I was touched because I could see that she really cared. She didn't want a rhetorical answer, and she didn't deserve one.

"It's hard coming back here. . . ." I took a long sip of martini and sat back in the leather chair.

"So many people will be thrilled to see you."

I laughed, but it came out as more of a snort. "Yeah."

Piper raised her eyebrows. "Truly, they will."

Mr. Hamilton walked into the room. "Anything I can do for you ladies?"

"Where can I get one of those drinks?" Piper asked.

"And one more for me," I said.

Mr. Hamilton swept his hand toward the bar. "At your service."

Piper settled back in her chair and chatted with Mr. Hamilton until he served our drinks. She took a sip. "Hmm . . . I can't remember the last time I had a drink with a girlfriend."

I thought she might cry, but then she leaned toward me.

She wore jeans and a tank top, as though she were a teenager on her way to hang out in the parking lot of the Tastee-Freez. "Please tell me all about your life," she said.

"No," I said, "tell me about yours. Mine is boring."

"Oh, no, don't tell me that. Tell me all about your exciting life in a university town with friends and parties and—"

"Oh?" I said. "Okay, I'm single, still live in Cedar Valley, and I work for the university where Dad worked. I work for the media relations department—assigned to the Athletic Office."

"Which means?"

"I work with the coaches to schedule interviews, send out press releases, that kind of stuff. Boring, I'm sure, compared to your full life."

"Boyfriend? Love?"

I waved my hand through the air. "I've been dating the same guy for almost four years now. His name is Thurman— he's the basketball coach at Southern."

"I know who he is. Thurman Whittaker—basketball coach extraordinaire. They say he's poised to coach at UNC someday."

I shrugged. "I'm sure he'd love to hear that."

"Four years," she said. "You must really love him to date that long. I gave Parker an ultimatum long before that . . . I hate wasting time."

I stared at her for a moment. On some level I couldn't believe I was sitting in Seaboro having a drink with Piper, talking about my life, my boyfriend. "I guess it is a long time to *just* date. But every time I think about leaving him, he does another adorable thing. He swept me off my feet from the very beginning and somehow always knows the right thing to say or do to keep me around." I touched the circle of diamonds on my neck. "We have a crazy life with our jobs, but we figure it out. I'm content just as it is. So, tell me about your life."

"Well, you met my three wild boys—twelve, ten, and seven. I married Parker Barber . . . do you remember him?"

"Parker?" I laughed and touched her arm. "You had a crush on him in kindergarten. You kissed him behind the monkey bars in what . . . fifth grade? And got grounded from Mary-Lynn's birthday party. . . ."

Memories flooded in like a spring tide.

She nodded. "I was determined, wasn't I? Well, this goes under the category of 'Be careful what you wish for.' "

"Oh?"

She waved her hands in a curled-finger, dismissive gesture. "Not in a bad way . . . just now I have this entire family to take care of. I still adore him—it's just busy and crazy, and I'm exhausted ninety percent of the time." She glanced away, then back at me. "Are you still a major bookworm?"

I laughed and took a long swallow of the martini. "Oh, you think I'm not married because I'm a nerd? Reading my life away?"

"No . . . that's not what I meant. I am just trying so hard

to picture you in your life . . . and all I can see is the Cappy I knew here."

I stared off at the books lining the shelves in neat, color-coordinated rows. "No, I'm not so into reading anymore. The job is crazy and . . . Oh, enough of me."

Piper sat in silence for long moments, then released a deep breath. "Can't you just stay a few days? Come on, Cappy. I'll pawn the boys off on my neighbor and we can spend a whole day together. I'll take you to all our old haunts . . . we can talk."

"No," I said. The thought of staying sent me free-floating—maybe my oxygen was running out. Then the sensation passed and I was back in the chair talking to my once best friend.

She must have heard the resolution in my voice, because she turned away and didn't ask me again. We talked of old friends, of Seaboro gossip, and we laughed. The conversation wrapped around until she asked about Ellie.

"I went to see her today," I said.

"Did she recognize you?" Piper leaned toward me.

"I don't know," I said, ran my finger along the top of the martini glass.

"Really?"

And I remembered this about my best friend: You couldn't fool her, you could not lie to her and she always found the right word for any and every situation.

"She did—but I was eleven in her mind," I said, and I couldn't tell her that Ellie had asked for Sam.

"Yes, that happens with her. Boyd can sometimes get through the haze." Piper leaned back in her chair and stared up at the ceiling. "Jim never knew her like this."

"What really happened with Jim?" I asked. "Mother only told me he died in a boating accident."

"I don't think anyone really knows what happened to Jim except Jim. There are many theories: He ran out of gas and didn't have a radio; he passed out in the sun when the boat broke down. Or he killed himself . . . ." She bit her bottom lip as if to stop the remainder of this particular theory.

I finished it for her. "Because he lost his son."

"Well, nobody knows, really. Some campers found his body a couple weeks later on a barrier island. His boat was found a month later by a shrimp boat up in the Outer Banks. If Boyd or Ellie knows exactly what happened, they don't say either." She brushed the air with her hand as if to clear the subject away. "You know Boyd married Camilla and moved to Savannah—he has his own handmade boat company."

"Camilla? I remember her trying to catch Boyd since first grade. Wow—I never did know what happened to him."

"Remember when he was the golden boy, the one we all wanted?"

"I never wanted Boyd."

"Oh, how we forget, my friend. How we forget. You had a huge crush on him."

The pine floors moaned and a voice came into the room.

"Cappy once had a huge crush on someone? She doesn't do crush."

Piper and I both turned to Forrest standing in the door frame, leaning up against it as though he were holding the room upright with his shoulder. He walked toward us, held out his hand to Piper. "Hi, I'm Forrest Anderson."

Piper stood and looked down at me with a twist of confusion on her lips. "Hi," she said to Forrest, "I'm Piper Barber."

I stood to join them. "Forrest, this is an old friend of mine." I pointed at Piper. "Piper, Forrest is a professor at Southern. He's here to do some research on Dad for an article he's writing about his life and how his teachings affected his students."

"You're kidding," Piper said.

Forrest nodded at her. "So you knew the Cappy Leary who lived here in Seaboro?"

"That is not—" I stopped my words and looked at Piper. "That is not my name now."

"Oh?" she said.

"It's Catherine."

"Hmmm, Ms. Fancy-pants." She rolled her eyes. "Sit down," she said to Forrest. "Join us."

"Oh," I said, "I'm sure Forrest has things he needs to do, papers he needs to grade. Right?"

"No, not really," he said, and sat in the opposite chair. "Since I was alone all day, I got a lot of work done."

Piper tilted her head at me. I held up my hand in self-defense, then pointed at Forrest. "He was not alone all day—I dropped him off this afternoon before I came to the dock." I made a scrunched-up face at Forrest.

He held up his hands. "No problem at all. I got to talk to Mr. Hamilton and learn a lot about Seaboro, took a long walk on the beach, and read a history book on the town. I actually got a good bit done. I just want to drive around tomorrow and see your old house, the courthouse exhibit, which Mr. Hamilton says is a must, the docks and marina, some of your old hangouts." He grinned.

Piper laughed, and I hit her. "What *is* so funny?"

"I just realized," she said. "You can't do any of that tomorrow. You'll have to stay an extra day."

"Why?"

She smiled the little smile I remembered—one when she was about to talk me into doing something that would surely get me into trouble, but she would escape unmarked. "Everything is closed tomorrow—Sunday."

I groaned.

"Guess you have to stay, girlfriend."

"Can you get me into the courthouse? Do you have a key or something?"

"I married Parker Barber, not the mayor," Piper said. "Nothing will be open. Not the stores, the courthouse, Morgan's Grocery." She smiled at Forrest. "All those places you want to see—except for the docks and marina—will be closed until Monday, which is Memorial Day, and by then you can come to the picnic, parade, shrimp boil. . . . Tomorrow you can go to church with us and come over for lunch—"

"Whoa." I cut her off with a sharp word. "We are not going to any parade, picnic, dinner, church, or lunch. Forrest is here to do research; I'm here to scatter Dad's ashes, and off we go."

Forrest leaned forward in his chair. "Why, thank you, Piper. It all sounds great. I accept the invitation."

"Forrest." My teeth slammed down on one another as I bit the inside of my cheek. The metallic taste of blood filled the back of my throat. "We are not doing all those things."

He shrugged. "You don't have to go. I can do this research alone without much problem."

"Didn't you learn enough today from Mr. Hamilton and the books?"

"One has to see things, feel them, to be able to write about them, Cappy." He grinned again, and I scowled.

"Did you get a lot of information?" Piper asked Forrest. "Mr. Hamilton and his descendants have been here since the beginning of time, if he is to be believed. I think the first Hamilton was a shrimp that evolved into a man." She laughed at her own joke.

Forrest laughed with her. "Yes, he was full of information." He turned to me. "I gather he was quite good friends with your dad."

I nodded. "Yes, they went fishing together back in the day."

"Well, he loved remembering those days, and it sounds like your dad wasn't much different then from when I knew him."

"I told you . . . nothing new here."

"Oh," he said, "but I did learn some new things—didn't know you were once a tomboy, or that you were an expert horseback rider, excellent swimmer, and all-around troublemaker."

"I wasn't," I said with closed lips.

"Oh, yes, she was," Piper said. "And the fastest runner in fifth grade."

"And," Forrest said, "I just learned from you"—he motioned to Piper—"that she had a crush on a boy named Boyd."

I stood, stomped my foot. "That is enough. Stop it."

Piper grabbed my elbow. "What's wrong, Cappy? Come on . . . ."

"Listen, I've had a really long day. I want to go to bed." I looked down at Forrest. "In the morning I'll show you around town a little bit—you can see whatever is open. We'll take a long drive."

Piper stood up too, hugged me, and whispered in my ear, "Church is at ten thirty in the morning. See you then."

I shook my head in a definite no response, bade her good night, and told her I'd call before I left. I nodded at Forrest. "Sleep well."

Mr. Hamilton came into the library. "I hate to interrupt, but your room is ready now," he said to me.

"Thank you."

"You're Catherine Leary," he said, and it was not a question when he handed me the key.

"Yes, I am." I nodded.

After I entered room four—the Lighthouse Room—I yanked on my Lilly Pulitzer jammies, fell into bed, and ignored the spinning ceiling brought on by martinis without food. "Yes, I am," I said to the empty room. "I am *that* Catherine Leary indeed."

Sleep was whispering over me when I heard a knock on the door. I jumped up—maybe, just maybe Thurman had received my message and come to see me in Seaboro. I threw open the door, only to see Forrest. I dropped my shoulders. "Do you need something?"

"I really am not here to make you mad."

"Okay," I said, "let's just get some sleep."

"Did you throw the ashes?" he asked in a soft voice, touched the side of my face in a gesture I remembered from years ago—a gesture he'd once made when he wanted me to soften up, talk about something I refused to discuss. I closed my eyes and felt his hand run through my tangled curls.

I almost, but didn't quite lean into his hand. Instead I backed up, put my hand up in defense. "No, I didn't toss them yet. Piper showed up and . . . I'll do it tomorrow before we leave."

"I'm not leaving tomorrow," he said, dropped his hand, which hung in the air. "If you want to leave, go ahead. I can rent a car. But I wanted to let you know I have no intention of leaving. I'd love it if you'd stay here with me. Really, it is such a gorgeous place. But if you feel like you need to go, I understand."

"I do feel I need to leave tomorrow. I've got to get home to Murphy and Thurman. . . ."

He nodded. "Good night."

He turned and I shut the door, leaned my back against the wood, and slid to the floor. I sat for long moments before I heard his footsteps walk down the hall to his own room, and even longer before I stood to return to bed.

# SIX

*"The meeting of two personalities is like the
contact of two chemical substances: if there is
any reaction, both are transformed."*
—C. G. JUNG

I awoke to the naked sun forcing its way into the room: I'd
forgotten to close the red-white-and-blue gingham drapes
before I fell asleep. The morning fog that so defined the area
still hung in the air like a curtain: It was still early morning. I rolled over and faced the window without lifting my
head from the down pillow; the belly and legs of a small
green tree frog splayed against the glass French doors. Thurman would've told me not to have that second martini last
night—and he would've been right.

I untangled myself from the covers on the sagging mattress, dropped bare feet onto the old pine floors where my skirt lay crumpled in a pile next to the bed, and then shuffled to the French doors. I tapped the window and scared off the green frog, then pulled the doors wide to step out onto the small picketed porch facing the beach. The splintered wood tickled my feet; I pulled at the peeling paint on the pickets, which didn't look sturdy enough to hold a child's weight.

Ah, a nice, long, head-clearing walk on the beach was the answer. That might bring some peace. Maybe in solitude with only the waves and tide I had once loved, away from Forrest's or Piper's spying stare, I'd understand why Dad had returned here, and what Forrest meant by "missing pages."

I stepped back into the room and smiled when I thought about how much Thurman would hate this room, with its cutesy coastal accessories, its life preserver–and-anchor wallpaper in the bathroom. I changed into a pair of jogging shorts and a top, slipped my sneakers on without untying the knots, and walked back onto the porch while pulling my hair into a ponytail.

The boardwalk stretched over the dunes and the flagged sea oats and thick grasses containing the small round sandburrs that would stick into my feet and legs if I dared to cross the sand without protection. I told myself to relax, take a stroll on the beach, and let the sea do its job. I strode down the planked walk. The wind pulled at my hair, dragged it from the rubber band, and slapped strands into my eyes, where I swiped at just one more nuisance. I was frayed at the edges, as if parts of me were thrashing in the wind.

I moved across the sand, dug my toes below the shifting surface. The beach changed personalities with each turn. Oyster shells cracked and broke under my shoes, shattering with the sound of thin glass. Cleanly swept white beach then changed to masses of shells and seaweed, eventually blending to marsh and creek.

I walked with my shoulders hunched up to my ears. My nails dug into my palms, and my footsteps were so heavy they thrust deep footprints where the ebb of the sea had left a narrow strip of wet earth. Bleached tree trunks protruded ghost-like from the sand in a distorted memory of the forest they were before the ocean surged inland. Uneven waves broke the white crust of foam. Flat, low pewter clouds held rain the sky was not ready to release. Underneath my parched throat and too-heavy head I felt an emotion that did not resemble either understanding or peace.

This I remembered—how standing at the sea's edge as a child, I knew things with visceral understanding before the literal truth came to me. I turned my mind to the good, to the situations I did understand: Thurman and his safe love.

I closed my eyes and saw us at a basketball game while he held my hand and took me onto center court after a huge win over UNC, lifted me up, and hugged me in front of a full crowd. The picture had ended up on the front cover of the sports section of the paper the next morning, so it was easy to see in my mind's eye, to remember.

I satisfied myself with other images—ones that filled the empty, unsure places that Seaboro had opened inside me: Thurman taking me to his family's house in Asheville, me falling asleep on his shoulder while we watched a movie at his town house, Thurman burning my birthday dinner last year because he forgot to set the timer on the oven; the two of us walking through the university village with his arm over my shoulder, his eyes turned only to me while he laughed at my story about the media interviewing one of his players.

Fortified with these memories, I turned my back on the ocean and jogged across the shifting sand, entered my room, and grabbed the cell phone to call Thurman. I closed my eyes against an expanding headache and visualized his cell phone ringing in some lonely hotel room in Nowhere, Alabama. Finally his voice mail picked up, and I left another brief message—irritated and clipped.

I leaned back on the lighthouse-print covered headboard and thought, *Where did he say he was staying? A Fairfield, maybe, or a Hilton?* I dialed information in Tifton, Alabama, asked for the number of the Fairfield, and was almost stunned when, moments later, someone answered the phone and connected me to Thurman Whittaker's room.

"Hello." A woman's sleepy voice drawled through the line directly to my gut. I coiled at the edge of the bed and squeezed my eyes shut, as if I could actually see her answer the phone. Surely the attendant had connected me to the wrong room.

"Shit, don't answer the phone." Thurman's deeper voice came through the line. My thoughts became a crazed ball in Alice in Wonderland's bizarre croquet game.

"Sorry, sorry . . . forgot where I was." Her voice was dreamy, slurred. The phone banged as it was dropped or grabbed; then there was the click of disconnection.

The sheer panic began below my navel, then slithered higher until I grabbed my throat to halt the sound. But just as I couldn't stop what had happened in that bedroom last night, I had no control over the arrival of panic and its accompanying gagging. I ran to the bathroom and emptied my martini dinner into the antique pedestal sink.

Deep breaths, deep breaths. My oxygen was running out now. I dropped onto the bathroom floor and rested my forehead on the cold tiles, next to the air conditioner vent, my arms splayed to the side.

I heard the question Forrest had asked, inside my head: *What do you want to be doing when you die?*

"Not this," I answered out loud. "Not alone with a hangover in an empty room while my boyfriend is in bed with another woman in Alabama. Not like this . . ." A sob crept up my throat—but I had kept my tears at bay for so long, for so many years, that the sob didn't make it past my pinpricked eyes.

I don't know how long I stayed there. Only thirst made me rise me to get water from the minibar.

I knew—as one knows anything deep down—that I hadn't dialed the wrong number, hadn't been connected to the wrong bedroom. I had not hung up, and I glared at the phone as if it had betrayed me. I picked it up with just two fingers, as if it were contagious, filthy with the remnants of what had happened. I clicked off, shut it, flicked the phone back and forth between my hands.

*Call somebody, anybody.* Instinct told me that if I called back, Thurman would answer, "What? You must have dialed the wrong number. I'm here." He'd sound sleepy, calm. I'd believe him, be gulled into believing that I had dialed the wrong number, that Thurman was actually drinking coffee in the lobby of the Fairfield with the Alabama newspaper on his lap. I could be lulled into ease—*Just be safe, be safe. Please be safe.*

I slammed the phone down and began to pack my bag; I'd drive to Alabama, catch them in the act, play the wronged girlfriend and shriek and accuse and scare the hell out of both of them.

*"Catherine,"* I told myself out loud in even tones, *"by the time you get there, all the tracks will be covered, all the emotion drained, all the proof gone as if it never happened."*

Light shimmered across the pine floors; I squinted into the sun pouring through the pane glass, and I understood that I had to finish what Dad asked me to do before I could go find what waited for me with Thurman.

This morning all of Seaboro would be at church—except for the few men who claimed nature as their church and were off fishing. This would be the perfect time to go to the dock . . . with Dad.

I slipped on a flowered sundress, brushed my hair back from my face into a slick ponytail, and then grabbed my car keys and the urn, and listened for the faint call of the river.

But it wasn't the river I drove to after sneaking out of the B & B. I didn't fully understand why I ended up in Ellie's driveway, but a faint streak of hope flashed across my temples: Ellie's peaceful house. What I found was a man leaning against a wooden porch pillar, smoke curling from his shadow. There was a glint of a cigarette when he turned and grimaced at me.

Boyd Loughlin.

When I was twelve years old, he had touched my cheek and opened up an entire new world of expectation. It had been a blazing morning when Ellie and Mother ran Saturday errands. Mother endured the Loughlin friendship as someone would tolerate a hyper puppy brought home as a gift for the kids. The children were best friends, the dads close friends, the families tied by the children and my affection for Ellie, the boys' bond with Dad. Mother vaguely tolerated the river family picnics, me running to their home, Dad bringing Boyd and Sam for dinner with all the fish they'd caught.

Mother had come along on these errands with a perfectly placed smile, a picnic basket packed and a thermos prepared. Later this morning Ellie was taking us down the Wahoo Creek, and Mother had made us lunch, which she said was probably complete mush by now, as Ellie had been late because she was helping clean the gardens at the church.

Boyd and I waited for our mothers while I leaned back on the vinyl seats of the wood-paneled station wagon. The town square was clogged with people doing similar morning errands before the day hit its expected 102 degrees, a hundred percent humidity. Boyd and I weren't willing to expose ourselves to the scorching pavement to spend our five cents at the drugstore on an RC or fresh-squeezed lemonade.

Boyd waved out the window. "Looks like they're almost done. . . ."

Mother and Ellie were in line at Morgan's Grocery. "Thank God," I said, turning to look at Boyd. He waved at someone I couldn't see; I leaned forward.

"Hi, Boyd. Hi, Cappy," Camilla Holloway said, leaned down to the car window, her long blond hair slightly greasy with a red slash of part down the middle. She would be pretty, I thought, if she didn't always look as if she'd missed a week of bathing.

"Hi, Cammie. Whatcha doing?" Boyd asked.

"Why y'all sitting in that hot car?"

"Waiting for our moms to finish their errands . . . too

hot to go outside," I said, fell back against the seat and closed my eyes.

"Oh," she said.

Boyd waved his hand. "They're coming."

"What you doing today?" Camilla pulled at her pigtail.

"Headin' to the beach, then up the Wahoo to see where it goes," Boyd said.

"Can't you just look at the map for that?" Camilla glanced at me when I opened my eyes.

I rolled my head back on the seat. Look at a map? It sounded like something my mother would say. Didn't she know a map would never show you where the creek really went, what you might find on the way? A horseshoe crab shell, a broken Indian pot, a shark tooth washed upstream, the sinking holes of bog that would swallow your leg to the knee. These treasures were not on a map. I didn't answer Camilla, just glanced out the window and told her, "Your brother is running in the street," then closed my eyes against her stupidity.

Camilla ran from the car and grabbed her baby brother from the cobbled road.

Boyd turned to me, shifted against the door, and lifted his left eyebrow. "You don't like her."

"Yes, I do."

"No . . . you don't."

"Do you?" I asked, curious, but not sure why I cared.

"She's nice, Cap. I feel sorry for her." That was Boyd—a

boy who could shoot a bow into a deer, yet feel sorry for a wounded chipmunk or shy girl.

I knew I should feel bad for Camilla too. She was always stuck in the house, helping her mother with her three younger brothers. Her father had disappeared after the youngest child was born, and the stories about where he went, what had happened to him, were as abundant as the oysters at the edge of the sound. But Camilla annoyed me, always sidling up to Boyd, trying be his buddy when he already had one: me.

I fingered the fraying edges of the appliquéd flower on my jeans shorts. Sweat dripped down my spine; my legs slid on the seat while my halter top skimmed against my back. Boyd reached his hand toward me, then ran his finger along the side of my face to withdraw a damp curl from my cheek. The curl fell onto my bare shoulder. "Your hair was stuck on your face," he said simply, as he put his head back out the window.

The simple touch of his finger drawn across my cheek fractured open something of my innocence and youth; the very thing that had been haunting my sleep and dancing with me in the summer mornings now pried the breath from me, causing my body to go limp, my legs to tingle as though I had been sitting cross-legged too long. It was a tangible impression that I had never felt before: a mixture of fear and expectation that had a name—desire.

Whatever the feeling was would change everything, and

I wasn't ready. But at least I knew whom I waited for, and I was content in this knowledge, patient.

When the chores and errands were done, when the fulfillment of obligations released us to the freedom of creek and tide, I ran from my kitchen as Mother called after me, "Be careful and be home before dusk, and try, Catherine, just try to act like a lady, not a tomboy today."

"Yes, ma'am."

I sprinted for the mouth of the creek beyond Boyd's house, where it dumped its frothed and sluggish water into Seaboro River with every outgoing tide.

Boyd's voice washed toward me; he was arguing with a friend, Ross. I stopped, listened while I hid behind the tall grasses.

"We need one more man on the team for a decent baseball game, Boyd. But no, you wimp of all time, you have to play in the creek with some girl. That is such a sissy thing to do. Sometimes I even wonder why you're my friend."

"Shut your piehole, Ross. I promised Cappy I'd go with her today. We're headed—"

Ross's voice interrupted. "I don't give a fish fart what you're doing. You act like a girl, wanting to play house. . . ."

"We are not playing house. We're building a fort, you moron."

I crouched lower behind the grass.

"What am I gonna tell the boys?" Ross asked. "That you wanted to play tea party with some girl?"

"Go on. I'll meet y'all in a while."

"Sometimes you really gross me out, Boyd."

"That's it, Ross. Shut up for good. Gross you out? I'll gross you out when I put this crab down your shirt."

Then there was the quick, wet sound of mud and running feet as Boyd and Ross burst from the wild sea grass and onto the lawn where I hid, Boyd holding a skittish crab.

I screamed and tried to step aside as Ross ran, but I couldn't move from my crouch quick enough and Ross knocked me over, Boyd following and falling on us. I wriggled my way out from under the pile and kicked at Ross. "Get off me, you idiot."

"You were out here spying. . . ." he said. "And I'm telling your mom you said the word *idiot.*

"Ross." Boyd's voice echoed across the lawn. "Go home."

Ross stood, turned, and walked past us to grab a ball of mud from the side of the creek. Then he splatted it onto the back of my head, mushed it into the tangled curls. I squealed and reached to hit him, but he ran until Boyd's hand grabbed the back of his shirt, tearing a hole from the neck seam to midback. Boyd spun Ross around. "Don't ever touch a girl like that. Don't ever hit Cappy again or I swear to God you won't have hands to touch a girl with when it's time."

"Let go of me!" Ross screamed.

Boyd released him to fall to the ground, his legs caving

underneath him as he fell into a heap. Ross backed away from us on his butt and then stood and ran just as Ellie came out holding the picnic basket. "What was that all about?" she asked.

I ran my fingers through the mud. "Moron Ross."

Boyd helped me up from the ground and I felt the earlier tug of unfamiliar want and I turned away from him, yanked up on my rubber boots to make sure they were tight against my feet. Here I was about to spend the afternoon alone with Boyd and I had mud in my hair and across my face. I ran my fingers through my hair in a poor attempt to fix the damage. "Moron," I shouted down the path he'd taken in his rapid retreat.

Ellie pulled some mud from my hair. "You need me to call his mother?"

"No, Boyd took care of it," I said with a tone of reverence.

Ellie laughed. "You two want me to come with you, or are you okay this afternoon while I finish helping at the church?"

"No, we're fine," Boyd said.

"Okay, then, don't go past the outskirts of the rice field," she said, and kissed my forehead.

"Yes, ma'am," we said in unison.

"Let's go," I said, and led the way, not turning to him for a full five minutes, afraid he'd notice the flush that had come to my face.

"I can't remember where we started the fort," I called over my shoulder, the familiarity of our friendship now replacing the odd pulse of his touch.

"About another ten yards past the bend," Boyd said, waved his hand toward the right.

"I hope it didn't wash away."

Boyd came up beside me, and our feet splashed together.

"There it is." Boyd pointed to a falling and warped structure of mud and sticks.

"Someone knocked part of it down," I said, and rushed to the side of the fort.

"Probably the wind or rain . . ."

"No," I said, "look, someone kicked a hole in it."

"Well, let's fix it." Boyd teased a clump of mud from my hair.

I sat down next to the fort that we'd spent weeks slowly building on the side of the deserted rice field, in the sheltered shade of a live oak. We had gathered the dry and hollow sticks of the grass and formed a plaster of pluff mud and sand, letting it bake in the sun to make a fort big enough to hold just the two of us.

I sat on the stump of a fallen cypress tree. "I bet Camilla did this."

"Camilla?" Boyd laughed and sat next to me.

"Yeah, she's madly in love with you."

"No, she is not." Boyd threw an oyster shell across the creek.

"Yes, she is. She follows you around like a lost puppy."

"She just doesn't have many friends." Boyd traced a line in the mud with a stick.

"Boyd and Camilla sittin' in a tree, k-i-s-s-i—" I started to sing.

"Stop it! You want to rebuild this or keep walking and see what we find?"

"Ellie said we couldn't go past the rice field. Let's just build this. I can't stand to see that hole."

Boyd looked at me, and I desperately wished I didn't have mud in my hair so he would reach over and touch me, touch my skin. But he didn't. He stood and sang a Beatles song about living in the USSR while he gathered sticks.

"Living in the USSR?" I asked when I stood.

"It's just a song. Got stuck in my head from the radio this morning."

"I never, ever want to live anywhere but here. Ever," I said.

"I won't," Boyd said, resolute.

I smiled at him, then poured all my energy into fixing our fort. In the few weeks we had left together, I stuck curls on my face, against my lips, and hoped Boyd would remove them, run his finger across my skin. The fear passed and only the hope remained.


As I sat in Ellie's driveway I understood that Boyd was now a man on the porch of his mother's home with a cigarette dangling from his mouth, and I wanted to close my eyes against this reality. Some things were better left as memories, and obviously Boyd Loughlin was one of them.

In a flash of something brilliant and full, I knew that all hope, all joy, and all expectation that had ever lived in me, had existed before Sam died. Why would I feel those things before his death, but not afterward? Did he take the joy with him? Did I give it to him? In a detached way, this realization was interesting, something to study and look at . . . later.

I walked toward the house with a treble vibration of fear in my chest. Boyd watched me until I reached him; then he dropped his cigarette, crushed it with his heel.

"So, it's true," he said.

"Hello, Boyd," I said, stopping at the bottom of the white-painted steps.

"Mom told me you were here, but I thought she was having a bad day. But just damn, it's true."

I nodded.

"What are you doing here?"

"Nice greeting, Boyd."

He came down the steps, stood so close to me I smelled the cigarettes on his breath. "Listen, Catherine. There is no need for you to come back here looking for some kind of resolution or redemption." He spit. "What an asinine word—redemption." He stared at me for a moment in the silence of rage. "You should leave. Please don't come in and confuse

Mom or make things worse. Just leave and get on with your life, like you have been."

"I love her, Boyd. I always have."

"Of course you do. Everyone loves Mother." He held his hand up like a halt sign, and I backed up two steps. "You need to leave before I say something I'll regret."

I stared at this man I'd once adored as a boy. I looked for the light around his head that in his childhood only I could see. Mother had told me I'd made it up—that no one had brilliance around their head except the baby Jesus. But I saw it around Boyd at various times: not a halo, but a diffuse light that winked and twisted in sunlight. Now all I saw was a leftover, faded man with lines of despair etched in his face.

"Okay, I'm leaving." I turned to the car, then changed my mind. If I didn't say the words now, they would stay in that place inside me where they'd lived for eighteen years, thrashing and rolling around, causing bruises I couldn't see, always wanting to be released.

"Boyd," I said, when he walked up the stairs.

He stopped. "What?" he said without turning around.

"I'm sorry. I am incredibly, outrageously, horribly sorry. Nothing I can do will make it okay, but I have never said sorry to you or your mother. I loved all of you, and I am sorry."

I wanted to keep saying it over and over and over—*Sorry, sorry, sorry. Forgive, forgive, forgive.*

Boyd twisted on the stairs and glared at me, pulled a cigarette out of his top shirt pocket, and stuck it in his mouth. "You think that is what I'm talking about—how sorry you should be?"

I stood still, waiting for what he'd say next, to discover what he was really talking about. But he turned away, walked back to the porch, and left me alone on the crushed shell drive.

I got back in my car and drove away. When I glanced in the rearview mirror I saw Boyd light his cigarette. The man who had just stood on the porch and turned his back on me was not the boy I'd known. I wanted a reminder of him: the boy who punched Ross in the mouth for calling me a prissy girl.

Still the word I'd finally said to him—*sorry*—tasted good. Really good. No matter what his reaction, I'd said the word loud and clear and numerous times.

I found myself in front of the white clapboard-and-stone church that I'd attended as a child. The church had been built in the seventeen hundreds, had survived colonization, revolution, slavery, civil war, World War I, World War II. It was where I'd been baptized, where Sam's funeral was held. Oak trees guarded the church like angels with wings of Spanish moss, reaching down to brush and shade their charges below. A peeling white picket fence surrounded a yard full of wildflowers. A white sign announced this week's sermon

along with a weekly inspirational quote for all passing by:
WHAT'S MISSING FROM CH__CH, UR. Announcements of
births, deaths, and other events were both typed and handwritten on crooked, taped pieces of paper. The wrought iron
gate was rusted to orange, and gaped open between the fence
posts: an invitation to walk up the granite stone walkway,
mortared by moss and grass, to the solid cedar doors.

I entered the dim-lit sanctuary and somehow found a
seat at the end of a crammed pew without making eye contact with anyone. Sunlight poured in through the stained-
glass windows, splashed everyone with the filtered purples of
Christ's robe, the watered-down brown of his cross. I pulled
the curls at the back of my neck and tried to smooth the
wrinkles from my sundress. The past rolled by in waves of
vaguely familiar faces and dusty memories. After I sat I stared
down at the pew, which was as scuffed as a worn shoe. The
kneeling benches were frayed around their red velvet edges.
The church appeared smaller, the stained-glass windows
dirtier; the air was too hot, too cold, too thick, too thin.

Then I realized Boyd had cut right through the scar of
my emotions—the wound I had thought covered and healed:
my sense of belonging.

I bowed my head; no one would bother a woman in
prayer. Boyd had just robbed me of whatever self-assurance I'd
carried with me from Cedar Valley. Or maybe I should blame
just being in Seaboro. Either way, I wasn't recovered enough
for another social encounter—friendly or otherwise.

Piper broke the thin barrier of anonymous haze when she barreled down the aisle and threw her arms around me. "You will not hide back here by yourself. Come sit with us." She waved toward the second pew.

"No way," I whispered. "I am not sitting in front. Go on, you crazy friend, go join your family."

She grasped my hand. "You either come with me or I stay here, and we can both watch how Parker handles all three boys by himself."

"That might be fun," I said.

"Not for me." Piper pulled at me. "My mother-in-law will give me a forty-minute lecture on children's proper behavior in a church service and I am not in the mood for that."

"Go, Piper," I said, gestured toward her family. Parker looked over his shoulder and nodded his head for Piper to come. She smiled and sat next to me.

"Mama . . ." Everyone in the church stopped picking up their hymnals, fiddling in their purses, or stuffing their donation envelopes to stare at Piper. "Come sit with us, Mama. Pleeeease . . ."

A few people laughed, and Piper smiled and waved at her youngest son over the tops of the pews.

"Go," I said, pushed at her.

"Not without you."

"You are exactly the same," I said. "I have no idea why I came here."

We stood and moved to the front. I walked straight and tall; you never knew who was watching, who was looking at you, especially when a seven-year-old boy was jumping up and down in a pew.

I nodded at Parker on the other side of the boys, who were wearing khakis and button-down white shirts, and had comb marks in their wet hair. Parker smiled at me, and I remembered one time he had held his breath underwater for so long we all thought he'd drowned. He was the biggest daredevil in the entire school. Now he sat in a church pew with his three children and smiled at me, mouthed, *So good to see you.*

We sat just as Father Rory stepped out and stood behind the pulpit. I swore he looked right at me, nodded, and smiled. I was at Sam's funeral again, cowering in the back corner of the church, understanding that even the man hanging on crosses all over the church, bleeding and wearing his furious crown of thorns, could not forgive me, just as the families and friends filling the church to overflowing that terrible day couldn't.

*Dad,* I thought, *why did you return here?*

Dad didn't answer, but Father Rory had us turn to hymn number 475, "Amazing Grace," just as I heard Forrest Anderson's voice whisper, "Move over."

I turned and forced a smile, released a long breath as Forrest slid in next to me. "What are you doing here?" I muttered behind my hymnal.

"Wasn't I invited to church last night?" He winked at me.

I didn't answer him, shifted away to stare at Father Rory—another person I had never said good-bye to who had been an integral part of my life there. He had always been around for the younger crowd—helping with the car washes, fund-raisers, and youth group meetings. He had never treated us as kids, but as people who would grow up and participate in "God's kingdom."

On that terrible day of Sam's funeral, he had found me under the back pew crouched all alone. The adults had been so wrapped in their own grief, in their own need to survive, that they hadn't come to look for me yet. I was alone and I deserved to be alone—I didn't deserve to be noticed by anyone ever again. I understood this fact with calm certainty.

But Father found me and murmured words of comfort that had something to do with mercy, with purpose, with forgiveness. I'd known they were merely what he was supposed to say. Not one word penetrated my newfound self: I was horrid, evil, black with sin.

What I do remember thinking was how amazing it was that I had spent the first twelve years of my life believing I was a good person, that I was better than poor, dirty Camilla or the bullies on the playground pushing the little kids off the jungle gym, or the boys who sneaked cigarettes after church. In fact, I was worse, much worse, and it had taken Sam's death to make me see this true self. Even as Father held my hand and told me I was valued, I vowed that from then on I would take the responsible steps that would protect me from this pain of loving someone who'd left.

Until the phone call to Thurman in that hotel in Alabama, I had done a pretty good job of keeping that childhood promise.

I shivered with the quick-flash remembrance of the call made only a couple of hours ago, and tried to focus on Father Rory's announcements for the week.

When the service was over, I slipped out the side pew to the ladies' room at the back section of the church. I remembered exactly where it was and how to sneak through the back choir loft to get there without being seen. I closed a bathroom stall and sat down, waited a decent amount of time for the crowd to thin and people to leave for their picnics and family gatherings.

Piper found me before I could exit with some dignity.

"Cappy Leary, I know you're in here. You could have at least been original and used a different hiding place than the one you used when you were little."

I opened the bathroom stall and stared at her. "What the hell is that supposed to mean?"

"I don't think you can say *hell* in church." She grinned at me. "Unless, of course, you are talking about where one could go after death."

"I'm not hiding."

"Yes, you are. Now let's go . . . the kids are starving."

Only two people remained in the front vestibule: Forrest and Father Rory in discussion, their heads bent toward each other. I moved forward with numb hands, my thoughts repeating the same phrase over and over: "Please don't be talking about me." How could my two lives, past and present, be colliding now, all because of Forrest Anderson?

I reached their sides and heard Father say, "Yes, he was a great man." Then he turned to me, and a smile spread across his face. "Why, look here, little Cappy Leary all grown up. Now, how is it that I've not aged a day, yet you're now a grown woman?" He placed his arm around my shoulders and squeezed. "It is wonderful to see you."

"You too, Father. And you're right—you don't look any older."

He laughed and nodded to Forrest. "This young man's writing about your dad, eh?"

"That's what he tells me."

Father offered another squeeze around my shoulders. "I am sorry for your loss. I loved Grayson Leary."

"Thank you," I said.

Piper clapped her hands. "Let's go . . . Parker is waiting in the car with all the screaming kids. Lunch . . ." She turned to Father. "Would you like to join us at my house?"

Father released me. "You're kind for asking, Piper, but I have promised the Cunningham family I'd join them." He patted his stomach. "Not that I couldn't eat two lunches, but you all go on and enjoy your afternoon." He added to

Forrest, "If you'd like to talk more, you know where to find me."

"Thank you," Forrest said. "I just might do that. I'd love to know a little bit more about how his ideas of story and God wove into his teachings."

"Well, for Grayson Leary, God was understood through story."

I turned to walk away; Forrest was poking his nose into every aspect of my past, and enough was enough. I spoke through clenched lips. "Let's go." I walked out the double wooden doors into the sunlight and expected them all to follow, yet I found myself standing on the cobblestone walk alone with the beating sun and a dizzying need for food.

On the left side of the church was an outdoor sanctuary framed by fir and cedar trees in a semicircle. Headstones of deceased founding members of the church were scattered across the lawn, the engraved letters worn so smooth I couldn't read the dates or names. Even when we'd have Sunday school in this outdoor chapel, I was afraid to enter the inner circle of the fir trees where the wooden pews lined up in front of a hand-carved altar. If ever God spoke to someone, or asked them to do something impossible like he did Moses, I figured he would do it there, in that courtyard.

A concrete bench with a winged angel engraved in the arms beckoned across the courtyard. I walked over to it, sat, and dropped my head into my hands. I still couldn't go in-

side that semicircle, and yet Forrest Anderson strode across
the grass, cut through the pews, and walked directly over the
gravestones set into the grass. He sat next to me, but I didn't
look up at him.

"Cappy," he said.

"Please stop calling me that. Please. You didn't know that
girl."

I expected to see the look on his face—the one I saw whenever he called me that name or wanted to get a rise out of me—
but what I saw was an expression of compassion, soft and real.

"Ah, but I do know that girl. I know her through her dad
and in the moments when, for five minutes, she stops being
the guarded and well-armored Catherine." He grabbed my
hand. "Come on; your friend is expecting us for lunch."

"I thought you wanted me to drive you around town
today. Besides, we've got to get home."

"It's just now getting fun. There's so much more to . . .
see, and I'd really like to see it with you."

These curious words came to me as if from a distance. If
only I could allow their meaning to wrap around me. Instead
I pushed their import far from me, stood up. "If we're going
to eat, let's go. I'm starved."

He smiled. "Do you mind if I come with you? Mr. Hamilton gave me a ride this morning."

"Mr. Hamilton?" I raised my eyebrows. "Have you ever
met a stranger?"

"Definitely not here. Nicest people you'd ever want to know—especially when I bring up your dad's name."

"I guess you don't say mine . . . you wouldn't get such a warm reception."

"That's not true . . . everyone here seems to adore you. Sounds like you were a funny and cute child who caused just enough trouble to be remembered, but not enough to cause rancor."

"Rancor? Is that your ten-cent word for the day?"

He laughed. "Come on . . . let's go."

I plucked my car keys out of my purse, then looked at Forrest. "I have no idea where Piper lives now."

"I do." He pulled out the church program with scribbled writing on the boxed-off prayer request section. "She wrote it down for me."

And as he walked toward the sole car remaining in the parking lot, I thought I saw, for half a moment, light around his hair, around him. Then it was gone and I was sure I'd imagined it.

We devoured steaks cooked to perfection on the grill, three-bean salad, and a peach cobbler. I saw Forrest trying to scrape the remains off the sides of the pan.

"Caught you," I said, came up behind him and pinched his arm.

He jumped, licked his finger. "That might be the most heavenly food I have ever put in my mouth."

Piper walked toward us. "Secret family recipe," she said.

"Yeah," I said, "the same one that's in the Junior League cookbook, I'm sure."

"Ah," she said, "can't you just let him believe it for one minute?"

Forrest took another swipe at the pan with a fork. "I don't care where it came from . . . as long as I can have some more."

Parker's voice hollered across the lawn, "Championship Wiffle ball game to start in five minutes."

Afternoon descended in the easy, light way it does on an early summer day as we walked across the yard. "Count me out," I said. "Major problems with hand-eye coordination." I flopped down onto a whitewashed wooden chair. "I'll cheer for Piper's team."

After two innings of zero runs scored, Piper's boys scrambled for the ball, attempting to get her out at home plate. Parker ran, laughed, and hollered at her to run faster.

Forrest's shouted response raised tears at the back of my throat. I didn't understand why. My long-held guilt about Sam revisited? Boyd's cruel words? Thurman's possible betrayal? If I was going to cause a scene and let the tears come in the convulsive way they were threatening, I wanted a very, very good reason for them.

Thurman had called five or six times since the girl answered, but I hadn't picked up the phone; I flipped it open—make that seven times.

Piper fell to the ground next to me, clutching her ankle.

"You okay?" I asked.

She winked at me. "You gotta make them believe you're hurt or you won't get the run. . . ."

"Faker, faker, faker," Zach yelled, jumping up and down. "We won, you faker."

She fell back on the grass. "Now, tell me how glamorous your life is while I have to face the Sunday dishes and three piles of homework still not done," she said.

When I didn't answer, she leaned closer, staring at me. "You're about to cry."

"I am not."

"Yes, you are. I know that look. . . . Did something happen?"

"I'm not sure. I think Thurman is with some . . . girl."

"What?"

"He hadn't answered his cell phone the past two days, so I called the hotel and asked for his room. A woman picked up, and I swear I heard his voice in the background saying not to answer. But I'm not positive."

Piper bit her lower lip while making dismissive movements with her right hand toward Zach, who wanted to show her a daddy longlegs crawling up his arm. "Is he that kind of man? I mean . . . has this happened before?"

"Not that I know of," I said, then gave a long sniff and a

quick glance at Forrest to make sure he couldn't hear us. He was on the far side of the yard in conversation with Parker. "This is ridiculous. I'm not even sure it happened and I'm about to fall apart."

"Have you talked to him?"

"No. I'm ignoring his calls—let him panic."

"Oh," she said, leaned back on her elbows. "Maybe it was the wrong room."

I shrugged. "Maybe." I watched Parker and Forrest drinking beers, laughing. "Sometimes I wonder how different my life would be if I'd stayed here. You know—the old *Sliding Doors* concept. How different would I be? One afternoon, one child, one mistake, and so many lives reshaped."

Piper stared straight ahead, pushed hair out of her eyes. "Would you have married someone from Seaboro? Would we still be best friends?"

"Yes and yes. But I'll never know. I mean, would Mother have finally gotten her place on the water? Would Dad have written that book he talked about? Would Sam have grown up to be as cute as he was when he was a toddler?"

"Yes, yes, and yes," Piper said. "Here I am wondering what my life would have been like if I'd *left*, and you're wondering what it would have been like if you'd *stayed*."

"If you'd left? Did you ever even think about it?"

"Well, I guess if you count yesterday, and the day before that . . ." She laughed. "I guess there's always that other road we wonder about. What if, what if, what if . . ."

"What is your 'what if'?" I asked.

"What if I had gone off to college instead of staying here? What if I had taken a wild chance and traveled? What if I hadn't said yes to Parker's proposal?" She sighed. "What's yours?"

"What if I hadn't said yes to Ellie?"

"Said yes to what?"

"Watching Sam."

"Oh, God, Cappy, are you still carrying that around?"

"How could I not, Piper? I lost a two-year-old child while goofing off with Boyd. Sam drowned. I'll carry that with me for the rest of my pitiful life."

She closed her eyes, and I could feel the speech she was about to offer me. The same speech I'd heard from Mother, Dad, and Alice—about how it wasn't really my fault. Wrong place, wrong time, Boyd was to blame too, blah, blah, blah.

I touched Piper's arm. "Don't say anything, please. I can't hear all that right now, okay? So tell me about your life and why you would even think about the 'what if' . . ."

She paused as though she were trying to decide whether to give me the old "it wasn't entirely your fault" pep talk despite my protestations. She must have changed her mind. "Well, there are ups and downs in a marriage—good and bad days. Sometimes I'm just tired, you know? And truthfully I'm a little jealous of your life—you can do whatever you want, take whatever path you choose tomorrow or the next day."

"No, I can't. I have a job, commitments. I can't just run off and choose new paths." But as soon as I said this, a glimmer of something I hadn't seen in a long time, a stranger to me now, glittered like cut glass in the corner of my eye and I recognized it: the possibility of doing something different in life.

I saw Piper realize it too: endless possibilities that were no longer open to her.

Her eyes were wet. "Having you here is a miracle." Then she whispered, "Have you spread his ashes yet?"

"No."

"I thought maybe that was what you were doing before church."

"No," I said. "I'd meant to, but then I ran into Boyd Loughlin . . . and got a bit sidetracked."

Piper stood and held her hand out to me. "Tell me what he said."

"Not much, really. He just told me I didn't belong here, that I should leave and not confuse his mom." I allowed her to take my hand and pull me to my feet.

"Don't take it personally. He's like that with everyone. It's so sad."

"Personally? He told me I didn't belong, that he didn't need my apologies, and not to come running back here searching for some asinine redemption."

"He said all that?"

"Well, I'm paraphrasing, but yes, he did."

"I hate that you had to see him. I should've told you he comes to visit Ellie every Sunday."

"It's okay. I got to say something to him that I've never been able to say."

She grabbed my hand. "What?"

"Just one word—sorry." I squeezed her fingers.

Piper closed her eyes. "Oh, Cap."

I made a motion to Forrest to come on, then hugged Piper. "I've got to go. Thank you so much for everything, old friend."

After elaborate good-byes to all the boys, Forrest and I set off. "Did you have fun?" I asked.

"Absolutely. Parker is a great guy," he said.

"Always has been." I turned off Piper's street and headed toward the inn as afternoon shimmied toward evening.

I pulled up in front of the B & B. "Forrest, do you mind if I drop you off? I'd like to go do something alone."

He shifted his weight back on the seat and squinted against the setting sunlight coming through the driver's-side window. "If I didn't know you better, I'd think you were running off to meet a lover every hour or two."

"Yeah, that's it." I smiled. "A secret lover I've kept in Seaboro."

He opened the door. "I'll be in the library reading if you'd like to talk when you get back."

"Thanks, Forrest," I said, then turned toward the river one last time.

# SEVEN

*"No one ever told me that grief felt so like fear."*
—C. S. LEWIS, *A Grief Observed*

The gray sequin curl of river glittered in front of me: the geography of childhood reflecting the same sky of Sam's last day—the day of the shrimp boil, a celebration of Seaboro's bounty. The land had given and then ceased offering cotton and rice, but the gift of shrimp was celebrated yearly.

I'd anticipated what became my last shrimp boil with joyous expectation. Dad brought the kettle to these parties: a huge cast-iron pot, round with hand-forged iron handles that clanked when Dad slid the pot from the shed in the back of Alice's property. I imagined that the building was made just for storing this kettle. There was a certain sacrament to everything associated with the boil, including the loading of the kettle. Dad and Jim got it onto the boat while Ellie and Mother took the kids on the Loughlins' Boston Whaler to Charles Island, where the festival was held.

I loved to listen to the yearly banter between Dad and Mr. Jim: a symphony of familiarity and contentment.

"Move it to the left, Jim," Dad said.

"Damn, Grayson, you're dropping it."

"You never lift your side high enough."

"You are going to slam my fingers against the hull."

Boyd and Sam ran around the men, trying to help, wanting to be part of the manly ceremony of fighting about the lifting and placing of the pot.

I twisted my hair around my finger while Sam pulled on Mr. Jim's denim shorts. "Daddy, up, up, up . . . pleeeze." Mr. Jim's hands and arms were wrapped around the pot, his left leg slightly raised to balance as they hooked it up and over the stern of the boat.

"Damn, Ellie, get the baby. This'll crush him."

I looked to Ellie, whose arms were full of towels and bags, her hands tangled in the ropes of the boat she was loading. "Jim, don't talk like that in front of the children, I'm coming."

"I've got him. . . ." I cooed as I moved toward him, crouched down to come to his level, convince him that I was a good substitute for his daddy. "Come here, I'll hold you," I said.

Dad thumped his side of the kettle into the boat, threw

Mr. Jim off balance, and sent him to the dock, hard on his bottom as the pot settled, lopsided, into the stern of the boat, where it nestled crooked in a pile of towels. Dad bent over and tousled Sam's hair, picked him up, and held him against his own skin, tickled the side of Sam's neck with his nose.

"No, no . . ." Sam laughed and buried his face in my dad's neck. Ellie let go of the ropes and watched; her face was smooth. I couldn't see her eyes behind the Jackie-O sunglasses, but I watched years fall from her face as Dad held Sam.

The sides of Jim's mouth turned down, and he rubbed his forehead before he reached his arms out for Sam, who now snuggled closer to Dad's neck. "I'm sorry I hollered at you, son. I didn't want you to get crushed," Jim said.

I was immediately and terribly sorry that I was not two years old, not a baby boy—I wanted that place on Daddy's neck. Jim's boys could go on hunting and fishing trips with my dad, but not take my place in his heart.

"I want to ride in the boat with Dad," I said, jumping in and sitting next to the kettle.

"No, Catherine," Mother said in a tight voice, "I don't like you with that kettle. If it tips over . . ."

"She's fine, honey," Dad said, and then handed Sam to Jim and began untying the ropes from the dock cleats. I studied Dad's face and what I thought might be sorrow on his features. I understood why he was sad: He had only me; no sons, no Sam or Boyd. Then he turned to me and smiled, and the look was gone. There was now merely the sun in his eyes, a kettle that was too heavy, and a child that needed attention.

"Pumpkin, sit up front with me, not next to that kettle," Daddy said, and hugged me as the wind whipped my hair around my face.

Boyd's complaint that it wasn't fair I got to go with Dad and he didn't washed over me. Daddy unhooked the boat and waved in exaggerated motions as he pushed the throttle down and exited the mouth of the river, ignoring the NO WAKE sign and Mother's commands to bring me back.

I wanted that boat ride to last forever. I wanted Dad's arms around me as I listened to the screeching seagulls, the slap of waves on the hull, the cry of a diving osprey. I tried to sneak a cuddle in his neck, but I was just too big.

Our families sat in the same place on Charles Island every year: an unofficial stakeout with blankets, coolers, beach chairs, and lanterns, a home base I ran to after each foray across the beach, a touch point of comfort. That last shrimp boil encompasses my memories of all feasts and roasts and boils. Sand, water, food, and love. I drifted in the moments: the cold lemonade with gritty sand on the edges of the cup, capture the flag played in the thick of the palmetto grove, the drunken mayor grabbing at the wrong wife, the hushed whispers of teenagers behind the trees as smoke—sweet and foreign—coiled into the air, the giggle of girls who chased Boyd in the hope of gaining his godly attention.

The annual kick-the-can game began soon after we ate. Piper and I hid behind the wall of a tabby ruin. "I have to tell you something," she said.

"What?" I glanced around the corner of the ragged walls.

"I kissed Billy Thompson."

"You did not," I said, turning back to her. "He says all girls have cooties."

"Well, I guess he changed his mind. You didn't come to Merritt's twelfth birthday party, and her mom went upstairs for, like, an hour. We all started playing spin the bottle."

"Oooh, I would've left. What if the bottle pointed to gross Pierce?"

"Yeah, I thought about that, but it didn't."

"Well," I said, "at least Billy is cute."

"Yeah, but it was disgusting, like a rubber snake in my mouth. I'll never do that again—unless I marry Parker."

"Well, I'm glad I missed that party," I said.

The wind blew across the tops of the ruins. Oyster shells scattered like tinkling bells.

"It's just the wind, right?" Piper said. She lowered her voice. "You ready to make a run for it? We can win this year; I know we can."

"Let's show this town." I said, and we bolted from our hiding place, kicked the can across the beach, and hollered that we were the all-time queens and winners of the Seaboro world.

Sated, I returned to the blanket in time to help our families load the boats and return home. There were only six more days until school started, and I wanted to soak up every single moment of that dwindling summer.

We reached the dock behind the Loughlin house, climbed out, unloaded the coolers, baskets, and then there was the matter of the kettle. I settled on the grass to watch the last ritual of the day—unloading and storing the pot. This was just like taking down the Christmas tree or putting away the blown eggs after Easter.

Ellie climbed from the boat—and this was the part I had gone over a million times and come up with the exact same memory, so I knew it was true. I knew I was to blame because this is what she said: "Cappy, darling, will you watch Sam for a minute while I get the baskets up to the house?"

And this was what I said: "Yes, ma'am." I know that is what I said because I still hear it in my own ears, in my own nightmares. "Yes, ma'am. Yes, ma'am." A simple answer.

Sam and I had wrestled in the grass, laughed at our dads while they tried to hoist the kettle and move it back toward the shed. Then Boyd ran toward us with a crab, a wriggling, angry blue crab snapping its claws. The recent and vivid memory of a crab holding on to my baby toe made me back away while clutching Sam.

"Noooo . . ." Sam and I screamed in unison, and ran behind an ancient log that had probably been there longer than anyone I knew had been alive—a massive tree that had fallen in one of the surging storms years ago. It had an opening in the rear—just the size of a two-year-old.

Sam crawled into the hole, and I sat in front of it, blocking him from Boyd and the crab—me, the almighty protector, right?

But when Boyd came too close, I ran. When he shoved the crab in my face and its claws opened in front of my eyes, I ran. I will always know this much—I did run. I did.

Boyd and I laughed while we ran, but only for a few moments.

Ellie's voice ripped through the evening. "Where's Sam?"

I looked up at her standing at the edge of the river, the picnic basket at her feet, sunlight falling on her like a blessing.

When Jim finally rose dripping from the river cradling a limp and wet doll, my thoughts, dull and numb, were, *Why would he come up with a doll when everybody else is looking for Sam?* My mind was unable to form the reality of Sam gone in his daddy's arms.

I promised God, Sam, and all the avenging angels that I would never again jump into the deep end, never say yes when I didn't mean it.

I grabbed Dad's urn from the front seat and walked down the public-access path toward the river and dock where someone had left an unlit hanging lantern that bobbed with the tide and my weight as I sat down on the far end. The urn dug into my lap, real, not vaporous like my memories of Sam and Boyd, but solid with the certainty with which I'd said, "Yes, ma'am," when Ellie had asked me to watch her little boy.

I stood and paced the length of the dock back and forth, never reaching either the water or land. How could I possibly do this thing, open this urn above the same body of water? This seemed as terrible as if I'd held Sam under the surface and refused him his last breath.

Sam.

I turned and squinted into the sun, up the river five or six houses away, toward Ellie's dock where I had lost him. Curiosity pushed me across the distance to the Loughlin dock as I wondered if the old oak log where Sam had hidden still lay on the ground, if the osprey had returned and nested there. I realized, of course, that I had lost more than Sam that day. Only Sam died, but we all lost a particular life we'd been living.

I moved toward that dock as the list of what I'd caused each person to lose grew inside me: home, husband, son, brother. . . .

Anger flooded in, masking and overcoming the grief. Briefly I was glad for this emotion. And I thought I understood—for one moment—why Boyd had chosen to hold on to the anger. It was easier. Truly easier.

I sank into rage, let it convince me that I did not have to

do what Dad had asked. That I did not, in any way, owe him this harsh request. I stomped and kicked and yelled across the lawn as I walked out onto the Loughlin dock. "No, I will not," I told Dad. And I hoped he heard me, wished he knew that this story—the one in which the dutiful daughter tosses the ashes in some demented mythological place of childhood—was over. This story was over.

As seething fury grew inside me like a twisting, enraged living being, I turned on my heels, slipped on a mossy board, and lost my balance. I wanted to scream, but I didn't. Instead I fell to the splintered wood and curled into myself, frightened I had released something that should have stayed locked up, secure in its fortress of disregard and neglect.

The heavy urn tumbled to the side before I realized I had released it; I reached for it over my bent legs, clawed across the slippery wood. Panic joined fury, and I was unable to command my arms or fingers to do more than grapple in ineffectual motions.

I watched the container roll, then fall into the river. The splash was imperceptible.

I knew, I absolutely knew, that this was the same sound that we had failed to hear when Sam fell in. The river was so alive with motion and its own clamor that the minute sound didn't register to the human ear.

I screamed with such innate dread that I didn't know it was my voice, only my breath escaping in fear. I crawled to the edge of the dock, and just below the murky surface I saw the top of the urn through the water, trying to decide whether to bob or to sink.

I bent over, reached for it. My fingers ran across the iron, but I couldn't get a hold.

Dreamscapes flowed over me: I was trying to cross the river, but wasn't making it to the other side, the safe shore. My whole life I had had this dream—running, swimming, and never reaching.

I rolled off the dock into the water because I knew it was all I could do: I couldn't let Dad sink like Sam. Not without the proper good-byes, the way he'd asked to go.

Guilt flooded me like blood in my mouth. I tasted it, swallowed it whole: Boyd was right—there was no redemption. I was there, I knew, to pay.

Water folded over my head as I sank beneath the surface.

The water was like silk; I released my breath in small increments. With each exhale I sank further and further to the floor of the river where minnows tickled my shin, where the unseen shrimp and fish swam past me in the tidal flow. The current drew me out—toward the sea.

I realized I could let go and everything would be released in me: guilt, shame, grief, everything our families had lost, all of them flowing out with me.

This huge, monstrous realization brought solace of such measure that I sank into it, exhaled one more time.

Underwater I didn't hear the words of blame I'd heard

inside my head my entire life. What I did hear was my name—over and over, my name.

*Cappy.*

I heard it again.

*Cappy.*

It was someone who knew my real name, my name before Sam died.

My oxygen was gone, the memories faded, and primal need forced me upward, away from this vision, to the surface of the water. My hands were empty—I hadn't found Dad's urn. My need for life pulled me up. Life where someone called my name.

I inhaled, my lungs filled with a burning combination of water and air. I reached for solid ground, but found only more water. I turned to float on my back, but my spastic attempts sent me back under the water.

My chest burned; my limbs were completely useless, ignoring all my commands to swim as I knew how to do.

I gasped and it was air I brought into my lungs when my body bounced back up. I understood that if I went down again, it would be for the last time.

I uttered a prayer I had not prayed in many years: "Please don't let Sam have suffered; let him have taken only that one breath. That one breath that was full of water and peace and sinking sleep."

But I knew it wasn't true—that he would have taken more than one breath, that he would have looked up and seen the surface just as I had, but not known how to get to it, not known how to rise to all those up there who loved him and waited for him, but would look for him too late.

This was too much for me to know—to take back to the surface with me.

I sank again.

A pain ripped through my scalp and I was no longer floating. I reached up to touch a broad hand.

I sputtered in the tight grip of this unknown hand. My head hit the edge of the dock, my teeth banged against one another, blood filled my mouth as I bit down on the side of my cheek. A snapping sound came from around my neck with a silver flash in the water: Thurman's diamond necklace. I watched it float, dance in a circle, and sink; I didn't reach for it.

I grasped onto the side of the wood; my left hand slipped off, then clutched again. I coughed, vomited seawater while someone held my hands to the edge of the dock. I wanted to empty everything in me; empty it into this river, into this blackness. I wanted to be so barren that I remembered and knew nothing but what was new and clean and whole.

But, of course, this was not possible. There was no way to abandon everything I was made of—everything that had formed me.

I crawled onto the dock and collapsed on my back, staring up at Boyd Loughlin, who was bent over me. His face wavered above me; the osprey flew in circles over his head.

She cried out in the high-pitched call of all ospreys, dipped low, then rose again on a current and disappeared from my vision. I reached up, touched Boyd's shoulder. He slid his hands under my back and pulled me to a sitting position.

He patted my back like one would a child, but harder. "Are you okay? What were you doing? Are you freaking crazy?"

My voice was gone, and I was afraid I'd left it down in the river. I pointed to the sky. "Did she get her nest back yet?"

"Whose nest? What?" He glanced around the dock, behind him. "What are you talking about?"

I released a noise that was somewhere between a sob and a choke, then dropped my hand to point at the water. "I left him down there."

Boyd placed his hands on both my shoulders. "Cappy, are you okay? Did you drop something down there? A nest? What were you trying to get?"

"God, I left him down there," I said, moving toward the water in a crawl.

"Stop," he said.

And I did. Just like when I was twelve years old and he told me not to steal second base. I stopped and turned my head toward where he sat in front of me, his face twisted as though he fought a thousand words and emotions and couldn't decide which ones to say or act on. He lifted his right hand and I thought he might hit me, and then I thought he might pull me toward him and hold me. But he dropped his eyes, then his hand, and shook his head. "Catherine Leary, what are you doing?"

"I dropped Dad's urn in the river. I didn't mean to."

"Your dad?" Then he stood and looked down at me, placed his palms on my shoulders. "You need to go home, Cappy. You shouldn't be here. Get up."

I stood and faced him, wiping water from my cheeks as footsteps shook the dock. Boyd and I turned to see an old woman half walking, half running down the dock. She carried a casserole dish covered in tinfoil, which she dropped as she reached us. Chicken, broccoli, and rice flew across the dock as her hands flew upward. "Oh, dear Lord, what is happening down here? What's going on?"

Boyd shook rice off his foot. "Alice," he said, "everything's fine."

"Alice?" I took a step toward the woman, touched her arm.

"Little Cappy Leary, what are you doing here? What is happening?" Her eyes filled with tears; her hands flew in circles as though she were trying to trace the osprey path from only moments ago. "Someone tell me what is going on."

Boyd took her hand. "It's all fine now. I was sitting on the back porch with Mother—waiting for you to bring dinner. . . ." He glanced down at the food, then at me. "When I saw someone on the dock. It was Cappy here."

Alice dropped Boyd's hand and looked to me. "What were you doing, dear? Why are you wet?"

"I was trying to . . . I meant to . . . but I lost him in the water." I wiped my face, bent over with a sharp pain in my lungs. "I have to go get it, Alice. I can't just leave him down there."

"It wasn't your fault, Cappy. You didn't lose him. It was *not* your fault. It was everyone's doing. It was everyone's fault. A horrible combination. You must not carry this burden of guilt anymore, child. You must not." Alice's voice shook.

I heard her words; I'd heard them before. They were repeating in my head and chest like those of an intimate lover, one I'd held close and used for comfort, but never truly trusted.

Boyd's voice broke through. "Please, let's get off the dock. Mother will come out here if she sees us."

His voice carried the blame and anger from years ago, and I took them in, allowed them to settle.

"Alice," he said, "don't worry about the dinner. Why don't you take Cappy back to your house while I check on Mother. She's especially confused tonight."

I wanted to grab Boyd, shake him, and make the empathetic boy I once knew come back onto this dock. I wanted to remove the anger and hatred I had obviously placed in him, on him. "Boyd," I said, "I am not confused. I dropped an urn; I saw the osprey; I am not confused."

He leaned toward me, squinted. "I am not talking about you—I am talking about Mother."

"Oh." I stood taller, took a deep breath. "I'm sorry."

He stared at me, then spoke softly. "Why were you in the water?"

I shivered in the heat, rubbed my hands up and down my arms. "I wanted to get the urn," I said, closed my eyes. "And then I just wanted to stay underwater. Just stay there for a while."

Boyd touched my elbow. "You scared the hell out of me. I saw you fall in, but not come up."

I opened my eyes and looked at him and saw the beauty of us before Sam's death. I turned away from Boyd, from all the exquisite possibilities of me, of him, of us. "I'm sorry."

"Get dried off and go home. . . ."

"Thanks for . . ."

He held up his palm, stopped my words.

Alice took my hand and I followed her across the lawn to her home. She left me alone while she put a kettle on the stove, then offered me chamomile tea in a delicate flowered teacup that reminded me of Mother, and wrapped an afghan over me, as if she were the stronger and surer of us two. She was smaller than I remembered, but her hair was the same brilliant white twisted on top of her head in a knot. She wore a pair of drawstring denim pants and a white tunic that now had rice and broccoli smeared across the front. Her tiny hands patted mine; her brown eyes looked at me with sympathy as she sat next to me.

"Alice," I said, "I need to explain something. I dropped . . .

Dad's urn of ashes. I wasn't trying to get . . . Sam." I leaned forward.

"Oh." She nodded and took my hand. "I see, dear."

"I can't believe I dropped it. What is wrong with me?"

Alice smiled. "Nothing is wrong with you, child. This is a hard place for you."

I took a sip of tea, leaned back in the flowered chair, and shivered. "You could say that. But it's good to see you, Alice. How have you been?"

"Well, quite well. Lost Mack about six years ago, and I miss him every day."

"He was a good man," I said.

"Yes, he was, just like your daddy."

I placed my teacup on a lace doily on the side table. "Alice, can I ask you a question?"

"Anything, as always."

"Did you see Dad when he came to visit here?"

She closed her eyes, settled into her rocking chair, and nodded twice.

"Where?"

"Oh, various places: Morgan's, Ellie's, the courthouse."

"You're the second person who has told me you saw him at the courthouse. What was he doing there? Why did he go?"

She shrugged. "I work there." She lifted her chin. "Seaboro has given me the keys, you know. And your dad had a favorite painting he came to see."

"Did you all talk?"

"Of course we did. What do you think? I'd be rude and ignore him?"

"No, I mean, did he tell you why he was there?"

"No, child. As nosy as I am, I wouldn't ask him something he didn't offer."

"Oh," I said. "None of this makes any sense to me."

"What do you mean?"

I twisted river-soaked hair away from my face. "Alice, I didn't even know he visited here. I always thought he went somewhere to study and work."

"Maybe he came *here* to study and work."

"But why didn't he tell me? Why did he hide it from me?"

"He was a private man."

I nodded. "He didn't tell me because I was the one who made him leave here and he didn't want to make me feel bad. That was the kind of man he was. He wouldn't want me to think he loved something I took away from him."

Alice stood, and she seemed taller, younger than she had only a moment ago. "I do not ever want to hear you talk that way again, Catherine Carrington Leary. You did not make your father or your mother leave this place. That was their choice."

I stared at her. "Alice, I am not a child anymore. I know what I did and did not cause—I can't fool myself or you or anyone else in this town about what came before or after

Sam drowned. I would have never, in my entire life, returned to this place if Dad had not asked me to bring his ashes. I don't need the consolation of childish assurances . . . not anymore." I stood, then bent over to hug her. "It is amazing to see you. You were an important person to me, and I think of you often."

"Cappy, give yourself some time here, try to discover what would bring you and your dad to this place."

"I know exactly what brought both of us: He loved it here; he made me come. Now I'm going home. He asked me to toss his ashes, and it might not have been the way he intended—but it's done."

"Done?"

"Yes, I'm finished." I clapped my hands together. "Thank you for helping me tonight. Weren't you always there to bail me out of trouble?" I tried to smile, but my mouth trembled.

She hugged me, held on to me for long moments, then leaned back and looked at me while still clasping my arms. I thought she had something more to say, but then she uttered, "I love you, Cappy."

"You too, Alice." I hugged her good-bye.


I drove back to the B & B and thought how Alice could offer words of consolation for hours and hours, but I knew why we had moved, why our lives had changed, and her simple solace couldn't remove the truth or my guilt. Mother had made it perfectly clear why we left Seaboro when she had come into my room three days after Sam's death, one day since his funeral: all time now measured by Sam.

I had spent each day trying to figure out how much longer I could wait until I ran to Alice's barn to sleep in the hay. Early in the mornings, the woodpecker knocked on the wide red door and dawn stunned me into running for my own bed before the sun revealed my empty room. My parents had been so out of it they hadn't noticed my absence through the long nights.

Mother and Dad had entered my room; Mother sat on the side of my bed, and then looked up at Dad. "Why don't you let me talk to her privately?"

"What?" I said, looking back and forth between them for some hint of what Mother wanted to tell me alone.

Dad leaned down, kissed me, and left without a word, obliging Mother with his absence.

Then she spoke. "Catherine, dear. These have been hard days for all of us. Very hard. I know we haven't been here for you. I'm sorry, but what I have to say will be difficult for you to hear." Mother leaned back against my headboard and closed her eyes, as if what she said next would take all that was left in her. My chest tightened, and I knew that whatever it was had to be terrible, twisting and horrid, and I didn't want to hear it. I covered my ears with cupped hands.

Mother opened her eyes. "Don't make this harder, Catherine. It's not that bad, not compared . . ."

*To what you did . . .*

I heard the blame in the silence.

There was no escape from what formed before me: as if an evil being had hidden in the shadows of my room and now stepped forward to bare his teeth.

"You know how Southern University has been begging Dad to come teach for years?"

I gripped the side of my quilt, pulled it up to my chin, then over my mouth, and spoke from behind it. "He always says no. Always. Every time."

"Well, they've asked again, begged your father to come use his expertise. . . ." Mother's eyes closed, and she fought an unseen temptation to give only the ending of whatever prepared speech she had begun. "We are moving to Cedar Valley, where our people are from."

"No, we are not," I said. "Daddy would never, ever leave this place, Mother."

"Yes, we are leaving in three days."

I didn't cry; I was sure that Mother was wrong. They would not rip the roots of my being from this earth. It was a simple fact: If I was removed from this place, I'd die. Wither and die. And so would Dad. And once again—death would be my fault.

"This is your fault!" I screamed at Mother. "You want to go back to your family. You are making me and Daddy leave . . . aren't you?" My voice rose with each word. I dropped the quilt, stood.

To inflict pain when I was hurting came as natural to me as running my horse through the sea oats. Push back, hurt back. There must be a place for the blame, and I found it: Mother and her heartless ways, her practicality without passion.

Then I saw something in Mother's eyes I had never seen before: tears. "It is not me, Catherine. Don't ever say that again."

And the unsaid words shimmered across the room in a wild dance—*It's your fault, Catherine. Yours. Yours. Yours.*

All of this was more than I could understand or absorb at that time. I ran past Mother, down the hall lined with family photos in sepia tones and cherry-wood frames, down the stairs, through the foyer with the mail scattered on the hall table and out the front door, where my feet didn't feel the ground until I entered Alice and Mack's barn.

When I shoved the doors open and launched myself into the hay, I landed on Boyd Loughlin, crouched and whittling an arrow from a piece of wood.

He looked up at me. "What the . . . ?"

"Get out," I said in a raw voice I didn't recognize. He had come into my sanctuary, my hiding place. I jumped off him, stood with my hands folded across my chest.

"This isn't just your place," he said, pushed his chest out in defiance.

The smell of wood, hay, and soil combined into an aroma

I wanted to wrap up, pack into my hands, and take wherever I went. "This is my place," I said. "I want to take it with me."

"Take what where?" Boyd stared at me, and it was there: the light—a thin shiver around his head that moved with him. I understood that the sunlight fell through the cracks in the barn, that evening was settling into our hiding place, but I saw the glow and this allowed me to fall to my knees.

I dropped into the hay, buried my face in his lap—something I had never done before. He laid his hand on top of my head, warm and comforting. I closed my eyes and waited for that word—redemption—without knowing the word, only the emotion it would bring if it came.

"Are you okay?" he whispered in the low voice of an older Boyd.

Blood pounded against my eardrums as I tried to find a way to tell him I was not, for once, crying about Sam, but from a new terror.

He ran his fingers through my hair, and this gentleness was as stunning to me as the fact that I'd dropped my head into his lap.

I didn't speak; I wanted to stay there with my eyes closed and his hand warm on my head and wait, wait a thousand days, a thousand years, until I was forgiven, until this pain went away.

A voice shattered our peace. "Cappy, Boyd . . . are you in here?" Alice called into the barn.

I sat up, looked at her as she came to us. "How did you

know we were here?" I asked, wiping my face in a quick gesture.

"I always know when you come here." She smiled. "Cappy, I just spoke to your mother. She wanted to know if you were here, if you were okay. I told her you were fine. . . ."

*Oh, God, no. No, don't say it.* Alice was going to say Mother's words.

"No, don't tell her where I am."

"She told me, Cappy—told me about moving."

"What?" Boyd's voice came quietly.

"Don't say it, Alice. Don't say it," I whispered.

"Catherine, you will be okay. I promise." Alice murmured words that only confirmed the horrible truth: I would be torn from this place, from Ellie.

Ellie—that was the answer. Why hadn't I thought of that already?

"If Mother wants to live in Cedar Valley so badly, she can go. I'll stay here with Ellie." I stood now, certain in my conviction.

Boyd stood and walked toward Mack's worktable, ran his hands through the sawdust where Mack had taught him to carve wood.

"Oh, Cappy." Alice pulled me against her chest. "You are a family. You must go with your family."

"Do you want to tell me what's going on here?" Boyd flicked his pocketknife back and forth between his hands, a picture of nonchalance contradicted by his tight mouth.

"Horrible Mother is making us move, but I am not going."

"Maybe it would be best if you left," Boyd said, snapped shut the knife.

It was then, truly then, that I understood how wide my sin had spread. I had already gone to the only safe place I knew. There was nowhere else to run.

"I won't," I said. "I won't go."

Alice sighed, and I saw the grown-up acknowledgment of childish denial. "You have three days until you leave. I would not spend these days pretending it won't happen. Spend them . . ." Alice didn't finish, and I thought that even she, with all the advice in the world, could not tell me how to use my last three days.

Boyd ran from the barn, slammed the door on my heart. Alice placed her arms around me so I rested against her chest. "You must go home now. You cannot stay here all night again."

"Please let me stay," I said. "Just tell Mother I'm spending the night with you. I cannot go home. I just can't."

Alice didn't hesitate. "Yes, I'll call her. You go home at first light, as you have been," she said.

"I promise."

The hay whispered beneath her feet as she walked to the door; then she turned and stared at me for the longest moment. It was the first time I saw unsaid words glimmer in the air: dancing, twisting to escape. Then she closed her eyes and they disappeared in a silvery shiver.

"What is it, Alice? What?" I stepped toward her, because whatever those words were, I needed to hear them.

"Oh, Cappy." She reached for me and hugged me once more. "I do love you."

And although these words were of desperate importance, I understood they weren't the dancing words I'd just seen above her.

When Alice left, I lay down on the hay and spoke out loud. "Daddy won't be able to stand Cedar Valley, and we'll come back. We'll come back."

I filled this balloon of comfort higher and larger with these words, with denial, as I drifted into the only sleep I knew those days after Sam: a sleep filled with deep, tidal waters, and fear.

Three days passed as my family packed. I rarely entered my home, unable to bear the cardboard boxes filled with bubble wrap and family belongings, men in overalls tromping through my house with packing paper, cigarette stubs left on the front porch. I couldn't listen to the talk of school applications, new neighborhoods, and our future house. In a factual tone, Mother informed me that our Seaboro house had been sold to the historical society, and that no one else would be living here—just more proof to me that we would come back.

Ellie was emotionally unreachable in those last days: gone into herself and the remote land of sorrow. I tried to see her. I ran to her house, a house so full of mourning that the air itself seemed thick and swollen with something larger than loss. Ellie rarely came out of her room, and when she did, her face was wrenched with pain.

My movements were slow, uncontrolled, as I fell at Ellie's kitchen table and sobbed. Ellie finally reached for me, wrapped her hands in my ponytail. I choked trying to stop the tears, the pain, the feeling that I was plummeting below the surface of life.

"It's okay to cry, Cappy. Okay."

"Mother says enough is enough. He wasn't my brother. Enough."

"We are all doing our own kind of mourning, each of us, Cap."

Now was the time to say I was sorry. I fell to my knees in front of Ellie. "It is all my fault. Oh, God, Ellie—you must hate me."

She lifted me from the ground, placed her hands on either side of my face.

"Never, ever forget this, Cappy: I love you. Whatever happens, whatever you know, never forget that." Ellie sighed, the longest sigh I'd ever heard, as if all the words she needed to say were trapped behind her heart—her large and beautiful heart. I waited for more—words of wisdom, of comfort. But she had nothing left to give except her embrace.

It was only after I left that I realized I had not said the words I had gone to say: *I'm sorry.*

# EIGHT

*"In the middle of difficulty lies opportunity."*
—ALBERT EINSTEIN

My clothes clung to me with the briny, tangy odor of the river when I walked through the front door of the inn, attempting to sneak past the library and down the hall to the Lighthouse Room.

"Cappy." Forrest's voice came from behind me.

I gritted my teeth and turned. He sat in a chair on the far side of the empty room, a book across his lap. "Hey," I said. "I thought you'd be upstairs by now."

"I was waiting for you," he said, but didn't move or rise.

I walked next to the bar. "Why?"

"Uh, because I wanted to." He squinted at me. "Have you been . . . swimming?"

"Not exactly on purpose," I said, wiped hair off my face.

"Did you . . ." He stood then, placed the book on a table, and came toward me.

"Did I what?"

"Toss his ashes?"

I stood still for a long moment and noticed details—small and trivial—all around me: Forrest's hair mussed and curled around his face, a lamp shade crooked on the side table, dust on the windowsill below the air-conditioning unit, a lace tablecloth with a coffee stain.

Forrest's face moved with concern, and I wondered if he would care if he knew what I'd done. If I walked toward him, held my arms out, he would hold me and allow me to settle into him, tell the terrible story of what had just happened on Boyd's dock. But instead I took a step backward, because although I knew he'd offer empathy and friendship, it would be false comfort; he didn't know the full truth of what I'd done, of who I was.

Forrest spoke again. "Are you okay?"

"I'm fine. Yes, I tossed his ashes. . . . I've got to go to bed now. We'll leave first thing in the morning." I turned away from him, from that room, from Seaboro.

On Memorial Day morning I went immediately to the courthouse to try to discover why Dad had come there. I'd spent the night searching for the answer and I couldn't find any reason beyond that he loved Seaboro.

The courthouse was one of the few buildings in town spared by Sherman's march of destruction, and it wasn't the courthouse anymore—it hadn't served that function when I lived here. The historic building housed a collection of Seaboro artifacts about the town and the surrounding Lowcountry, and I knew it would be open on a holiday for tourists.

I'd visited there on countless school field trips. As I walked up the wide wooden steps to the front door, I brushed away the stray curls that had found their way out of my low ponytail, smoothed my button-down blouse, and took a deep breath in which I felt the ragged ache of last night's plunge into the river. For the second morning in a row, I'd sneaked out of the B & B without Forrest. I needed to see this painting Alice had told me about without Forrest's observant eyes and probing questions.

Wilted flowers spilled out of the window boxes, and humid air washed in off the water only a block away. I pulled at the doors, but they remained shut. I leaned back and looked at the sign. SEABORO DISPLAYS WILL BE OPEN LATE TODAY—ELEVEN A.M. PLEASE COME BACK.

All down the main street American flags lined the walkways, front porches, and the sides of the windows for Memorial Day—the start of summer. In Seaboro there would be picnics and parades and parties, and here I was by myself. This isolation loomed larger than it would on most days, and I realized why—this had always been a day of anticipation for the carefree weeks ahead, for fun and sea and freedom. Today it was just another day.

I groaned and kicked at the brass plate at the bottom of the door. My flip-flop bent backward, and pain shot through my foot. I sat on a bench willing the person who was supposed to open the courthouse to hurry and show up.

When the quiet street and chirping cicadas were still my only company, I stepped down and stared across the street to the common area, where a statue of a Confederate soldier stood at attention. Unnamed, he represented all those from Seaboro who had died in the war between the states—a list was etched in a marble engraving.

The green expanse of the town square was filled with benches and magnolias and live oaks. Gas lamps stood guard on each corner, and the cloudless sun rested on my arms like my only friend. I glided down the sidewalk, ran my hands over the tops of benches, across the doorknobs of stores, the barbershop, the pharmacy, the boutique, and the used bookstore. I felt their familiar names on my tongue as I said them out loud and attempted the names of the new stores.

I stopped in front of Cloud Nine Café, in the same location it had occupied since 1932. There was still a metal bench in front, croissants and pastries in the window. Hunger prodded.

A handwritten sign hung crooked on the front door—IF THERE IS A LINE OUTSIDE, PLEASE TAKE A NUMBER AND WAIT.

IF NOT, COME IN AND FIND YOUR SEAT. I entered a room thick with the scents of yeast, sugar, and coffee.

The cracked Formica tables looked as if they'd been there since the founding of this café. The small room hummed with the mechanics of the air conditioner, stuck slanted in the window. The ceiling fans meant to circulate the cool air mixed the smells of bacon and biscuits and pulled heat from the kitchen to create wafts of cool and hot air around the tables. Nobody complained, as the food more than made up for any lack of atmosphere.

A young woman, no more than eighteen, stood behind the counter, a hairnet over her blond hair. "May I help you?" she asked.

"Yes, I'd love a cup of coffee," I said, and then coughed as my words came rough and raw. "And a cinnamon scone to go, please."

"Totally. Just give me a minute," she said.

I scooted back toward the wall and waited, but the silence overwhelmed me. I still hadn't talked to Thurman, and decided I wouldn't until I saw him in person. But I couldn't leave until I found out why Dad had been coming here.

Secrets: so many of them whispering around me.

I pulled out my cell phone; I had missed calls from a couple friends at home. The crowd Dad had called my "party friends." He didn't much care for any of them—said he'd bet not one of them had read Yeats or Hemingway or even a contemporary like Conroy.

I had never told him that he was right—they probably hadn't even read today's paper. But they sustained me with their boisterous laughter, playful antics, and grand gestures of frivolity.

At Dad's most frustrated moments, he'd ask me why I still pretended I was in college, why I couldn't move past the bars, concerts, and parties. I told him that I held down a perfectly secure job, made my own money, was responsible for myself, and that I was quite happy with the way things were.

I knew this saddened him, but we'd gotten into only one harsh disagreement about it. Dad needed to go out of town and asked me if I'd accompany Forrest to the Literary Awards at the university, as Forrest had won the Southern University award for a short story he'd written. I'd said no without further discussion. Only I knew that I was not good enough for a man like Forrest—he required something more than I could give. It was different with Thurman—I didn't have to be anything more than what I was; he didn't ask for anything deeper or more demanding than what we already had.

I was flipping my cell phone open and closed when I heard, "Ma'am?"

I started, dropped my phone. "Yes?" I stared at the young girl in the hairnet.

"Your order is ready," she said, handed me a white bag and a Styrofoam cup with a lid.

"Thanks," I said, and picked up the phone, then moved

out of the way of a woman who sidled past me to enter the store. Her silver hair was cut in a stylish bob, and the thin skin around her eyes told the story of age, but she was beautiful: a statue cut of thin, sharp lines and linear slashes. She carried her alligator purse in the crook of her arm and smiled at me.

"Excuse me," I said.

"No problem, dearie," she said.

She moved past me, her silk pants and shirt sighing a soft sound. Her crisp clothes and hair didn't hint at the morning humidity that soaked the back of my neck. Then she turned again and stared at me. "Is that you, Catherine Leary?"

I opened my eyes wide, reached for the stray curls around my face. I should have at least put on some makeup. I knew I looked a disheveled mess, but I'd expected to get in, look at the damn painting, get out. Go home.

"Yes," I said, nodded. "I am."

"Well, well. I'd heard you were in town from Mary-Belle Fortner. What a pleasure to see you."

I nodded again, wishing I could take one long, deep sip of coffee. Mary-Belle must have been the woman at Ellie's house when I'd first arrived.

"You don't remember me, do you?" the woman asked.

I hated that question. I smiled. "I'm sorry; it's just been so long."

"I'm Dixie Appleton, your piano teacher. . . ."

Ah, yes. She'd taught piano, dance, and etiquette, along

with the other niceties of Southern charm: how to walk, talk, hold a teacup, leave a calling card, write a thank-you note. Wouldn't she be sorely disappointed, her education obviously squandered on me with my chipped nail polish, wrinkled clothes, puffed hair? I almost wished I could pick up a teacup and take a delicate sip to show her that not all of her tutelage had gone to waste, tell her I always wrote prompt thank-you notes and I crossed my legs at the ankles when I sat. I had cross-stitched my dining room chair covers, as all good Southern woman did, while I'd sat at Mother's bedside during her last days.

Mrs. Appleton walked over and hugged me.

"Catherine, dear. I would know you anywhere—as usual, looking like you just came from some grand adventure."

Grand indeed—last night I'd dropped my Dad's urn at the bottom of the river.

From Dixie Appleton this was not an insult and was not taken as one. As a child, I'd tested her Southern patience and womanly charm, showing up for classes straight from the river, fort, or stables.

I laughed in the same rough voice I'd spoken with. "Adventure. Yes, I guess you could call it that."

"How are you? What are you doing here down from the mountains?" She made a pout with her lips. "I am so sorry you lost your mama, and now your dad. It must be hard for you."

I looked away, gripped the Styrofoam cup so that a

single crack appeared at the side. Coffee dripped down my arm, burned in a straight line from wrist to elbow. I gasped and dropped the cup as dark fluid flowed over the hardwood floors and onto Dixie's pointed leather high heels.

"Oh, God, I'm sorry," I said, wiped in spastic, frantic motions at my arm, then the floor.

A hand rested on my shoulder. "It's okay; I've got it." I looked up at the girl who'd given me the coffee.

"If you get me some paper towels, I'll clean this up," I said, glanced up to Dixie and expected to see a brutal stare, but I found sympathy. I stood. "I'm sorry for your shoes."

"No, it's my fault. I obviously said the wrong thing." She dropped her hand on my arm. She glanced around the room, and then whispered to me, "Did you come back to see your old home? Where you grew up with him?"

"No, I came to scatter his ashes."

"Oh," she said, and I saw that for probably the first time in her life, she was without an appropriate response.

All at once my throat closed up, my eyes filled, blocked with emotion I could not, would not release. I would not let it come full force. The young girl came to me, touched my arm, handed me a new cup of coffee. "Don't cry, ma'am. Here's another coffee for free. You don't have to pay for it or clean it up—just don't cry."

Dixie grabbed my arm and guided me outside, then sat with me on the bench in front of the café.

"She thought you were going to cry about the coffee."

Dixie's words were wrapped in laughter, like the loveliest gift.

"The coffee," I said, and laughed with her.

We sat on the bench with a proper distance between us, two women who used to know each other in a different life and time. "I am so sorry for your loss," she said again.

"Thank you," I said, then took a sip of the coffee. I lifted the cup to her. "Good coffee."

She laughed again. "Worth the tears?"

"Absolutely," I said.

We were silent for a few moments. A boy on a skateboard whizzed by; a woman younger than me pushed a baby stroller and smiled.

Dixie broke the silence. "How long are you staying?"

"I'm leaving today," I said.

"Oh, that's too bad. You'll miss the parade and the picnic on the green. I'm sure there will be many people there who would love to see you."

"I have to get back . . ." I said.

"Family?"

I shook my head. "Job, house, dog . . . friends. You know."

Dixie stared at me for a long moment until I was uncomfortable, itching under her kind scrutiny. "Is something wrong?"

"I am trying to decide whether to ask you something."

"Go ahead."

"Have you seen Ellie? She would just love to see you . . . know you're well."

"Yes," I said. "I stopped by and said hello to her."

She bit her lower lip as if attempting to stop the question that came next. "Did she remember you?"

"Yes," I said.

"Have you kept up with her at all?"

"No." But underneath that answer were all the other things I wanted to say: *I wanted to keep in touch, but Mother told me to move on. I called Boyd when I was in high school and he hung up on me because I couldn't get words out of my mouth fast enough. I called Ellie once—on her birthday—and got the answering machine and was too scared to leave a message.* But I didn't say any of these things to Dixie. Instead I stood. "I need to get going. It was lovely to see you."

"You too," she said.

I turned toward the courthouse, where a small woman was unlocking the doors. She turned and smiled at me— Alice McPherson.

As I climbed the steps, Alice said, "Well, well, hello, there, dearie."

I laughed. "That is the second time today that I've been called *dearie*."

Alice touched my cheek. "Are you better today? You know, you scared the life out of me last night."

I kissed Alice's cheek. "I just need to get in the courthouse for one minute; is that okay?"

"I had started to think last night was a dream. I'm thrilled to see you, Cappy Leary."

"Thanks, Alice. And I wish parts of last night had been a dream." I patted her arm. "I'm just here to see that painting real quick before I leave town. I want to see what Dad might have loved so much that he had to keep coming."

"Sure thing," Alice said, then stuck the key in the lock and wiggled it back and forth.

"Here," I said, "let me help you."

"No, someone might see you and think I can't handle the job." She winked at me. "Then they'll give the keys to old Mrs. McGillicutty. She's wanted this job since 1975. No way I'll give this key to that old biddy who tried to kiss Mack at a New Year's Eve party."

"You don't forget anything, do you, Alice?"

She squinted at me with her hand in midair. Then she spoke so softly I needed to lean in to hear her. "There are some things an old lady wishes she could forget."

Alice opened the door, but stood in the entranceway and stared at me. "You are still a beautiful young woman, even with the pain of the previous night etched in the corners of your mouth and a sheen of weariness settling into your green eyes."

"I guess that's a compliment," I said.

"Oh, don't mind me," Alice said. "Sometimes I don't even realize I've said things out loud. Getting worse and worse." Alice stepped into the foyer and flicked the lights on.

I ran my hand along the wooden banister. "Is the painting upstairs or down?"

"Follow me," Alice said.

My footsteps echoed behind her as she walked upstairs and down the hall on the right into the room where local artists' work was displayed: framed paintings, sketches, folk art, Gullah sweetgrass baskets, and other local crafts.

Alice stood in the middle of the room and pointed to the far wall. "Right there."

I walked toward the painting with hesitant half steps, then stopped and stared.

"It's one of my favorites," Alice said.

"Who painted it?"

"I don't know. . . . It's anonymous."

I laughed. "I thought you knew everything."

"I do, everything except that." Alice backed a few steps from me and sat down in a cane chair on the side wall.

I stared at the painting—an oil work on a piece of driftwood. The colors were muted, almost gray, but I saw evening in the painting—the end of a day. A man stood on the wet sand of a retreating tide and held out his hand to a woman who sat at his feet. He was pulling her to stand, this was obvious, but she just gazed up at him. Part of an oak tree entered the right side of the painting where a small, empty nest teetered on the edge of a branch. The background was full of turbulent waves against a line of low gray clouds. A brass plate hung below the painting: TITLE: *THE LAST DAY*. ARTIST: ANONYMOUS.

I turned to Alice. "This . . . was Dad's favorite painting? Are you sure?"

"Very," she said.

"Nice painting. Why do I feel as if I've seen it before—or something like it?"

Alice shrugged. "It only came to us about three years ago. It was an anonymous donation—left on the front steps with instructions to keep it here. Not to sell it or give it away."

"This is all so damn weird."

"You are too pretty to curse, dear."

"I wonder what he saw in this."

Alice walked next to the painting and ran her finger over the bottom edge of the driftwood. "When I first saw it, I thought it was beautiful in its art technique, but as I've spent time with it, I've found that it's beautiful because it is heartbreaking."

Alice walked away, glanced over her shoulder. "I'll leave you alone. Please let me know if you have any questions. I'll be in the office at the front of the building."

I nodded. "I'm done here. I have no idea why he loved a sad painting of a man leaving or making a woman leave—or a wicked storm ruining a day at the beach. I have no idea, but now I've seen it."

Together we walked out of the room, down the stairs, and across the foyer. I stared at Alice for a moment. "I want to say . . . thank you for last night. Truly. You saw me at my absolute worst. I don't understand anything that was going on with Dad, and I'm tired of trying to figure it out. I think I just need to go home."

"Cappy." Alice took my hand. "When you don't understand something, you don't have to run from it."

"Listen, this is all terrible for me. I've done what Dad asked."

Alice hugged me. "I'm here if you'd like to return or stay. Please remember that. Now, granted, I don't know how much longer I'll be here."

"Stop that," I said, released Alice. "I'm really glad I got to see you. I've never been truly able to thank you for all you did for me those last days here."

"No need, dear one."

I walked out the front door of the courthouse, but felt all the way down inside that despite what I had just said to Alice, my stay was not over, not over at all. Something unnamed had just begun.

# NINE

*"There is such a thing as sacred idleness."*
—GEORGE MACDONALD

I drove past the Memorial Day flags lining the streets of Seaboro. Each pole had a name written in bold black letters with the war in which the men and women had sacrificed their lives listed below. In the distance I heard a band warming up with offbeat drums, scratching horns, and clarinets. As if in a blurry watercolor painting, I saw my ten-year-old self as I sat at the edge of the sidewalk, Dad at my side, new baby Sam on my lap, Ellie and Jim behind us, Mother in the background. I held a bright red ice that dripped down my arm, melting faster than I could lick it. Boyd was jumping up and down trying to see the parade before it came around the corner.

This memory made me smile, and I wanted to pull the

car over, find that girl at the edge of the sidewalk, and tell her to say no when Ellie asked her, two years later, to watch Sam. Tell her, "Say no; tell Ellie to take him with her and then we will all still be here in twenty years. We'll all still be here at the parade, with one another."

But, of course, that little girl was gone. Long gone.

A song of ringing bells came from my purse; I grabbed my cell phone. When I glanced at the number, I let out a long exhale before answering. It was a local number.

"Hello." I forced the cheery phone-answering voice I'd perfected over the years at work.

"Hey, where are you?"

"Oh, hello, Forrest. I'm just fine, and you?" I rubbed the bridge of my nose. "I just ran out to get some coffee. . . . I'm on my way back. Can I get you something?"

"No . . . just come on back so we can drive around. I'd love to go see your old house today."

"This is my last day here . . . and . . ." My words echoed in the car: *last day, last day.*

The painting—*The Last Day.* A stricture in my throat told me there was more, something more. I pulled the car to the side of the road, pushed the gearshift into park, and stared out the windshield.

A single chill ran down my arms, over my neck. An opening appeared inside my chest.

I knew exactly where I'd seen that painting—or another in a style just like it. Ellie had painted that picture.

"Last day," I said again.

"What? Are you okay?" Forrest's voice came from the phone I'd forgotten I held.

"I've gotta go . . . gotta go see Ellie. I'll check in later." I hung up on Forrest.

*The Last Day.*

Whose last day was it? I closed my eyes and attempted to recall the painting—the man pulling at the woman: Dad making Mother leave her sea, her home, her dreams? The man didn't look like Dad, or the woman like Mother. I remembered Dad's advice about a novel I didn't understand—I mustn't descend into literalism; I needed to feel the themes and emotions before I could apply the meaning to my life.

Or maybe it had something to do with *my* last day. Was there a hint?

On our last day in Seaboro a man from the local newspaper had come to take a family photo to place on the mantel of the house for the historical society. Every family that had lived in the home would have a portrait—ours was to be taken on moving day. Mother had made me wear an all-white linen dress with a scratchy petticoat underneath, as though she could convince anyone who ever looked at our photo that I was an innocent, pure child: clean and white.

When the last flashbulb went off, I ran past the boxes and paraphernalia of moving, jumped on my bike, rode past the horse stables to the tip of the land, to the beach.

I stood on the outcropping of rock above the water, stared out, and lifted my dress to keep the sand from dirtying it. "I'm sorry," I said to the water, to Sam, to life. "I will never, ever do anything wrong again. I promise. Just don't make us move; please, God, don't make us move."

But no one answered me, and I realized that it didn't matter what I said now. I ran down to the beach, burrowed into the sand, no longer caring if I ruined the dress. I needed comfort and didn't know where else to find it. The tide was at its lowest ebb, the sun descending. I laid my head on the sand, felt the telltale scratch of a sand dollar below the surface. I lifted my face and came to my knees, dug up the sand dollar and flipped it upside down to watch its cilia legs wriggle in a vain attempt to return to the life-giving sea. There was a crack down its middle where I'd laid my cheek. I had killed it. I choked on another sob, desperate now to save this sand dollar.

"I'll get you back there; I'll save you," I cried, crawled toward the water with the sand dollar in my hand. I reached the slurping edge of the water and laid the sea creature on top of the waves. "There, there, you'll be all right now."

The wave grabbed the sand dollar, took it into the sea.

I scuttled away from the water, where hundreds of sand dollars and starfish blended into the sand, just under the surface, a toe scrape away. They were stranded sea life, carried to shore by a high tide and left to bleach and die on the drying sand.

I dug furiously, threw handfuls of sand dollars and star-fish into the water. I continued as the strip of sea receded with the tide. My hands were raw, my fingertips bleeding as I scraped and clawed to save these animals stranded between the tides.

I felt no pain, or I had lost myself in it; I wasn't sure in the memory. It was Boyd who finally came up behind me, grabbed my arm. "Cappy, stop." He said my name louder and louder until I paused and held my hands up, tried to focus on him.

"You're bleeding," he said. "What are you doing?" His hair slashed in the wind, his face white below the low gray clouds.

"Can't you see? I'm saving the sand dollars and starfish. Saving them," I screamed, held up my bloody hands. "They were wriggling their teeny-tiny legs, kicking and trying to get back to the water. I'm saving them. What else would I be doing?" I pushed Boyd's knees so hard that he fell onto the sand next to me. I picked up the sand dollar, held out my hand, an offering.

Boyd took the sand dollar, turned it upside down. "See, it's alive. You're scaring me, Cappy. You're bleeding; your dress is ripped. Stop it. They're not dying . . . they'll be fine when the tide comes in."

I pushed him again, but this time he was prepared and grounded in the sand. He grabbed my hands, held them.

"They're gone. Sam's gone. I'm gone," I said.

"You'll come back, Cap. Stop it; you'll come back," he said in a cracked child's voice.

I pulled loose from him and fell into a fetal position on the sand. I felt but never saw him run away from me. Sam should be here and I should be gone. Something had gotten backward, been mixed up.

When I knew Boyd had truly left, when I would not have to see him leaving me, I lifted my head to the lonely dent in the sand that told of his presence. I lay down again and waited. I didn't know what I waited for—maybe the incoming tide or Dad, who eventually came running onto the sand, took me in his arms, and held me so tight my breath came in small gasps. He pried sand dollars and starfish from my hands and murmured words I've never remembered, took me home, and hid the ruined dress from Mother.

Maybe the painting was of Dad and me, or Boyd and me on the beach—not the parents at all. Or maybe it was all of us— all six of us leaving in our own way on the last day. Mother, Daddy, and me in a literal leaving; Boyd to his anger; Jim to his death; Ellie to her Alzheimer's.

Rain dropped on my windshield at the side of the road. This vivid memory told me no more than I already knew—I had killed Sam and we had moved. So, was this all about forgiveness? Moving on after remembering? No. There definitely had to be more than that.

Sam.

Boyd.

Ellie.

My eyes flew open and my heartbeat fluttered in a quick moment of something combined of fear and knowing. I flicked the windshield wipers on and shoved the gearshift and drove straight to Ellie Loughlin's house.

Palmetto branches brushed the side of my car as I pulled into the driveway. Tires sank into mud as I drove too fast into the parking spot at the side of the yard. Sweat trickled down my neck despite the air conditioner pumping full force onto my face. My palms were wet, and I'd bitten my bottom lip raw in the five-minute drive to the house.

I sat in the car and stared at the pickup truck parked to one side: Boyd's truck. Panic prodded my gut. I walked up to the porch and knocked on the front door, remembering the days when I would have run inside calling Ellie's, Sam's, or Boyd's name.

No one answered, and I called, "Hello . . . anyone home?" Raindrops grew larger, plopped on the pine straw off the porch, ran down the gutter in a song of metal and water.

I paced the porch, then sat on the wicker swing. The air was swollen, mist rolled off the river, a warm blanket that evoked a sense of dread. I was aware of an immense loss that didn't have anything to do with my present life, but of childhood, innocence, what was, what should have been.

I understood that if I or my family had stayed here, I'd be different: I'd be able to identify the sounds that surrounded me at that moment: what bird, or frog. The naming of the sounds was a lost corner piece of a large puzzle, which had a completely different image from the one I had lived since I was twelve years old.

The front door scraped across the porch; I jumped up to face Boyd. Maybe it was the memories I'd had about him moments ago, but I softened to his hard face, his bloodless lips.

"You're still here?" he asked.

"Yes," I said, stepped forward. "Please let me see your mom one last time."

"You've been sitting out here since you knocked?"

A breeze came from around the house, flung hair in my face. "Yes . . ."

"You still don't give up easily, do you?" he asked.

"Please, Boyd. You won't ever have to see me again. I know you hate me. I know that, but I'll never come back. I'll leave. I just want to see your mom once more."

He sat on the swing and looked up at me. "Okay, then here are the rules. Do not mention your family. Do not ask her questions about the past—she is confused enough about the past and present without trying to answer questions that mix the two. Do not cry—this only sends her into a state I can't calm for hours." Boyd looked up at me now. "Do you understand?"

"Yes."

"Do not apologize for something that happened a long time ago. Just sit with her and talk about whatever she wants to talk about."

"I get it, Boyd." I dropped my hand on the door handle, then asked, "Do you remember my last day here?"

"That is exactly the kind of question I'm talking about. Don't ask it." He stood, took a step toward me.

"I'm not asking her; I'm asking you."

He yanked a cigarette from his back pocket, shoved it in his mouth, but didn't light it. "Of course I do."

"Remember, you thought I'd move back?"

"Hell, I knew you weren't coming back." He lit the cigarette, and then released a plume of smoke from his nose.

"No, you didn't. You said it—'You'll come back.' I remember."

"I just wanted to calm you down. I thought you'd gone crazy crawling through the sand, bleeding and crying, trying to save sand dollars that weren't even dead."

"How'd you know I wouldn't come back?"

Boyd took one long inhalation of his cigarette, then blew the smoke up toward the blue bead board ceiling. " 'Cause Dad told me that your family would never step foot in Seaboro again."

I dropped my hand from the door to stare into Boyd's eyes. "Do you know why he said that?"

He shrugged. "Not unless you do." He turned away

from me and walked down the front steps onto the circular driveway. "Go on, go see Mom. I'll be down on the dock. I need to wrap the sails—got a storm coming in."

I stepped inside the house and Ellie's voice echoed. "Boyd?" Footsteps came down the hallway, and Ellie appeared around the corner. "Well, hello, Cappy." Confusion fluttered across her face in slow movements as she tried to decide whether to smile.

"Hi, Ellie," I whispered, then walked across the space between us and hugged her.

She held on to me for a few moments, then stepped back. "Are you in town for long?"

"Just a little bit longer. I wanted to come see you before I left."

"Boyd told me you were here."

"I came a couple days ago. . . ."

She closed her eyes and leaned against the wall. When she opened them, she stared at me. "Did your mom allow you to come? You know you'll be grounded if you didn't ask first."

"Yes, I asked first." I scanned the walls for artwork, something on driftwood. "Let's go sit in the living room by the fire," I said. The sweet smell of burning pine came to me.

She smiled. "Boyd made us a fire because there's a wicked storm coming in. You want to play Scrabble until your daddy comes to get you?"

"Great idea." I reached for Ellie's hand and took it in

my own. I lifted her hand to my cheek and held it there, then kissed the middle of her palm. God, I loved this woman.

When we reached the living room, Ellie turned in circles. "I can't remember where I put the Scrabble board."

"Sit down," I said. "I'll get it. It's over there, on the dining room table."

I took small steps toward the Scrabble board and artwork hanging on the dining room wall. I touched a painting of sea oats and a single osprey on a ragged piece of driftwood. I took a deep breath and turned to Ellie; she settled herself into a chair, tucked strands of hair into her bun.

"Ellie?"

She looked up at me. "Yes, dear one?"

"Who painted this?"

"Why, I did, of course." She stood and walked toward the wall, touched the edge of the wood. "It is my favorite surface to paint on. The rough wood against the smooth paint. The texture the wood adds to the sea and sand makes me look like a better painter than I am."

"You're a brilliant painter, Ellie, always have been."

"If you think so, then you must see my favorite painting." Ellie made a circle around the room, once, then twice. On the third trip I touched her elbow.

"I don't have to see it today," I said.

"I can't find it. Where is it?" Ellie turned to me, her lips shaking, panic spouting from her eyes in large teardrops.

I found nothing to say because I knew exactly where it was: the Seaboro Courthouse art exhibit.

"We'll find it." I took a deep breath and made a decision inside the smallest moment—between the intake and release of a breath. "What is the painting of?"

"Oh," she said, and smiled. "Me."

I wanted to know where she dwelled at that moment, confusion or reality.

"Really?" I said. "Who else is in it?"

She looked left and right. "I hung it over the fireplace; I swear I did. Where is it?"

I pulled a side table next to Ellie's chair, placed the Scrabble board on top, but Ellie threw her head into her hands and began the slow, hiccupy sobs I'd heard from only small children.

I moved to sit on the end of her chaise and took her hand. "Ellie, don't cry. I'll find it for you."

"Everything is lost now. You can't find it."

We both looked up at the scrape of the screen door across the back porch. Boyd came into the room and glared at me. "What did you say to her, Catherine?"

"Nothing. We were looking at her paintings when she said she couldn't find her favorite one."

"Damn," he said, and kicked the door frame. "I knew I shouldn't have let you in here."

"Boyd, where is her painting?"

Ellie stopped crying now, glanced up. "Boyd doesn't know. I'm the one who lost it."

I stood and moved toward him. "The courthouse, maybe?"

Boyd's eyebrows shot up, and then he hollered for the nurse, who came running around the corner and went straight to Ellie. Boyd grabbed my arm. "Shut up," he said between clenched teeth. "You have no idea what you're dealing with here." He led me onto the back porch, then kicked the door shut with his heel.

We faced the backyard, where weedy wildflowers had infiltrated Ellie's once tidy, now overgrown garden. Early-blooming wild mustard cast a bronze haze before the strip of river.

I remembered Boyd, Sam, and myself as children moving through those grasses. Sam's small body would be hidden, and he'd laugh his belly laugh, which originates in the soul of children.

I turned away from the lawn and river toward Boyd. "Tell me what's going on. Now."

"I don't know." He said each word as if it were its own sentence.

"Yes, you do."

"No, Catherine, I don't. Why don't you tell *me* what's going on. Why are you here? Why are you bothering Mom, and how do you know about the painting?"

Something of the love I had once felt for the boy this man had been crept up on me now, and I sat in the peeling white rocker and told him what Dad had asked of me.

Boyd dropped into the chair next to me. "Why would he do that?"

"Trust me on this, Boyd—I have no idea."

He yanked another cigarette from his pocket, stared at it, then put it back and gazed at me, his eyes dead and dark, and I realized he was gone too—the Boyd I knew was as gone as Sam.

When he didn't say anything, I asked him, "Who is in the painting?"

"I don't know," he said. "I just know that when she stared at it she would cry for what seemed like hours on end—I had to take it out of the house."

I closed my eyes and the wind increased, tossed rain into our faces and laps. But we didn't move.

"I hate you, Catherine." He said it as simply as if he'd told me the temperature. "I hate your dad, your family, and everything that happened after the day Sam died."

These words should have cut deeper than they did—but I realized I already knew them to be true. These were words that had lived inside me for so long they were part of me. "You should hate me," I said. "I lost your brother."

He looked up at me. "You think I hate you because of that?"

"Of course." My face was wet. I wasn't sure how much of it was rain and how much of it was my broken spirit.

"Shit, Catherine. *I* lost Sam. Not you. *I* chased him away."

These were words I had never thought to hear. Their import took long moments to reach me, as if they were traveling a great distance of years and geography.

He stood, looked down at me. "I hate you because when you left, when your family left, we all fell apart. You, on the other hand, got to go on and have a nice, new life in the mountains. We had to stay here and deal with the looks, the whispered comments. I knew what I'd done—I knew it was all my fault—but your family got to run away while we were left with the misery." Boyd paced the porch, then walked out into the rain, lifted his face to the sky. "*That* is why I hate you."

When he finally turned to me, he said, "Now Mother has left too, retreating into this dementia."

"And you lost your dad," I whispered, calculating loss as a never-ending equation for all of us.

"Ah, yes, that too. Brave man that he was, he couldn't take the pain of losing a beloved son and he killed himself. I don't care what anyone else says about him getting lost in the boat, or in a storm, or passing out. I know he left without any intention of coming back."

I rose, joined him in the rain, took his hand. "I lost Sam.

I told your mom I'd watch him. I said, 'Yes, ma'am.' You can't blame yourself when you know it was me."

He yanked his hand from me. "You didn't chase him off. You didn't scare him into running into the river. I did that. At least one of us has to have a life without blame."

I walked in a circle; my feet made sucking noises in the wet grass. "We had to move; we left here because my family couldn't face the shame—the shame of me."

He squinted through the rain falling into his eyes. "The shame?"

"For God's sake, Boyd—it was in the newspapers. Remember? 'Loughlin boy lost while being watched by neighbor.' Remember that? And Dad gets a job offer that week. Coincidence?" I shook my head. "I don't think so."

His face seemed to soften, but it might have been only the water that blurred the anger. "You believe your family moved because of you?"

"Of course. What else was I supposed to believe? That Dad magically landed his dream job that week? That Mother suddenly didn't want a house with a water view or to be admitted into the Daughters of the Confederacy?"

"Do you really want to know what I know?" Boyd asked.

"Yes, I do."

He turned, and his wide back was a wall I couldn't climb or bust through. Then he spoke. "My family asked your family to leave."

Nausea washed over my stomach like a storm-force wave. I bent over with the power of this new truth. Boyd's hand came to rest on my shoulder. "You asked."

The rain had lessened, but we were both soaked. I straightened. "You're telling me that your family asked my family to leave."

"Yes," he said.

"How do you know this?"

"I heard it."

"Where? When?" I wiped at my face.

Boyd turned and stared over the water to a place I couldn't discern. "It was the day after Sam died. Mother and Dad thought I was out in the boat."

I nodded.

"But I was in my bedroom. They were in the kitchen, so I didn't hear all the words. But Dad told Mother to deliver some ultimatum. That's all I know."

I walked down the lawn toward the river. The rain had pulled back like a curtain to expose a deeper blue. Clouds hung above the horizon like a blanket to the sea, covering the water and all it held. I longed to crawl underneath these clouds, into a safer place. This was too much . . . and not enough.

Boyd followed me until we reached the bank over the torn-edged oyster shells. I sat and pulled my legs up to my chest. "That's it? We were asked to leave because your dad made us?" Boyd didn't answer me, and I continued in a blur of words and confusion. "Why would he do that when we all needed one another so much?"

"I don't know, but I do know y'all got to go on, start a new life. Not us—it was finished for all three of us."

"We all could've helped one another through it, you know? I needed Ellie. I did. Why didn't you tell me when you heard this?"

"I was thirteen years old. I didn't know what to do."

I sat silent feeling something out on the horizon, crouched and quiet—curled into itself and unable or unwilling to show its form yet. I squinted and thought there was something I was missing, something about the edges of the water, the waves at the top.

"Boyd." I jumped up.

"What?"

"Come back to the courthouse with me."

"Listen, Cappy, I know exactly what that painting looks like."

"Please."

Boyd stood and squared off with me. "Why?"

"I think there's something . . . there. Some hint or some answer."

"The answer is right here." He waved toward the house. "A family ruined by loss. You know your dad did come here to visit . . . not until my dad was gone, not until your mother died, but he did come."

"What?"

"Maybe more often than I know, but enough that I saw him at least three times over the past four years."

"When was the last time he was here?" I asked.

"About a year ago."

I dropped my head into my hands. "Boyd, that was right before he died." I walked back toward the house, wanting to get through to Ellie, ask her so many questions.

"Stop. Let me get your stuff out of the house . . . if you don't mind—I'm afraid Mother will start back up with the crying and . . ."

"Okay," I said, and Boyd walked off.

When he returned he handed me my purse, my keys. "She's sleeping; I've got to finish wrapping the boat. Just go home and forget all this. What's done is done; leave it be."

"Yes," I agreed. "What's done is done."

With one last look he disappeared into the house as the sky began to sprinkle rain again.

The path around the house was overgrown with wild-flowers, and I did my best not to crush or kill a single flower as I picked my way to the driveway.

I stopped, stood frozen, stared at a figure under an umbrella: Forrest had found me. He moved toward me, since I couldn't seem to find my footing or command my legs to walk. He reached me, placed the umbrella over my head. "Are you okay?"

I tried not to look into his face, where I'd stumble on compassion. I needed to get Forrest out of here before he found out about the painting, about Ellie and Sam and the mystery of our families. Above all, our sordid story did not need to end up in his article. Forrest needed to go home with his fairy-tale version of Seaboro and our family intact.

"How did you know where I was?" I asked, smiled in a mask that felt fake to me. It must have looked the same to Forrest, because he tilted his head.

"You said you were going to Ellie's, and you sounded so weird and scared. So when you didn't come back to the inn, I asked Mr. Hamilton where Ellie lived and he drove me here."

"I hate small towns," I said, tried to laugh, but only a rough sound came out.

"I was worried about you," he said. "You didn't sound right."

This time I did look up into his face. "Let's get out of here. . . ." I motioned toward the house. "I thought I'd stop by and visit some old family friends, but she is sick now . . . and you do not want to meet Boyd."

"Ah, the old crush."

"Let's go."

We climbed into my car and I started it, backed from the driveway. "It's time to go home, Forrest. All the parties and picnics have been canceled by now. The weather is terrible, and I think you've found out everything you need to know."

"Will you please show me your old house?"

This seemed like the absolute perfect ending to his fairy tale—our antebellum home. "Yes, I'll take you there right now. I'm sure it's open for tourists."

"Tourists?"

I nodded. "Yep, it belongs to the historical society now and is decorated in period pieces to show how old homes looked when the town was founded."

"You might be the only person I know whose childhood home is on a tour."

"Oh, lucky me."

# Ten

*"We are generally the better persuaded by the reasons we discover ourselves than by those given to us by others."*
—BLAISE PASCAL

*I* had avoided every turn or circle that would've led to this house. I stood on the sidewalk with Forrest and didn't want to enter, but I saw no other way to get Forrest out of Seaboro.

He touched my elbow. "Is this weird for you?"

"A little." I stared up at the house, which sat like a grandmother with her glasses low on her nose, inspecting me for proper dress and behavior. The windows had the same curtains—I could almost smell the dust and feel the tattered gold fringe on the edge of the yellow-and-green toile draperies inside.

"Does it look different to you?" he asked.

I shook my head. "Not much. I feel like it's looking at me—making sure I've done something decent with my life." I rubbed my hands up and down my arms. "Gives me the chills." I pointed to the magnolia tree at the left of the stairs leading to the front door. "Dad planted it the day I was born."

He nodded. "I know. He'd put a pink ribbon on it for your birthday every year."

"Yes, and Mother would remove it the next day so the place didn't look tacky." I laughed, but it was not a sound of joy. "Displaying a large bow one day a year was almost more than she could bear. I remember thinking that the color would change—maybe to red or bright blue or orange—for my thirteenth birthday. I thought surely Dad would notice I was going to be a teenager and would choose a different color."

Forrest dropped one arm over my shoulder; I scooted out from underneath its weight.

"Okay," I said with a deep breath. "Let's get this over with."

We walked up the front stairs and I read the brass plaque on the side of the front door: THE WHITFIELD HOUSE. SEABORO PRESERVATION SOCIETY. EST. 1842.

"You know," I said, "the entire time we lived here, Mother still called this the Whitfield House. Never the Leary home. It's like we never lived here."

Forrest ran his fingers through his hair and smoothed the front of his white button-down shirt and I knew he felt as I always did—you must be presentable to cross the threshold of this house. We entered the front foyer, and I was dizzy with rushing memories, remnants of emotions associated with my former home. I heard voices, I swear I did, of Mother calling my name, of Dad laughing, of Piper running up the stairs; I heard the clinking teacups at Mother's various luncheons and dinner parties. I could not imagine how horrible it was for her to be yanked from this place where she thrived.

"Hello . . ." Forrest called to the formal living room on the left, while I stood fixed and staring at the familiar chandelier. I used to imagine jumping from the top stair and grabbing onto the light fixture to swing to the foyer. I should've done it the day we left. I smiled, thinking of what Mother's reaction would have been.

A woman wearing an antebellum dress came into the foyer. "Hello, I'm Mrs. Whitfield. Welcome to my home." She twirled in her crinoline skirt.

Although I knew this was an act for the tourists, I stood with eyes wide, mouth open.

Forrest laughed. "Hello. We were wondering if we could have a quick tour."

"Yes," the woman answered. "Would you like the self-guided tour, or would you like me to come with you and explain the history?"

Footsteps echoed above us: other tourists wandering through Whitfield House.

Forrest looked up, then at the woman. "Do you live here?"

She shook her head. "No, but for a few hours a week it is fun to pretend that I do."

Forrest touched my arm. "This is Catherine Leary. She actually did live here years ago."

I punched the side of Forrest's bicep, forced a smile for the tour guide.

She spread her arms wide. "What an honor to have you here—a Leary. Would you like me to show you around?"

"No, thanks," I said. "I think I can still find my way."

"Go ahead, then." She smiled. "Nice to see you." And she disappeared behind the door at the end of the hall, which I knew led to the brick-floored kitchen.

"I swear to God, Forrest, I think I'm having an out-of-body experience. I should not have come here. This is too bizarre for me." I tried to sound breezy and light.

"Come on. . . ." He took my hand, winked. "Let's go see your room."

"Let's start with the bottom floor," I said, and began the slow tour of my childhood home now decorated in period pieces from 1845 to 1860.

Forrest stopped in the dining room. "Is any of this furniture yours?"

"No." I shook my head. "I don't even recognize much

of the interior stuff, except the curtains and chandelier. If you wanted a feel for it, I'd have to dig up pictures. It was always this formal, but we had more artwork than they have here."

Forrest held his hand up to the fireplace, where six framed family photos were lined up on a cherry-wood mantelpiece. He pointed to the last photo on the right side. "You?"

I placed my fingers on either side of my temples and rubbed. "Wow, yes. I remember having that picture taken, but I've never seen it." I picked up the frame and stared at Mother in a long peach-colored skirt with a white silk shirt. She wore her family pearls, which I now owned and had never worn. Dad stood on the other side of the photo wearing a blue pin-striped suit with a yellow tie and a white button-down shirt—an outfit he would've never worn in real life. I stood between them in my white dress with its petticoat. My hair fell in soft curls, which would have lasted about fifteen minutes before they fell into their usual disarray. Dad had his arm around my waist; Mother's hands were folded in front of her waist. We all smiled into the camera.

Forrest touched the glass over the photo, ran his hand across my face. "You sure were a cute little girl."

"I was?"

He placed his right hand under my chin, lifted my face to his gaze. "Of course you were."

"Oh," I said, placed the photo back on the mantel. In a

distant echo, I wished Forrest had been there eighteen years ago to tell me the exact same thing. I watched him cross the room, point to the library.

"Your dad's office."

"Yes," I said. "He had piles and piles of books in there. We never had enough bookshelves—drove Mother crazy. She would go in, alphabetize them, stack them, restack them, until she finally just closed the door to his office and never let anyone in."

Forrest entered the library through the open glass French doors. The room held a single desk and a few leather-bound volumes, knickknacks of fake sailing trophies on the shelves.

I looked around for a place to sit, but all the chairs had green ribbons across them with DO NOT SIT signs.

Forrest walked toward the window, pulled out his notebook, and jotted down a couple of notes.

"What are you writing?"

"Describing the view."

"Ah." I joined him there. "Now, that hasn't changed." We stared out to the cobblestone street, the gas lamps, a pink house with a wide white front porch across the way. The rain had abated, but the sidewalks and street were wet. "Except that the trees are much larger, and there used to be a red Firebird in the driveway from one of the teenagers who lived there." I smiled that I remembered this detail. Now I was giving Forrest what he needed.

He turned back to me. "Did you ever hang out with your dad in here?"

"Oh, yes." I pointed to a marble plant stand. "There was a huge leather chair over there, and I'd sit and read while he worked. *Charlotte's Web, The Chronicles of Narnia, Alice in Wonderland, The Secret Garden.*" I clapped my hand over my mouth to stop the rising emotion, the deep joy I'd once found in books; an emotion that threatened to turn into an even deeper sorrow for their loss. I walked from the room and cut through the hall into the kitchen.

Forrest caught up to me before I reached the door. "I didn't mean to make you upset; I'm sorry."

I spun on my heels. "You did not make me upset. I'm fine." I pushed open the swinging doors. "This is the kitchen."

He sidled past me. "Did you spend much time in here?"

I rolled my eyes. "No, Forrest, we never went in the kitchen." I walked toward the front stairs, waved up them. "Three bedrooms upstairs. One for Mother and Dad, one for me, one for guests. The end."

Forrest came up behind me, placed his hand on the small of my back, and gave a gentle nudge up the stairs. "Come on; we're almost done. Don't bow up on me now."

"Bow up? What does that mean?"

"You know how you get defensive and sarcastic when you can't handle your feelings."

"I do not. And this is not, by the way, fun for me," I said.

"Well, then, thanks for doing it for me." He grinned, and I followed him up the stairs to my bedroom, where the glass doorknob was the same.

"I remember Mother ordering the housekeeper to clean the cut glass on every door once a week."

Forrest entered my room first. The walls were painted moss green—not pale pink like when I lived there—and there was a four-poster twin bed with a wedding ring quilt on top—not a queen-size sleigh bed with my grandmother's quilt. "This isn't my room," I said.

A rope surrounded the bed, but Forrest moved it and sat down on the quilt, which made me laugh.

"Now, don't get body oils on that quilt, darling. We don't want to ruin a family heirloom." I ran my hand across a dresser on the far wall on which a framed document listed how old each piece of furniture was and what antebellum plantation it came from.

"Your room."

"Not anymore," I said. "Let's go. I've seen enough." I walked down the stairs and out the front door. I sat on the porch in a wicker rocking chair and waited at least fifteen minutes until Forrest came out with an, "Okay, I'm ready. Let's go."

"Yes," I said. "Let's go home."

"Oh, not home yet. At least five people have told me I

must see the courthouse exhibit if I want to understand the history of Seaboro."

"Maybe, Forrest, but you aren't here to understand the history of Seaboro. You're here to understand a little about Dad's history."

"They are intertwined. Stories are always braided together—one affecting another."

I stood, faced him. "Now you sound like a teacher."

"Ah, my sweet, you never know what you'll learn when you hang out with me."

He reached out and pushed a strand of damp hair off my face, his expression full of pity.

I turned away from his touch, his look, and walked back to the car. "Where to now, Professor?" I asked.

His voice came down the stairs. "The courthouse, please, ma'am."

I drove the longer way to the courthouse, passing historic landmarks and the infamous lighthouse, some of Dad's favorite places, including Bud's Shrimp Shack.

"Hey, let's eat lunch there," Forrest said.

"No way. Not on a rainy holiday—it'll be packed with drunk tourists and screaming kids."

He smiled. "Like you're not a tourist now?"

"I'm not a drunk tourist."

"Maybe you should be," he said.

"To be with you, you're probably right." I slapped the side of his leg.

"You're so funny, Cappy Leary. So very funny."

"And voilà," I said moments later, and held out my hand and waved. "The courthouse. Have fun." I parked the car and leaned back against the seat.

"You're not going in with me?"

"No, I think I'll walk over and get a cup of coffee at Cloud Nine, wait for you there." I stepped out of the car and flipped open an umbrella. "They have fantastic cinnamon scones."

Forrest came around the car as wind whipped his hair; I withheld the urge to run my fingers into his curls, fix them.

"Come in with me," he said.

"There's a docent, Alice McPherson. She'll tell you everything you need to know. I promise she knows much, much more than I do."

He squinted at me. "What are you avoiding?"

"What?"

"You're avoiding something or someone."

"Yeah, the bogeyman. Now go have fun. I'll be over there." I headed toward the coffee shop.

The same young woman who had served me earlier smiled at me. "Coffee and a cinnamon scone to go?"

"You got it, except for here, please," I said, held out my hand, fanned myself. "It's hot in here."

"Yeah," she said, pouted out her lower lip and blew her bangs upward. "The air-conditioning system got hit by lightning a couple hours ago."

"Ah. By the way, my name is Catherine." I held out my hand.

"I know." She smiled, shook my hand. "I'm Allie. Mrs. Appleton told me you used to live here. She said, 'You know, they always come home.' But I told her that when I leave, I'm not coming back."

I laughed. "Always come back? My, my, she's mighty sure of Seaboro's allure."

"You think?" She handed me a scone wrapped in paper.

"I do." I took a big bite.

"You know, Mrs. Appleton said that your old house is the one on Seventh Street where the Preservation Society shows the house and has its offices and such." She leaned against the counter.

"Yes." I nodded. "That was my home—a long time ago."

"What was it like growing up in such a grand house?"

"Grand?"

"Yes. I'm saving money for school—architecture school— and your old home is one of the finest examples of the antebellum era, with some elements of Georgian Colonial and Greek Revival."

"There are plenty of ghosts in there."

Her eyes opened wide. "I thought so. I really thought so." She lowered her voice. "Is that why you moved—the ghosts?"

I smiled. "Maybe," I said. "And where is that coffee?"

She laughed and moved to the machine behind her, poured a generous cup, and handed it to me. "Nice to meet you, Catherine."

"You too, Allie," I said, and then wandered over to sit at a table by the window. Had we moved away because of the ghosts? If we had, they'd followed me all the way to Cedar Valley and back here again in a circuitous journey.

A sky blue VW convertible Bug drove up to the curb and stopped. The woman inside stared at me: Piper. She jumped out and ran into the café to wrap her arms around me. "Yahoo, Catherine." Coffee splattered across my wrinkled T-shirt.

"Whoa," I said, attempted to stand.

"I thought you left." Her smile covered her entire lower face; I saw her molars. "I am so glad you're still here." Then she pouted. "Why didn't you tell me you stayed?"

"It was a very, very last-minute decision. There was just some . . . unfinished business."

"Like what?" She held her hands wide.

I glanced off toward the courthouse. "Forrest wanted to see my old house, then the courthouse. I'm waiting for him now." I glanced up at the sky. "Bad weather. I'm sure it ruined everyone's holiday plans."

"Just our way of getting tourists out of town."

My laugh felt warm all the way inside. "It didn't work this time."

"Ah," she said. "Proof that you belong." She hugged me

and sat down, motioned for a coffee from Allie. "I'm on my way to the grocery store, but if the choice is you or food, the kids can order pizza."

"You're insane," I said, then leaned across the table. "I thought about you today when I went to my old house."

"How was it?" She threw her head back, closed her eyes. "We had so much fun there. So many plans and wishes."

"Yeah," I said, "and all your wishes came true: marry Parker, have babies, live on the marsh. You asked for it and you got it—like a fairy tale."

Piper straightened in her seat. "You think that just because I got exactly what I thought I wanted, everything is perfect? That I don't have days when I wonder what else could be out there for me? Or when I wish I didn't have to deal with Parker's cranky mama, or wish I weren't so outrageously tired I could die, or wish I could sleep in and then go out with a girlfriend for drinks? That I wish I didn't always have to clip coupons or look for sales? Everyone, Cappy Leary, everyone has their struggles. No one lives a fairy-tale life. At least, not anyone I know."

I hugged her across the table, almost tipping over the coffee, which she rescued in one swift move. "I wish I could have been a part of every minute of every struggle," I said.

"Me too," she said. "But there is—what does Father Rory say?—joy in the journey."

"That, my friend, is what Dad would say. But the only joy I've found in this confusing journey to Seaboro is seeing you."

Piper laughed. "Then you're just not looking in the right places."

I took a long sip of coffee, a bite of scone, then asked Piper, "Why do you think my family left here?"

"I don't know. And you never told me. In any of your letters, you never told me. You just said that your dad got a new job and that you were sure you'd eventually move back. Which, of course, you didn't. And"—she took my hand— "you quit writing."

I squeezed her hand. "I had to, Piper. I'm sorry. I just had to—I had to make myself forget."

She whispered, "Why did you leave?"

"I've always thought it was because of what . . . I did. But now I think there might have been more to it." I stood, walked over to the window, and stared at the courthouse. "I think it has something to do with Ellie. Okay." I took a deep breath. "I'm ready to hear this: What was the gossip about why we left?"

"I was only twelve years old, don't forget. We, the kids, only thought your dad got a new job and that you felt too terrible about what had happened to stay—so your dad took the job. We all knew that it wasn't your fault, but we also knew that you thought it was."

"No other gossip?"

"Oh, definitely. Your dad got in trouble with the law. Your mom was discovered to be a descendant of Sherman, and Seaboro asked her to leave. Or a Whitfield ghost chased you out because you didn't behave like a proper lady."

My laugh was sudden and loud. "Really?"

She nodded.

"That's it?"

"Pretty much."

I traced my finger along the rain pattern on the window. "Forrest's taking too long. . . . I'm going after him." I turned to Piper. "Go on and get your family some food. I promise to come by before I leave."

"Promise?"

"I just did."

She gave me a squinty look. "You two want to come over for dinner tonight?"

"You're sweet, Piper, but no, thanks. I really am trying to get Forrest out of here as fast as I can."

"You don't want him to know . . . about Sam." She said this with such loud certainty I was sure that Forrest could hear it all the way across the green.

"No, Piper, I don't want him to know. This paper he's writing is about Dad, not me, and I don't want what I did to . . . affect that."

She opened her mouth to speak; I held up my hand. "Please, old friend, no more right now."

"Okay," she said, and hugged me.

I walked into the foyer of the courthouse, and the doors shut behind me with a swish of air. Dust motes twisted in the sliver of light falling onto the pine floors. Alice and Forrest had been in here for too long to be talking about Civil War bullet heads and sweetgrass baskets. I glanced around, listened, but heard only the hum of the air conditioner threatening its last breath, and decided it was a good time to take one more look at the horizon on that painting—something I had seen, but didn't really *see* the first time.

I climbed the staircase on the tips of my flip-flops. Forrest and Alice appeared at the top of the stairs. "Hey," I said. "What's taking you so long?"

"I got interested in the pottery collection," Forrest said. "Sorry, were you waiting too long?" Then he grinned that smarty-pants grin that told me I'd done just what he wanted—shown up looking for him.

"Yes, I waited too long. If we want to leave before dark we need to get going."

"Leave before dark?" He bit his lower lip. "Hmmm . . . I don't remember those plans."

"They're new plans," I said, came to the top of the stairs. "Hi, Alice." I squeezed her hand. "I'm sorry if this nice gentleman has been bothering you."

"No bother. He is incredibly interesting to talk to. And he is writing a fascinating article about your dad. Isn't it brilliant—one novel for each changed life? My favorite is the one where *The Heart Is a Lonely Hunter* makes a young girl reconsider her choices, makes her realize how she has isolated herself."

"Pottery, eh?" I said to Forrest.

"Oh, yes, he loves the Indian pottery made from the silt and pluff mud. And I showed him your dad's favorite painting."

I spun toward the stairs, lost my balance, and grabbed the newel post before stumbling.

"You okay?" Forrest asked, held on to my arm.

"Let's go," I said. Whatever was on that damn horizon would stay on that horizon—for good and all.

"Hold on," he said. "I left my notebook in the art room." He turned and walked toward the room where Ellie's painting hung.

I followed with Alice behind me.

He picked up his notebook, flipped open the pages, and scribbled a few notes while I shifted my weight from one foot to the other, averting my eyes from the painting five feet away. Then, as if responding to a magnetic force, my eyes lifted to the horizon of the stormy sea on driftwood.

I squinted and inspected the space between earth and sky—what was I missing? What was hidden in plain sight?

Then I saw an oblong tear on the woman's face; I pointed to it without realizing I spoke out loud. "Is she crying?"

Alice let out a whoosh of air, as if her lungs had just collapsed. "You're the only person I've known who's ever noticed."

"You see it?" I asked her, turned.

"Yes," she whispered. "It's barely there, isn't it?"

"Now it seems obvious," I said.

Forrest looked up from his notes and took a step toward the painting. "Things aren't obvious unless we see them. I don't see a tear."

His words ran along my skin as if they'd left his mouth and crawled over me. *Things aren't obvious unless we see them.*

I took a step back, then another, until I'd separated myself from Forrest and Alice. Forrest leaned into the painting, and then squinted at the woman's face. Alice crossed her arms, straight and sure in what she saw.

I stared until the art blurred, then refocused into a hazy melding of water and horizon, of oil paint and ragged wood. Then I saw it; a round bundle of waves formed like a blanket wrapped around a child's form. There was no face inside this shape.

I lost my breath in a single release of air; my oxygen was gone. I reached out for something to grab onto—I found nothing solid and stumbled forward. Forrest came to my side before I saw him move, grabbed my arm and held me upright. I pushed him away and took an unsteady step toward the painting, and then touched—with just the tip of my pinkie finger—the bundle at the left corner of the horizon. "You see that?" I whispered.

Alice spoke first. "Dear Lord, yes, I do. How could I have not seen it before?"

"A child," I said.

"Where?" Forrest whispered. "Show me."

I pointed again. "Right there."

"I only see waves, water, sky." He looked again. "What are you talking about?"

"It's Sam," I said.

Alice nodded. "Sweet baby Sam with his green eyes."

I saw Sam in my mind's eye, in the shadow of dawn with white hair against skin darker than mine, round feet that dug in the sand, small hands that reached for Ellie with primal love. But I couldn't see his eyes. It was strange, I thought, to have such distinct memories of the rest of him but not the shade of his eyes. I waited for Alice to fill the gap of memory.

"He was part of you," she said.

"Of course he was," I agreed, and finally felt the lack of oxygen level; I was surviving on ancient air. "I loved him."

Alice stared at me, and exactly like that evening in the barn, when her unspoken words danced and moved in front of me, the words that were born on that day wanted to arrive now.

"Say it." I lifted my hand in supplication.

She nodded, closed her eyes, and then opened them to me. "*You* must say it, Cappy."

"I can't." I spread my hands apart. "I know there are unspoken words. I've seen them in front of you twice now, but I don't know what they are."

"Turn, look, feel," Alice said.

But when I spun around I saw only Forrest with a curious expression, his hands in a knot behind his back. I lifted my eyes to the painting again—and spoke as if my own words could wrap themselves around Alice's unspoken ones. "Dad, Mother; Dad, Ellie; Jim, Boyd, Sam."

I stopped.

"Green eyes," I said, stepped forward, turned to Alice. "Leary eyes."

Alice offered me a nod, and then dropped her chin to her chest, where it stayed—an affirmation almost like a prayer.

"What?" I asked through numb tongue, bobbing head. Electric shocks ran down my arms. "Dad and Ellie's Sam?"

"Yes," Alice said, stealing the last solid ground of childhood on which I had stood.

"Did my mother know?" I looked over to Forrest. "Did you?" I waved my hand, frantic and wild-winged, through the air. "Did everyone but me know and no one had the courage to tell me?" My words became louder, fuller. "I had to come on this stupid trip to find out that I killed my half brother?" I screamed this, and Forrest rushed to me; I pushed him away.

"No," he said. "I didn't know." Then he too bowed his head. "These must be the lost pages of childhood your dad talked about."

"Lost pages?" I took a long, deep breath and found that I had not, after all, run out of oxygen, but found a new source:

my own. "Lies. Call them what they are: lies. Not freaking lost pages. Let's not make this a family drama, Forrest. It's a horrid lie."

He stared at me without making a single movement.

Alice touched my elbow. "Only I have known, Cappy."

Maybe, I thought, maybe I'd just stay angry and mumble over and over, *I don't care, I don't care.* But the truth flew through me, past me, carrying me in drenched fog and darkened air to the place that had left all of us with shattered lives, sharp pieces that each of us carried, and I *did* care. We had each formed new lives out of those broken shards. This new piece, this knowing, had been Alice's, and she now handed it to me.

She stood next to me, grabbed my hand.

"How much more of my life is a lie?" I asked. "Have I been living in some kind of fantasy world since I was twelve? This changes it all, Alice, yesterday, today. Knowing this changes . . . everything."

I looked at her and felt a small, firm thing shift into place: truth, and I wanted more.

"How do you know all of this, Alice?"

"I was there that terrible night when your broken families crowded into the emergency waiting room. It was the worst night of my life until I lost Mack to a sudden aneurysm. Your parents and Ellie and Jim were huddled on plastic chairs around the room.

"This is the thing about grief: It spares no one. No one

was there to be strong for Ellie or Jim. They were all four so lost in their grief and pain that they couldn't reach out to one another. They isolated themselves until the young doctor walked through the door and told them they'd done all they could, but Sam was gone.

"Ellie wanted, needed to know exactly what caused the death. She was frantic and wild in this need to know the details, and she wouldn't let anyone leave until she found out.

"When the doctor brought a lab report out to Ellie, handed it to her, she fell to the ground and wept in the wild, incandescent way of the lost. Jim took the report from the doctor and read it to himself with a swollen and broken face. When he'd finished, he tossed it onto the floor and walked from the room, leaving Ellie and your parents alone under the fluorescent lights with empty Styrofoam coffee cups and leftover crumpled tissues scattered on the metal side tables.

"It was your dad who finally stood and picked up the report, read it. He looked up at your mother and told her, 'It was the drowning.' He said it with such force that Ellie stopped crying, stood and faced him with a resoluteness I'd never seen from that quiet, still woman. She told your dad to really read the report, and he told her he had. They stared at each other for a long time until your mother stepped between them, grabbed the paper from his hand. I hope to never see another night like that one." Alice stopped speaking, sat down in a chair as though it had taken all of her energy to tell this story that she'd withheld for so long.

"The report," I said, "what did it say?"

"Sam's blood type was noted in large red letters and was not Loughlin blood."

I said nothing, waited for the rest.

"For a short time, Ellie was so consumed by grief that she seemed to have gone with Sam. During this time, nothing of consequence mattered to her except her son." Alice paused, looked at the painting as if she could see that day against the paint strokes. "She told your dad, told your mom, in the waiting room, on plastic yellow chairs and black and white checked linoleum floors, that Sam was his, that Sam had been his child."

I tried to envision it. What I knew, what I remembered, what I cherished about Ellie: They were not in the picture Alice was forcing on me. I couldn't see it: Ellie falling apart, admitting to a betrayal so complete that nothing would ever be the same.

"Did Dad already know?" I whispered, amazed how I was asking for details in this blurry, unfocused room.

"No," Alice said.

"I must not have really known Ellie," I said, completely forgetting Forrest's presence in the room.

"Yes, yes, you did. You knew all of her. Grief wraps around people, Cappy, takes them to a place they would not go otherwise. Ellie told all of us and then she couldn't take it back."

"Does Boyd know?"

"I don't know. He thought more, heard more innuendo. He was always lurking, listening, demanding more and more of his mother, and he might have figured it out."

"Secrets," I said.

"Yes." Alice's voice sounded hollow, emptied out, like one of the pottery vessels across the room.

"What if I'd never seen this in the painting? I'd never have known . . . I would have gone my whole life and never known."

Forrest came to stand next to me. "I believe this is what your dad was going to tell you in that letter—the letter about the lost pages of childhood. I also know he believed that everyone sees what they are supposed to see in any piece of art. If you didn't see Sam—it could be because you weren't supposed to—yet."

I spun to face him. "Stop it. Stop pretending to know my dad better than I did. I didn't ask you to come. And neither did he. I didn't ask for your opinion, and I don't need it."

He placed his hands in his khaki pockets. His shirttail had come out of his shorts, and he looked young, vulnerable. I tried to turn away from him, but my heart wouldn't let me move, and before he could walk out of the room I was in his arms with the side of my cheek against his chest.

He placed his hands on the back of my head. "Oh, Cap."

His heartbeat echoed over and over in a metronome of comfort. Maybe I could stay here forever and the sound of

Forrest's heartbeat would drown out the words Alice had just said.

Forrest ran his hand down the back of my head, shifted his weight.

"Don't move," I said. "Stay. . . ."

"I am, I am," he said.

I stood against him, allowing him to take my full weight until Alice's voice broke through. "Cappy . . . ?"

The rain had resumed in full now, as if it had waited for Alice to release the truth so it could all come pouring down. The storm pounded on top of the metal roof. I turned my head and stared at her. "You've kept this knowledge to yourself all these years?"

"Yes, it wasn't mine to share."

"To share . . ." I said, dread replacing the calm of Forrest's touch. I grabbed his arm, squeezed. "You won't write . . ."

". . . this in the article? No, Cappy. No."

Fatigue fell on me like a thick robe I wanted to sleep in until the rain stopped, until I was home in Cedar Valley without any of this new knowledge.

I looked up at Forrest. "I'm tired."

Alice took my hand. "Give yourself time to understand all this."

"Oh, I understand perfectly," I said. "We moved because Sam was proof that Dad and Ellie loved each other—that they were unfaithful. Whatever Mother could fool herself into believing before was gone with that lab result. Jim couldn't look at Dad every day and know. There was only one option—to leave.

"I always, always thought we went to Cedar Valley because I had lost Sam. That we had to separate ourselves from Mother's beloved town and our best friends because of me."

"I could have told you that wasn't it," Alice said. "No one here ever blamed you. If there were ever any whispers, it was about Boyd and how he ran after both of you—how he scared his brother."

"It doesn't really matter what was whispered then . . . or now. We left. The Loughlin family was destroyed. Now I understand why Boyd hates us—he thinks we were able to escape and continue with our lives while he stayed here with the blame, the horror, the remnants of his family."

Alice dropped her arm over my shoulder. "I think this is quite enough for one day. Why don't you come over for lunch and—"

I held up my hand. "I don't want to know anything more about the past."

"Sometimes," Alice said, "just sometimes we have to know the truth about the past to discover our future."

I stared at her for long moments as my heart warred between anger and grief; then I looked to Forrest. He took my hand, wound his fingers through mine, and we left the courthouse. I could almost hear what Dad would say now: *Give the story time to settle inside you. Let it move and twist around until you see what it has to say to you.*

Outside the wind had increased, slanting and brutal against the windshield for the short drive back to the inn. Forrest drove in silence. There was nothing to say, and he must have known this.

Anger mixed with pain, grief with mistrust, and yearning with disgust. My mind and body were unable to take in these new revelations about my family.

Dad had an affair and a child—a child named Sam whom I lost to the river. The facts were clear, the implications as gray as the painting I'd just seen.

If I hadn't known this fact of Dad's life, what had I known of him? He loved literature; he believed in the power of story; he had integrity and honor; he loved me. I reached back farther, to childhood, and remembered a time on the beach.

Dad and I had been crabbing off the old footbridge until our bucket overflowed with the large crabs that would turn blue in the boiling water. We'd wandered down to the beach at an extreme low tide—the sand spreading like a rich, wet carpet all the way out to the second sandbar. I remembered thinking that the water was racing for the horizon, and told Dad this. "The water is running away—trying to get to the other side."

He laughed, loud, long. "Now, there is a beautiful analogy, my brilliant daughter."

"What?" I said, too young to understand what an analogy was or how I'd made one. I'd thought maybe it was a sea animal I didn't know about.

He hugged me close, rubbed the top of my head. I couldn't have been more than six or seven, because my head reached only to his waist. "The lowest ebb brings the highest tide," he said.

Even as a child I had understood what he'd meant—when it all looked like it was gone, at the lowest point, soon it would come rushing back in.

I had believed him then.

After living more of life I no longer believed him: A low tide was nothing but a low tide. High tides were guaranteed in nature, but not in my life.

In all the battling feelings, one rose to the surface. I touched Forrest's arm. "I'm hungry," I said, pointing to Morgan's Grocery.

He pulled the car up as close to the front door as he could. "You run in and get whatever you want. I'll wait here." He held out a twenty-dollar bill, which I waved away. I ran under the blinking rain-shrouded outside light, then stepped into the pine-scented store, with its unorganized shelves, its randomly placed merchandise. And I'd been correct—on the front counter was a display of *Farmer's Almanac*s.

I wandered to the back of the store, dripping rain onto the hardwood floors. Homemade sandwiches, cookies, and brownies wrapped in cellophane lined the left wall. I chose a tomato-and-mayonnaise sandwich for myself, a roast beef–and-cheddar for Forrest, then two monstrous double-chocolate brownies and two Coca-Colas in glass bottles. I plopped it

all on the counter, then threw in an almanac just to prove
to Forrest that I'd been right. To the left of the register was
a crooked plywood shelf full of dried and painted shells decorated with various themes: angels, Santa, crabs with real
faces, and fish. The shells were shellacked to a shine.

I picked up a sand dollar with a thin crack down the
middle where it had been glued together. A white angel was
painted on the top and over the crack. A thin wire was glued
to the back of the shell so it could be hung. I placed the sand
dollar on top of the sandwich, then called out into the empty
store, "Hello, is anyone here?"

A gray-haired man popped up from below the counter
to my left. "Hello, missy. Sorry, I was fixing the shelves back
here." He walked toward me, rang up my merchandise, and
then picked up the sand dollar. "You know, these are gathered and made locally—got yourself a wee bit of Seaboro to
take home with you, you do."

"Thanks," I said. "It's lovely."

"Now don't go a-tryin' to do these yourself. You can't col-
lect live sand dollars—it's illegal. You can only take the ones
that've been left for dead and dried on the beach."

My heart pinched at the remembrance of the cracked
sand dollar under my cheek so long ago. If only it were so
easy to pick up the broken pieces of life, glue them back
together, and cover them with paint like nothing had ever
happened.

# ELEVEN

*"The heart has its reasons of which reason knows nothing."*
—BLAISE PASCAL

The B & B appeared to settle into the rainy afternoon—
warm and secure. Forrest and I entered in silence, and I followed him into the library, where we sat at a small round
table in the back corner of the room.

I placed the bag in the middle of the table, tapped the
wood. "Forrest," I said.

"Yes?"

"Please do not take what you heard today and . . . use
it. You don't . . . understand all of it, and it has nothing to
do—"

He held his hand up in the air. "I told you earlier, whatever I heard today has nothing to do with my article." He

leaned across the table. "But everything to do with you and who you are now."

"What?" My hands dropped in my lap, twisted into a knot.

"All these years I've known you, all the times we've talked and gone out and spent time together, and you never once told me about a little boy named Sam."

"I couldn't."

He released a long breath. "Have you ever told anyone?"

"Do you want to know because it might be a really good story, or because you give a flying flip?"

He stared at me, didn't blink, and I swore his eyes turned darker. "After all these years do you really need to ask me that?"

"I am not a story. This is not a story. This is real life—my life."

"No, Catherine." He looked away, and I realized he had finally called me Catherine and it sounded wrong, like an off-tune note in a song. He took off his baseball cap, ran his hand through his curls. "This was your father's life. There is something about his life he wanted you to understand—and maybe that will translate into something in your life. But for once, it is not all about you. This is about him."

He could have punched me in the face and I would have felt better than I did. I turned away from him and swallowed the tears rising at the base of my throat. In forcing down this blow from Forrest, I answered in defense, "I think I knew the man better than you did. I grew up with him; he was my dad, for God's sake. How do you presume to know what he wanted or why he sent me here with his ashes?" I turned back to Forrest, the tears falling down my throat, anger rising. "You always think you know what is right for everyone else—like you're the God-ordained authority on my father?"

I thought he'd break eye contact, maybe even apologize. But he bent so we were eye-to-eye. "What was his favorite book? His favorite quote? Who was his best friend?"

I didn't back away from Forrest, but leaned closer still. "What was his favorite bridge for crabbing? When did he catch his first shark? Where did he keep the shrimp boil pot? What kind of Boston Whaler did he like the best?" I stomped my foot. "You didn't know him, Forrest Anderson. Just because you sat with him and talked about literature and collected quotes on a bulletin board doesn't mean you knew him like I did."

"You're right: I don't know those things about him. But those were all from another life—the one he lived here. I'm talking about his life in Cedar Valley."

"His favorite bridge was the one behind Seaboro Creek— once, we caught fifteen crabs in five minutes. He caught his first shark with Boyd Loughlin; he kept the iron pot in the shed behind Alice's barn; his favorite Boston Whaler was the 1972 sixteen-footer with the outboard motor."

Forrest moved closer. "His favorite book was Graham Greene's *The End of the Affair,* his favorite quote was 'The heart has reasons that reason knows nothing of,' and . . ." He took a long breath in, then out. "You were his best friend."

"Okay," I said. "You want to know the missing part of the story? The part you don't understand about our lives? Here it is—we moved from this town when I was twelve years old because I was watching our best friend's two-year-old son, Sam, and I lost track of him. He drowned. We moved. The end. And to top off the horrid nightmare, I lost Dad's urn in the same place and never tossed his ashes like he asked. Some great story, eh?"

Forrest looked up, whispered, "I'm sorry."

"So am I. But you wanted to know the whole story, didn't you? The entire story . . . you've got it now, don't you? I have no idea why Dad made me come back here—I was finally living my life separate from this place."

"Were you?" He took my hand, ran his finger along the palm. "Were you really?"

I couldn't find an answer behind my twisting thoughts; I closed my eyes.

"Ms. Leary?" Mr. Hamilton stood in the doorway.

"Yes?" I realized the mayonnaise from the sandwiches had soaked through the grocery bag I'd clutched to my chest and was staining the front of my white linen shirt.

"There's a phone call in the hallway for you."

"Me?"

"Yes," he said, nodded.

I rose: Thurman. I was sure it was Thurman—he missed me; he had an explanation for the other day; he needed me; he loved me.

Those were the thoughts rambling like lost children through my head as I walked in slow motion to the phone on a wobbly cherry-wood table in the hallway. I lifted the receiver. "Hello?"

"Ms. Leary?" It was a woman's voice with the sound of tears caught behind the words.

"Yes?"

"This is Cedar Valley Animal Clinic. I've been trying to reach you all day. I'm calling to tell you that we believe Murphy had a stroke. Our night girl heard some banging around and found Murphy . . . well, convulsing. Right now her right side and rear legs are paralyzed."

The sobs rose; all the ones I'd withheld for days, for months, for years, climbed to the top of my throat, my eyes, my heart. I dropped the phone and slumped against the wall and allowed the tears to fall.

I heard Forrest take the phone and speak softly. "Yes, yes, okay, I'll tell her. We'll be home as soon as we can." Then he pulled me to him. I wept for Sam, for Dad, for Mother, for Ellie, for Boyd, for Murphy. And I wept for myself and the years I'd gone without feeling any of this sorrow, anything at all beyond surface sentiment.

Forrest didn't murmur, "It's okay," or "We'll fix this," or

"Now, now." He didn't say anything at all, just held me while I emptied myself of so many sorrows.

With a swollen throat, I finally asked, "Tell me what else they said. Tell me. Is she dead?"

"No, she's not. They want to watch her and make sure it was a stroke and not just a seizure. They'll know in a day or two if the paralysis is permanent. Cappy, she's fourteen years old. That is a long life for a golden retriever."

"I know . . . I know." But, I thought, two years was not a long life for a boy.

Forrest held my face between his hands. "Let's go . . . there is something we need to do."

"Go home," I said. "We have to go home, get Murphy."

"We will, but there is something else we have to do first."

"What?" I followed Forrest to the library, where he grabbed my keys off the table.

Mr. Hamilton stood at the bar, glanced back and forth between Forrest and me. "You know there is a hurricane watch out there, right? If there's an evacuation, they ask tourists to go first."

"A hurricane watch?" I repeated with upheld hands.

Mr. Hamilton nodded, then walked over to the TV I hadn't noticed above the bar. He flicked on the Weather Channel, but turned the sound off. A thin man with a comb-over hairdo stood pointing at an electronic screen, which animated the projected path of a hurricane. This path led directly to the South Carolina coast.

Mr. Hamilton nodded at Forrest. "You two will probably have to evacuate in the morning," he said.

"Evacuate?"

"Yes," Mr. Hamilton said. "You'll hear lots of banging—we'll be putting the hurricane shutters up. I'm sorry if it wakes you."

Forrest had his hand on the small of my back and I felt empty, smoothed out like the inside of an empty shell left to bleach on the sand. I allowed him to guide me into the passenger seat of the car as calm descended over me.

Afternoon spread her wings as Forrest stood on the dock where I'd lost Sam, where I'd lost Dad's urn, where I'd lost my childhood. It was a cloudy and disjointed scene I took in a little at a time: The tide came in; the dock slanted to the left; a plump jaybird watched from the oak on the right; the scent of newly blooming jasmine filled the wet air. The horizon was hazy with fog, the clouds so low and dense that it looked like the sky melted into the sea. The swollen clouds held their breath and left us dry for the moment.

Forrest turned to me. He still wore his khaki shorts but had skimmed off his T-shirt, tossed it into the puddle-strewn lawn. He looked over his shoulder where I stood with one foot on the wooden dock, the other foot on the grass as if my body and feet couldn't decide whether to go forward or backward.

A T-pole, which Piper's son had erected with the help of his osprey committee, now stood nearby. I glanced up, noticed the remnants of the osprey nest, but the bird wasn't there. I looked back to Forrest and felt a sorrow I blamed on the empty nest.

He nodded at me. "This is where the child drowned."

He said it as a fact without emotion, a fact that had nothing to do with me. I nodded and wondered at the vacant impact these words had on me—as if I'd gotten used to them.

"Where did you drop the urn?" he asked.

I pointed to the left of the dock. "It has to be gone; I tried to dive for it and couldn't find it."

"It was heavy iron; it would have sunk."

I held my hands up in surrender, a sweet, round bubble of denial protecting me from more emotion. I found what he was doing more curious than upsetting.

Forrest stood poised above the dock as if he were about to dive.

"Forrest!" I hollered.

"What?" He turned to me.

"Don't dive until you know how deep it is. That is the number one rule of swimming in the river. You need to go in safely. . . ."

A part of me knew I was talking backward, to Sam, giving him instructions. "Don't jump, not now."

Forrest cannonballed into the water. A large splash

washed over the dock. He rose above the surface, shook his head, made small droplets shimmer and dance in the air. Then he submerged, rose, and sank again. I held my breath each time he dove, until the final time when my lungs burst and I had to take a breath. He'd been down there too long, way too long. I took another breath, held it until my chest burned, my heart pounded. I ran to the end of the dock. "Forrest!" I screamed.

I lay down on the wood and my voice burst the protective calm around me as I screamed for him. My voice vibrated across the water, over the pearl-shimmered oysters, the black pluff mud, until finally it sank into the white-crested waves riding out on the tide.

Pain like molten liquid poured over me. I couldn't separate one emotion from another—grief from guilt, loneliness from loss, fear from expectation, and finally love from hate. I felt them all—combined in one tight braid as I shouted over the river.

"I'm over here. . . ." I sat up, swiveled to see him kneeling on the far bank.

"Don't stand up," I told him. And my voice sounded different, as though something had been added—or maybe taken away. "You'll slice your feet to shreds." I pointed to the shells. "Those oyster shells are like razors."

He gasped for breath, bent over to take in another breath.

"Are you okay?" I asked, stood.

He nodded. "I felt it down there . . . and I couldn't leave it. I had to bring it up, but it was stuck in the mud, heavy."

Then I saw it: the urn resting on the shells covered with sand, black mud, streaks of green moss.

"Oh," I said, placed my hand over my mouth. I ran over to him and reached the edge of the grass, looked down at him. "You found it."

He nodded. "I figured I would—it was too heavy to just float away. But once I felt it, I was afraid I wouldn't be able to find it again, so I stayed until I could pry it from the sand."

He lifted the urn. "Here, take it. I'll swim over to the dock."

I lay on my stomach, leaned over the urn, and wrapped both hands around the container, lifted it and placed it on the grass. Forrest swam to the dock, climbed the crooked ladder, and came to me.

The grass dented with his weight when he sat next to me. I stared at this man whom I'd known for eleven years and saw another man: a man who loved Dad, who dove into the river for me.

I whispered, "No one has ever done anything like that for me."

"Do you want to do this now?" he asked, tapped the top of the urn.

I shook my head. "I want to be alone. You understand, right?"

"You don't have to do everything alone, Cappy. I'm here."

His words held so much comfort that I wanted to crawl into them. But I wouldn't let myself go there again—to that place of beauty and expectation where disaster inevitably followed. "Why are you trying to make me feel so much? Things I haven't felt since before Sam died?" I slammed my fist on the soaked ground; mud splattered across my shirt. "I don't need to feel all the things I felt before our world fell apart. I've been just fine without all that hope and fullness . . . stop making me feel everything I used to . . . before. I don't need any of this. I was perfectly fine without it."

"Perfectly fine?" Forrest stood and looked down at me. "You haven't truly felt anything in years and years, and you call that perfectly fine?"

"Yes, I do." I stood to face him.

"I've always seen the potential in you, for greatness, for deep love, but you always back away when you get too close." He slammed one fist into his opposite palm. "But you know what? It's good that you don't feel, Cappy. It's good that you don't allow anything inside that would make you say yes to life, because you'll never know what this feels like" —he spread his hands wide—"to love someone who will never love you back."

I bent over, dropped my hands on my knees. "Oh, God, what is wrong with me?"

He touched the top of my head, but didn't answer.

"I don't think I can do it," I said, and stood and wiped at my face. "I don't think I can take Dad's ashes and spread them across this river."

Forrest leaned forward and put his hands on my shoulders. "Yes, you can. You cannot stay stuck here—in what your dad called *medias res*—right in the middle of things."

I remained still beneath his hands and I wanted to lift mine, touch his face, his arm, but I held tight to the urn. "What middle?"

"The middle between past and future. That middle."

"That's called the present, Forrest."

"But that's the thing . . . that's what I mean. You're never really present, fully present, because you haven't let go of the past and because you won't look to the future. You've never, ever told a soul about Sam—you've carried it around your entire life. And you won't answer your dad's questions, which are all about the future. That, right there, is what I'm talking about."

"I can answer those questions, Forrest; I just don't want to. And have you ever thought that maybe, just maybe, I didn't tell you about Sam because it was none of your business? None of anyone's business?"

He shook his head, put his hands on both sides of my face; I couldn't move. Rain began falling again in large drops that landed on our faces, made dimples on the river. "Just because Sam and your dad are gone doesn't mean they aren't part of this story."

He ran his hand down the back of my head, behind my neck.

I mumbled, "I bet you can't answer those questions either. What would you regret not doing, Forrest Anderson?"

"That is the second question . . ." he said, pulled me closer.

"I know that," I whispered.

"I can't answer that until you know the answer to the first question."

And then I didn't say anything else as he drew me to him, wrapped me in his arms.

I wanted, furiously wanted to fall into this feeling of protection, to allow what grew between us, but my heart turned the other way; I nudged Forrest back. He released me. "Let's finish what we came here for," he said.

I looked up at him and saw it: clear and brilliant even without the sun, a shimmering light that vibrated all around him. I took his hand, stared at him, but when I blinked the light was gone.

"No," I said, "I can't do it here, not where . . ."

"Yes, you can." He placed his hand on my shoulder. "No guilt rests here, none."

I tilted my head toward the water. "It does live there though, and always has."

We were soaked now; Forrest with river water, both of us with rain, as the strengthening wind yanked at our hair, our clothes.

Forrest took a step closer. "No, it does *not* live there either. It is gone. Long, long gone. Right now the only place guilt lives and grows is inside you. There is not one person who condemns you. How long can you be sorry?"

"Forever. I can be sorry forever and ever." But when I looked at Forrest, for the first time I believed I might find something other than blame in anyone who learned about Sam.

"How long can one girl pay for a mistake? How long?" His voice was part of the wind and rain.

I looked at the urn, thought of Dad. Sam was part of me in more ways than I'd known; he was Dad's child. I thought of the picture on Ellie's desk, of the bond between them, of the grief that overtook Dad when we left. Now I knew that Dad's deepest sadness had come from a loss I could never have fully understood.

I reached down for the urn, walked to the end of the dock. I sat on the splintered wood, and although Forrest was behind me on the grass, I understood that this task was mine alone to complete. I unscrewed the top, turned the container upside down.

The wind, the rain, the ebbing river combined in one force to carry Dad away from me, to the place where he'd asked to go. I knew I should speak profound words of love and goodbye, but all I had inside me was a clean and barren place.

I rose and walked to where Forrest stood. I buried my face in his soaked shirt and tasted briny river, clean rain, and grass combined in an earth-taste of redemption.

When I lifted my head, he waited for me to kiss him.

As we fell to the grass I was lost in his touch, gone in the comfort of this man who knew what I'd done and didn't judge me. In Forrest I found rest from regret.

His hands wandered up my spine; his mouth was warm on mine. Thunder broke us free.

He stood, lifted me. "Let's get back to the inn." His voice was full, swollen with whatever we had started on the grass beside the river.

I nodded, agreed.


He drove with the slap of water and leaves against the windshield. Then we stood in the hallway of the B & B and stared at each other. "We should drive home," I said.

"No, we shouldn't," he said, pulled me toward him.

In the harsh light and stark reality of the inn, I returned to who I was. Rational thought filled my empty, hollowed-out center.

*Thurman.*

*Murphy.*

"Murphy . . . we have to get home for her," I said.

"It's too late, and the weather is bad. We'll leave first thing in the morning."

I sought the energy to argue and found only a deep need for rest. "Okay," I said. "First thing . . ."

I wanted to give something back to Forrest, some kind

of offering for all he'd done for me that day. I took his hand, brought it to my mouth, kissed his palm, then his wrist.

He lifted my face, tilted my chin to look at him. Then he stared at me, searched my face for something I didn't understand and couldn't give him.

He touched my cheek, whispered, "The right thing at the wrong time is never the right thing."

I shivered. "What book are you quoting now?"

He shook his head. "No book. Just me."

Then he yanked his key out of a soaked pocket and leaned against the banister. His hair dripped water onto his shoulders, and between the two of us small puddles formed, and I thought how the water was merely traces of the river that had followed us home.

"I'm so, so tired." I closed my eyes.

"Go take a nap. I'll catch up on reading. Come find me when you wake up." He kissed my forehead as though I were a small child, then turned and was gone.

# TWELVE

*"I have spread my dreams under your feet;*
*Tread softly because you tread on my dreams."*
—W. B. YEATS

I'm swimming across the river, looking for something important. I am tired, so tired, until I remember that I don't have to swim or struggle, because I know how to breathe underwater and drift while the tide carries me to where I need to go.

The water is brilliant, shot through with prisms of light, and I see shrimp, whiting, and trout swimming by. I am one with them; they accept me. I am free and peaceful. Light winks and dances above me; nothing can harm me here, and isn't it beautiful? I am amazed at all the grace we believe is on top of the river: the rippling waves, the jumping fish, the grasses and shells at its edge. Ah, it is much more exquisite below.

I let myself sink, free-float until I feel the tickle of sea life and then shells at the bottom. I reach my foot down, and the thick black sucking mud pulls me deeper. Then I know I'm wrong; I can't breathe underwater, but now I'm tangled in the plants and mud with Sam, trapped and reaching for the glass surface. Through the blurred water I see something wrapped and bundled—far away toward the horizon and on top of the waves. An osprey cries over and over as she flies above the waves.

Damp and panicked, I burst through the surface of sleep, claw at the sheets, struggle for air.

I tore at the bed; the comforter fell to the floor. I hadn't had this dream since the night before my first date with Thurman. I had always thought of our relationship as the magic formula that had banished my recurring dream of Sam's drowning and how I eventually went with him. I never knew, still didn't, what I was looking for, what I needed on the other side. Whatever it was, I had swum for it, then given up to float with Sam, sink with him.

I curled into a fetal position on the bed, pulled a pillow to my middle, and rolled my feet up from the footboard, as if it contained the plants and mud that reached for me. I didn't want to dream this nightmare again. I wanted the past to stop reaching up to torment me.

The storm outside the inn came in gasps of air, blew against the windows. I rose from the bed and went to the French doors. The sky was the green-black of a storm, of a bruise. Palmetto branches whipped sideways in the wind like someone had rotated a picture of the beach forty-five degrees. Dune grass lay flat in the shadows of the sand.

I walked closer to the door as a gust forced its way around the corner of the house, whistling a high-pitched sound, like someone calling a dog in from the beach. With a single exhalation of the storm, my door burst open. Sand, grass, rain, and one large palmetto branch flew into my room.

I jumped forward, slammed the door shut, and locked it, then backed away. Then it was quiet, still, the storm holding its breath. I moved away from the glass, not wanting to be standing in front of it if the storm came to life again.

I must have slept through the afternoon and evening under the newfound weight of this Leary family knowledge. I wanted to run to Forrest's room upstairs, but I crawled back into bed, pulled the covers up to my chin, and waited for the storm to pass and the night to end.

I stared at the shadows on the ceiling and waited for morning; thought of Murphy and Thurman, of the many possibilities awaiting me at home. We had been gone for only three days, and yet life had been turned inside out.

Sleep finally washed over me until dawn sneaked into the room in streaks of pink light. I rose inside a fatigue that spread across my back, my insides.

I took a quick shower, dressed, and left a message at work that I wouldn't be back today—Tuesday. I made my way down to the library, where I found the remote control and flicked on the TV. The electronic curve of the hurricane had whispered across the South Carolina coast, then been pushed out to sea by a western wind. Seaboro had received a sideswipe of rain and wind, but nothing to harm the coastline.

The TV showed scenes of cracked trees, crooked docks, downed power lines. Far off I heard the thin cry of a bird: the osprey. I jumped off the bar stool and grabbed my purse. I needed to check on the osprey—had the storm ruined her home that had finally been reconstructed?

The B & B was hushed in the quiet of early morning, and I knew I was the only one up. I drove as fast as I could navigate past the downed palmetto branches and around large puddles until I reached the river. As the sun rose, I ran down Ellie's side yard to the wooden T-pole erected by Zach's committee. The pole stood straight, and my gaze traveled slowly up its length to the top. The mother osprey sat in her nest, looked down at me with her yellow eyes impassive and sharp.

"You're okay?" I asked as if she might actually answer.

A thin, high cry startled me, and I turned to see the male osprey on a branch above me, watching.

I sat on a log, exhaled as though I had been holding my breath for years and years. The ospreys had returned to their destroyed home, found twigs and pieces of their old nest and formed a new one in which to rest, raise their family; their new-formed home had survived the storm. I stayed there and watched until I knew what I needed to do next: make something new of the remnants I'd retrieved while I'd been here. Before I went home I needed to see a few people, mend a few broken twigs.

I drove back to the B & B, ran into the library to find Forrest. But only Mr. Hamilton stood there. "May I get you something?" he asked.

"Do you have any coffee?"

"Yes, and my wife made a lovely egg-and-cheese casserole this morning."

"That would be great," I said. "I need to check out also."

"Oh, Mr. Anderson already did that for you."

I gripped the edge of the counter. "He already checked out?"

"Yes, and paid both your bills."

"Did he leave?"

"I guess so. My wife checked him out. I didn't see him. I had to make a run to the docks this morning and check on the boats—she talked to him." He shrugged.

"How did he leave?" I asked.

"My wife said he had a rental car delivered about an hour ago."

Forrest had left—paid the bill and sneaked out, so he

wouldn't have to face me, face what had almost happened between us the afternoon before. I called Mr. Hamilton back into the room. "Just the coffee is fine."

"Are you sure?" He looked over his shoulder as he walked from the room.

"Yes, I need to get on the road."

I reached into my purse, grabbed the cell phone to call Forrest and find out why he had left, where he was. Then I realized I had only his work and home numbers.

In the brief moments it took me to throw my bag in the car, I'd formulated a plan: say good-bye to three people, go home. The end. I would not think about Forrest leaving me here, about Thurman's betrayal, or about my precious dog.

The Barber house was dark, empty. The driveway was full of puddles and bikes, the sound of small boys distinctly absent. I glanced at my watch—it was nine a.m. Where would they all be this early on a summer morning?

I scrawled a note on the back of an old bank statement I found in the bottom of my purse. *Piper—finally finished here. Will call when I get home. Love to your adorable family. Love you. C.* I added my phone number and took the note to her front porch.

I stepped over a plastic play set, a rusting tricycle, and a beheaded G.I. Joe. I stuck the note in between her screen and wood doors. There was evidence of her family everywhere—as if she was more real, more genuine than I had ever been. These possessions kept her grounded and safe. I touched the post of her porch—a touchstone—and climbed back into my car.

Ellie's front porch was still wet—the leftover rain in puddles of silver-white reflection. Only one car was parked in front of the house, with a round blue sticker stating, SEABORO HOME HEALTH CARE. Boyd must have returned to his wife and work in Savannah.

I took a deep breath and knocked on the door. There were some things that needed to be said even if the person you were saying them to didn't understand; words that must be released from their trapped place where their flapping to get out could cause internal damage.

The nurse opened the door, the same woman I'd met three days earlier. She smiled at me. "Hello again. Come on in." She swept her hand into the house. Her scrubs were done in an all-over print of Band-Aids.

"Thanks," I said, entered the foyer. "May I be alone with Ellie for a few minutes?"

She bit her bottom lip so hard I thought she might need one of those printed Band-Aids from her clothing. "Well, Boyd told me not to leave her alone with anyone for the next few days. She's been . . . out of sorts this week."

I nodded. "Okay."

I walked toward the living room, to where a pair of feet in slippers were perched on the end of the divan. I marveled at how quickly something could become familiar: a coffee shop, a glimpse of feet on a lounge chair, the slap of wave against a dock.

I walked to the side of her lounge and sat, grasped her hand. Her eyes were closed, and small puffs of air came from her half-open mouth. I squeezed her hand and she opened her eyes, smiled at me. "Hello, Cappy."

"Hi, Ellie." I leaned toward her.

"What are you doing here today?"

I gazed into her eyes and they appeared wiped clean, as if the rain had entered this house, her soul, and washed the confusion from her. I took the chance that she was in present time—that she knew me at thirty years old and understood why I was here.

"I have to leave today, Ellie, but I wanted to come and say good-bye. I need you to know how much I love you and that I never meant to disappear and not keep in touch. I was scared of all the blame I would feel, of all the pain I would bring to you and Jim and Boyd. But, of course, I see now that I should have called, should have come. I want you to understand I love you. You were more important to my life than anyone I've ever known outside my family."

Her eyebrows moved together and I wondered if I'd said too much, if I'd lost her.

"Cappy, my dear, I know all this. I love you too. I always

have. You have never left me—I understood you would re-turn when the tide rose, when your heart healed." She nod-ded, and a small tear came to the corner of her eye, one oblong tear she didn't seem to notice. She wound her fingers through mine and lifted our hands to her face. She kissed the back of my hand, closed her eyes, and recited a line from a poem: " 'The silver apples of the moon; The golden apples of the sun.' " I allowed her lips to say these words against my skin, each word a whisper across my hand, and then she added, "That was his favorite poem."

My heart turned toward Ellie. "I wish I'd known—"

I'd started to say that I wish I'd known about Sam, about Dad and Ellie, but then I realized, as surely as I'd ever known anything, that I could not have known then, that it would have been the final beat of my child heart.

"What, dear, what do you wish you'd known?"

"That you still loved me," I said, and knew these to be the truest words I'd ever spoken. I wish I'd known I was still loved after Sam's death.

"You have always been deeply loved, whether you were able to feel it or not. All these years. All of them."

I allowed slow, large tears to fall. I stayed this way for long, long minutes, allowing this truth to fully arrive. I had always been loved, even if I hadn't been able to feel it.

A hand fell on my face and Ellie's voice sounded differ-ent now—cracked. "Excuse me, why are you leaning on my chair?"

I sat up and stared at her, but she was gone. The confused woman I'd met three days earlier had returned. "I'm Catherine Leary," I said.

"Oh?" Ellie twisted her head in rapid movements, then stood, called out, "Boyd . . . Boyd . . . Cappy's here."

"Boyd's not here today," I said, and stood with her.

"What do you mean, not *today*? He lives here."

I remembered the nurse who said she wouldn't leave us alone; I turned and saw her in a chair in the corner, sitting straight, her stethoscope hanging from her neck. I motioned to her and she came to us, stared at me for a moment.

"What?" I asked.

She took the stethoscope off her neck. "That was one of the few times I've seen her fully alert and in the present."

I looked at Ellie, who was now walking into the kitchen calling for Boyd.

"Really?" I asked.

She nodded. "The other time was with . . ." She glanced into the hall. "I am probably breaking all kinds of confidentiality here, but it seems important for you to know. The only other times I've seen her vaguely alert was with . . . your father."

"What?" My heart skipped a beat, a bloom of some new knowledge starting just below my heart. "How do you know it was my father?"

"Boyd told me. When he came to visit—sometimes she knew him and they could talk, sometimes for an hour or more before she disappeared again." She took a step to the hall, called Ellie's name, but spoke over her shoulder at me. "She especially knew him when he read to her."

I held my hand over my chest as if I could stop what washed over me. Pure love. For Ellie. For Dad. For life. For hope. For Dad's conviction that words and literature bring us to ourselves, return us to our true self, that they connect us to one another.

I wanted to run to him, throw my arms around him and absolutely make him understand how much I had loved him.

Instead I found Ellie in the kitchen, hugged her one last time. Before I left I asked the nurse for Boyd's work address and directions to his boathouse. I stuffed the directions in my back jeans pocket and ran out to the car.

I touched Sam's headstone, traced my forefinger through the dates. I sat on the thick grass and pulled weeds from around his grave, smoothed the black dirt, and cleaned the area free of rocks and debris.

The gravestones around me were decorated with small trinkets, shattered plates, broken clocks, and cracked mirrors. I had learned on a field trip in seventh grade that leaving these things was an African tradition amongst the Gullah of South Carolina. A favorite object of the deceased or the last item they held was placed on their grave.

The Gullah believed that the shells embodied the spirit of the sea and transported the deceased to the next world. At eleven years old, I had imagined spirits crossing the ocean in clam-shaped gray-striped shells, or riding on sand dollars like rafts, over the horizon to home. This image came wrapped in Sam's green eyes, his laughter, his short, yet beloved childhood.

I had spent all this time wondering what my life would have been like if he hadn't drowned. Now, at his grave site, for the first time I wondered what *his* life would have been like. Would he have ever known his mother's secret? Would his Leary eyes have finally been obvious to us all?

I reached into the bottom of my purse, removed the dried and painted sand dollar I had bought at Morgan's Grocery, and held it out as an offering, then placed it on the clean and flat ground in front of Sam's grave. It was all I knew to do—leave a final vessel to take him to the other side, release him in mind and heart.


The directions to the boat shop where Boyd worked were written on a scrap of baby blue paper in the nurse's handwriting. The hour's drive along winding, marsh-lined roads ended at the Savannah River. For one moment, I thought to call Thurman, but didn't.

I drove up to a warehouse with LOUGHLIN BOATS stenciled on the side. I entered the rear door and inhaled the sweet aroma of sawdust—a scent memory of Boyd as a child. Four men turned to me and all stopped in the midst of their sanding and sawing.

"Yo," called out one of them with dark, curly hair. "You need something?"

"Yes," I hollered over the sounds of a grinding machine coming from somewhere in the back of the building. "I'm looking for Boyd Loughlin."

The man laughed. "Figures. All the good-looking ones are for Boyd." He threw his arms wide. "What about me?"

The short man standing next to him punched him. "You're married, and so is Boyd." Then he glanced at me. "But I ain't."

I laughed. "Okay, where's Boyd?"

The short man pointed up the metal stairs in the back. "Up there. I think he's finishing a final varnish."

"Thanks," I said, and walked toward where he pointed. My flip-flops slapped against the metal stairs in a loud announcement of my arrival.

When I reached the top, I ducked under a swinging metal lamp and stared at Boyd. He was bent over a handmade wooden sloop of beautiful craftsmanship. A brush hung in his hand, and the sharp tang of varnish permeated the air.

The boat glimmered where he had already painted. He turned to me, then propped the brush on the can and wiped his palms on his smock. "Catherine," he said.

"Hi, Boyd." I didn't know what to do with my hands or feet.

He glanced around. "What are you doing here? How did you know where I work?"

"Ellie's nurse gave me your address and directions."

He smiled, and for the briefest flicker of time I saw the old Boyd.

"I just came to say good-bye and . . ." Then I lost all the words I'd meant to say to him. All the profound utterances that had formed inside me on the drive here dissipated into the varnish-thick air.

He spread his hands out. "What? You came to say what?"

"Sorry," I said, and my voice cracked.

"You already told me that. No need to tell me again. Really, there is no need for any of this. Let's just get on with our lives like we have been."

"That's it," I said, moved closer to him. "I don't think either of us has really gotten on with our life. We have carried this . . . thing with us for far too long."

"Maybe you have, but I haven't. Don't be putting your crap on me."

I took a long breath. "You can't hate me any more than you already do—so I've got nothing to lose." I paced around the boat, touch the unshellacked area. "Did you make this?"

"Yes," he said.

"It is beautiful. An amazing piece of craftsmanship. Mack would be proud." I took a deep breath. "Ellie knew me today," I said.

"Those are the best days of all—when she knows—but they can also be the worst."

"It was all mixed-up in there, wasn't it?" I asked.

"What was mixed-up?"

"The best and the worst—all mixed-up in those childhood days."

Boyd stared at me and said nothing. His mouth was straight and bloodless.

"I think," I said, "you and I have chosen two different ways to deal with this terrible tragedy. I stopped giving and receiving love. You chose anger."

"And this is any of your business because . . . ?" Spit came from the corner of his mouth and landed on the sawdust-covered floor, making a small wet spot.

"Because I once loved the boy you were. Because I love Ellie. Because I am leaving now and will never have the chance to say this again. Because I am part of the reason you are so . . . angry. And I want to take what piece of it that I can away from you. I want you to understand what I now understand."

"And what—exactly—do you understand now?"

"There was more to it than you and me not watching or scaring Sam. More than that failure that tore our families apart."

"What, that Mom and Grayson had some kind of love affair? You think you're telling me something I don't know?"

"No, Boyd. I'm telling you that our family moved and yours fell apart—not because of us, but because of Sam."

"Because he was their son?"

I opened my mouth but nothing came out.

"Shit, Catherine, you think I don't know that? I figured that out a long time ago." He stepped closer, poked my shoulder with one finger. "You got to pretend nothing happened and just continue on with your life—your pretty-face, happy-go-lucky life."

Now I was the one who stepped closer. "You are out of your mind. My *what* life?" Anger rose in me as if his were contagious. "You have no idea," I said.

"And"—he took a step back—"neither do you."

"I give up," I said, threw my hands up in the air. "I thought we could talk about it."

"You were wrong." His breath reeked of cigarettes.

"I've been wrong before." I turned to leave, then glanced back. "Boyd Loughlin, it's like you're in that river with Sam."

I turned and walked to the stairs and down them, wanting to run, but taking careful steps all the way to the front door. I closed the door behind me and heard one of the men holler up to Boyd, "Damn, what'd you say to that pretty lady? You crazy, man?"

If I'd had any guts at all, I'd have returned and told those men that it was I who'd said something. I had pulled out my keys when a viselike grip covered my upper arm. I spun around to Boyd; he released me.

"What the hell do you mean by that, Catherine? That I'm at the bottom of the river?"

"There are more ways to be dead than actually dying, Boyd."

He rolled his eyes, walked away from me. "You're utterly insane, just like your father was."

I watched him walk away and thought he would turn around, apologize. But he slammed shut the warehouse door without even a backward glance.

I got into my car and turned the air conditioner to high. The Savannah Bridge lay down the road, reaching toward the sky in a marvel of human engineering. I'd drive over it—feeling as though I could fly—and return home.

Everything I had learned these past three days was like the crazy quotes pinned all over Dad's bulletin board—haphazard, with no real theme or direction, just random pieces of scattered childhood memories and half-forgotten truths. But I did understand that the below-my-breast sorrow I felt wasn't for myself, but for Boyd. I would not stop trying to reach him, not stop searching for the softer places I knew hid inside him—where at one time love had lived and moved, and might yet once again.

# THIRTEEN

*"How many a man has dated a new era in his life*
*from the reading of a book!"*
—HENRY DAVID THOREAU

By the time I drove into Cedar Valley, the animal clinic had closed for the night, but I stood at the back door and banged until a weary, beard-stubbled teen came to the door. "We're closed."

"My dog," I said, "is really sick . . . Murphy."

His eyes widened and he stepped back, let me in. "That's why I'm here—I was staying with her until you could get here. I'm the vet tech."

"How is she?" I pushed past him to the kennels. A wet-dog smell mixed with animal food, ammonia, and fur made me dizzy.

"Follow me," he said. "She's in medical."

I followed him down the hallway to the medical clinic and fell to my knees in front of the large kennel where Murphy lay with her nose wedged up against the gate, her hind legs spread as an afterthought. "Oh, Murphy." I lay down on the floor, pushed my hand through the fencing, and rubbed her nose.

The tech spoke in a whisper. "Wow, she must have dragged herself to the front when she heard your voice. I had her settled on that bed back there." He pointed to a round sheepskin bed I had brought with her.

He reached above his head, unlocked the kennel, and I crawled inside with Murphy, buried my head in her fur and cried. She licked my face, threw her left front paw over my head. The tech went to the back of the run and pulled her bed forward.

"Can she come with me?" I asked, looked up at him.

He shook his head. "I have the shots and medicine she needs in case—"

"I'm staying with her until the doc gets here in the morning."

"In here?" He swept his hand across the kennel. "I'm here to watch over all the dogs. She'll be fine."

"No," I said, "just help me get her back onto her bed."

He bent and together we lifted Murphy onto the round bed; I settled myself next to her on the stained linoleum floor and laid my hand across her chest. "You can go now," I said to the tech.

"I'll be right out there if anything happens. Just holler."

"Thank you," I said and lay down with my head next to Murphy's and rubbed her ears, her neck, her face until her breathing settled into the soft sounds of sleep and her frantic movements subsided.

Our breathing combined into one rhythm while I held my hand over her chest, whispered what an amazing dog she was, how she had been Dad's best friend. I smoothed her gray muzzle, cried until tears soaked the corner of her doggy bed, until sleep came over me and I awoke to her still chest, a calm puppy look on her face. Morning light filtered through the miniblinds. Cats began their morning cry for food; dogs barked to be let out.

I stayed on that floor with my dog, with Dad's dog, until I heard footsteps approach. I sat up, but didn't remove my hand from her chest. Dr. Morrison stood over me in green scrubs, his hands held together in a prayerful pose.

"Ms. Leary," he said. "Are you okay?"

I shook my head. "She's gone," I said, and felt my face screw up in the withholding of a sob.

He unlocked the kennel, knelt down next to me, touched Murphy's chest. "Yes, she is."

"She was the best dog in the entire world—you know that, right?" I said.

"Yes, I know that. Your dad thought so too."

I nodded. "He was right. About so many things, he was so right."

"This was a blessed dog, Catherine. She was loved and adored and died with you right next to her. Would you like another minute to say good-bye?"

"No." I stood, stiff and achy from sleeping on the floor. "I've spent the night saying good-bye."

I followed the doctor down the hallway, and he turned to me. "You need to go home and sleep; then call me and we'll talk about . . . what you want done with her."

I nodded, then ran back, kissed Murphy's muzzle one last time, and left to face an empty home.

The house felt as though someone had left the windows open while I was gone, but instead of air and light coming in, everything had emptied out. I gathered the mail and sorted it into junk and must-do piles, threw the newspapers into the recycle bin; the front page of today's paper showed how the edge of the storm had impacted Cedar Valley, grabbing a few trees on its way, crushing a couple cars, and smashing a roof.

In a daze of sleeplessness, I called work to say I needed to take a personal day, ate a toasted bagel with jelly, and crawled into bed, allowing sleep to wash over me in a thick wave of relief. Through the morning, I dozed off and on, heard the distant ringing of the phone, the buzz of life outside my window: cars, neighbors, birds. Thurman's voice came on the answering machine over and over. Once I thought I heard Forrest's voice, but then again, it could have been a dream.

Hours later, I knew what I had to do—read Dad's favorite book. This had seemed the only option available to me in the dark night with Murphy when I counted all that was lost to me. I wanted to find what Dad loved, what touched his heart.

I showered, dressed in jeans and a white linen tunic, pulled my hair back, and drove to the Cedar Valley Public Library. I hadn't been there since high school. I inhaled the pulpy smell of paper, of books. I remembered how in summer Mother would take me on weekly trips to the Seaboro Library. I would return the five or six books I had borrowed the previous week, and then choose five more. The air conditioner had hummed in the corner by the desk where Piper had carved *I love Parker,* and I had once kept a list behind the counter of which Nancy Drew books I'd checked out so I didn't accidentally take out one I'd already read.

I had spent hours choosing which books would be my constant companions and best friends during the next week. I'd loved the crinkle of the plastic covers, the soft texture of well-read pages, and the thrill of finding a new book—one in which the spine cracked with the first opening.

The Cedar Valley Public Library was much more modern than Seaboro's: Computers stood in banks along the left wall. Coloring books had been spread on low-lying tables for children while their mothers browsed the stacks.

I headed toward the fiction section. When was the last time I had read a novel—something other than required reading for school?

A sudden thought caused grief to flicker like lightning you see only out of the corner of the eye. It must have broken Dad's heart that I didn't read novels anymore. He never said much more than, "Read anything good lately?" and I'd tell him that the latest *Allure* magazine had a fantastic article on how to keep your hair from frizzing in the summer humidity.

I figured he had his friends, the other professors, and Forrest to satisfy his need to discuss books. He'd had his students. But it occurred to me now, standing in the library, that maybe I was the one who had missed out. And it seemed only right that the first fiction I read in years should be his favorite. I didn't want to get the book from the bookstore, where I knew I had a strong chance of running into Forrest or one of Dad's associates.

I found the Gs on the last row, moved down the shelves to find Graham Greene: *The Power and the Glory; Brighton Rock*, but *The End of the Affair* wasn't there. I leaned against the shelf, dropped my head back.

"May I help you find something?" I heard.

I opened my eyes to see Mrs. Parson. I wouldn't have known her anywhere but standing behind a row of books, her glasses hanging from a thin silver chain. I knew her immediately, although I hadn't seen her in years. I smiled. "Yes,

I'm looking for a Graham Greene novel that doesn't seem to be here."

She nodded. "I'll look real quick. It might be checked out."

"Thank you. *The End of the Affair*," I said.

"I'll be right back." She turned, then glanced over her shoulder. Her panty hose rubbed together in a swishing noise as she made her way across the library.

When she returned, she held out a tattered copy of the book. "Someone just checked it back in—it was in the stack to be reshelved."

"Thank you," I said, took the book from her and flipped it over. I glanced up at her. "Have you read it?"

She nodded. "Yes, it is a sad story, but beautifully written."

"What's it about?"

"Oh, this book has a lot of answers to that question. It explores themes of love and God and loss."

"What was it about for you?" I asked.

"You read it and tell me what you think." She smiled at me and returned to the reference desk.

I made my way through the stacked shelves to the poetry section, grabbed an anthology of W. B. Yeats poems, and dropped both books on the checkout counter. Mrs. Parson punched at the computer, then glanced up. "Library card?"

"Oh . . ." I said. "Not anymore."

"Do you have a driver's license?"

"Yes." I smiled. "I'm Catherine Leary."

"I thought I knew you. Catherine Leary. Don't you re-member me?" She tapped her chest. "I'm Mrs. Parson."

"So good to see you," I said.

"It is very nice to see you again—it's been years."

I nodded. "I'll be around more often, I promise."

Mrs. Parson's tongue stuck out the corner of her mouth while she keyed information into her computer and then handed me a new card and both books. "We miss your dad."

"So do I," I said, then tucked the card into my purse and walked through the front doors of the library with my two books and a free day before me.

I entered my home, fatigue still throbbing behind my eyes, the books under my arm. I stared at the flashing light of the answering machine and pushed play to hear messages from work—they hoped I was well and not to worry about missing another day, as I had plenty of vacation coming to me. Then Thurman's voice came on three times in a row, his voice escalating with frustration as he asked me to please call him back. He was still in Alabama until that night. Then Forrest's voice—soft and wounded in a confusing message. "Hey," he said, then paused until I thought the message was over. But just before I hit erase, his voice continued. "Why'd you leave like that? You could've at least told me you wanted to drive home alone." And then the pause turned to a beep—message over.

I sat at the kitchen table and dropped my head into my hands. What did he mean? He'd left—not me. I picked up the phone, dialed his office and then home, but got voice mail at both places. I left identical messages: "It's me. I didn't leave . . . you did. Where are you?"

Then I didn't know what else to say or do, so I climbed the stairs to my bedroom, tossed my shoes in the corner, dropped a bag containing a scone and coffee from Starbucks on my bedside table, and curled up beneath the down comforter to read *The End of the Affair*. Oh, how I wanted Murphy to jump up on the end of the bed and sleep on my feet while I read. I swallowed tears and flipped open the cover and read the first line: *A story has no beginning or end*. I closed my eyes and knew this was true. And I kept reading, which was, astonishingly, all I wanted to do.

I was starving for words, for story, and I hadn't even known it. Crumbs fell onto the bed as I ate without notice; the coffee was cold before I remembered to sip it. I fell into the book, into the words and emotions, and remembered how a story could take me to a different place. I craved nothing else over those next hours. The sun moved across the sky and the phone rang downstairs.

And when it became too much, when the emotions of this story of love and secrets washed me in despair, I slept.

That evening, I rose with a deep ache along my back

and wandered downstairs with the sad love story still moving inside me, blending with thoughts of Dad and Ellie, of Sam, Thurman, Murphy, and all love gone awry.

I carried the Yeats collection into the kitchen, nuked a frozen pizza—the only food in the house—ignored the blinking answering machine, and took the book into Dad's office. I settled into his desk chair and realized I'd only stood in this room; I hadn't sat at his desk since his death.

It seemed right, with a poetry book in my hand, to do so now. I set the pizza on the side and opened the book, searched for the poem with the line about silver apples, golden apples, yearning to decipher what it meant.

When I found it, my heart stood still for long moments as I read the last stanza of a poem entitled "The Wandering Aengus."

> *Though I am old with wandering*
> *Through hollow lands and hilly lands,*
> *I will find out where she has gone,*
> *And kiss her lips and take her hands;*
> *And walk among long dappled grass,*
> *And pluck till time and times are done*
> *The silver apples of the moon,*
> *The golden apples of the sun.*

When my heart found its beat again, it was a different one. I had gone, for the briefest time, inside this poem, lost myself and returned with a new understanding: Dad had wandered until he found her, till time and times were done. Until the end. It was, and forever would be, pure love: a sad love story. And, for a time unknown to any of us, Ellie was still in the place where he took her lips and hands and walked with her among the dappled grass.

My heart grew, expanded, and I twirled around in the chair, stared at Dad's bulletin board.

Maybe deep inside my locked heart I had known about Dad and Ellie, but instead chose to shoulder my own burden of guilt, carrying that knowledge in the inaccessible places of my heart.

This scared me with a panic-stricken thought: What if I had not loved at all?

The bulletin board with Dad's random quotes and notes confused me. I leaned back and stared at it, held a slice of cold pizza in the air until my eyesight blurred, yet I found no pattern as I searched for something, anything by Graham Greene or Yeats. And then I found it: the opening line to the book in the middle of the board: *A story has no beginning or end.*

I tore a piece of paper from a blank notebook, wrote, *"Whereof what's past is prologue"—Shakespeare* and then tacked it onto the bulletin board—right in the middle. I smiled. *In medias res*—in the middle of things.

I had now added to the bulletin board, to the collection of quotes that meant something in Dad's life, in mine. And I would continue to add them.

This I knew—I did not want to live one life yet love another. "Thurman," I said his name, tasted it for what feeling remained for him after discovering how deeply and how long my dad had loved another woman. I jumped up with sudden purpose.

The Athletic Office was dark and empty, since most of the staff had used this lull in the school calendar to take some vacation. Thurman's last message said he had returned from Alabama, and he had a surprise for me. Regular business hours were over, and night settled over the offices like a net. I felt as though I must tiptoe through the halls, although I had entered with my key.

I reached my office and unlocked the door. The room was full of . . . nothing, although it was overflowing with papers, notes, phone, fax, copier, and a photo of Thurman and me on the basketball court before a UNC game.

I walked around the office, ran my hand across the desk, the phone. I grabbed the messages off my desk and shoved them into my purse. I'd answer them later. I flung through the keys on my key ring until I found the one with a big T on it: Thurman's office.

I didn't turn on the lights there, but headed for the room with the filing cabinets. I reached the recruiting files and held my breath. I had been standing right there the first time Thurman asked me out.

"Hey," he'd said. "Want to get a drink after work?"

I'd hesitated, but for only a moment. Dating where you worked was a big taboo, but here was Coach Thurman Whittaker asking me out.

He'd stared at me while I searched for an answer. "Okay," he'd said, "I've tried to build up the courage to ask you for over a year now. You have to say something."

And that admittance—that this coach revered by men needed courage to ask me out—made me smile and say yes, but for the next night.

I opened the filing cabinet. What did I think I'd find here? Thurman would not be so stupid as to keep proof of his guilt—if there was any. But he would keep it about someone else. It was a thought that came to me unbidden and from a source I hadn't known before—a source of doubt about Thurman's character and integrity.

I rifled through the files in the blinking overhead fluorescent lights. After an hour, my back ached and the clock said eleven p.m. All I had found were the names, addresses, and notes about the chances for each recruit. *Mother wants him at UNC—need to convince Mom more than player.* Or *DUI in high school.* Or *Best free throw in state.*

I carefully kept each paper and note in the files where they belonged. I finally reached the last file with only meager hope of finding anything. It was the file for the player he had gone to see this past week: Darius Williams.

I found all the information I already knew about this

player—he was leaning toward a smaller college in Alabama to be close to his family, whom he helped support, as there was no dad. I reached my hand back and found one small scrap: a money order for a year's rent on a house on Tyndale Lane. I knew this road, of course—a lane of suburban houses at the base of the mountains where families of university professors lived and played in the sidewalk comfort of large trees and clean streets with a park at either end.

I inhaled as I stared at a scribbled note: *125 Tyndale Lane. One year's rent.* Then there was a signature, indecipherable, that started with a C and had either an L or S in the middle.

I knew the recruiting rules well—anyone in media relations for the athletic department must: A booster for the university could invite a recruit to dinner, but only once a month; he could hire a recruit to work for him, but only for fair pay. But renting a house for his family to have somewhere nearby to live—this was an absolute violation. Even if Thurman didn't have anything to do with it, the misdeed could take down the basketball program.

I breathed slowly in and out. I took the paper with me to my office, made a photocopy, then returned the original to Thurman's files. I understood this was merely a scrawled note inserted into a file, but it was all I had, and my deep need for the truth made me shove the copy into my purse.

# FOURTEEN

My office held little appeal that morning, but nevertheless I headed to work on Thursday. If I concentrated on the multiple tasks I needed to accomplish, I wouldn't have to feel anything. I was embedded in the busy aftermath caused by being away for a few days when a cough came from my office door. I glanced up from my desk, stared at Thurman. He looked down at me with a smile that seemed half-cocky, half-apologetic grimace. "Hey, darling," he said.

I lifted my eyebrows. "Aren't you talking to the wrong girl?"

He smoothed his khakis with his palms and then sat on the chair opposite my desk. "Catherine, I have missed you so damn much. Why haven't you answered your phone in days? I've been worried sick. I didn't even know you'd come into work today until I saw your light from down the hall."

"I came home two days ago," I said. "Didn't you get my message?"

"That you'd come home?"

"No, that I enjoyed talking to the girl who answered the phone in your hotel room."

"Catherine, you must have dialed the wrong room."

"I heard your voice."

He closed his eyes, breathed deeply, as if he were dealing with a player who didn't understand zone defense. "It wasn't me. I was working my ass off in Alabama trying to get this player to come here. I wasn't with a girl. I wasn't out having a good time. For God's sake, I was working, Catherine."

"Thurman, this isn't the place to talk about this."

He touched his neck. "Where's the necklace I gave you?"

"At the bottom of the Seaboro River," I said.

His entire face furrowed into a scowl. "The diamond necklace I gave you is at the bottom of a river in some backwater town?"

"Yes," I said.

The room filled with his blazing anger. "Just great, Catherine. You get mad at me and throw away a thousand-dollar piece of jewelry. Brilliant."

I leaned over the desk, my palms flat on it. "I didn't

throw it in the river. It fell and I couldn't find it. I didn't do it on purpose. I'm sorry. . . ."

"Yeah, I can tell you're real sorry."

"Thurman, please, it's been a rough few days."

"I know. I know. We've both had long days. Mine were spent beggin' this player to come here, then when I went back to Alabama my car was totaled and I had to get a rental."

"What?" I stood up. "Was anyone hurt?"

"No, I'm fine. My point is, I've had a hell of a time—not a great way to start the summer. Listen, I didn't come here to fight with you. I love you, Catherine. I missed you while you were gone. I really did. It went well, though. Darius changed his mind and will be playing for yours truly. So I guess all that hell was worth it."

I lifted my eyebrows. "What about his family?"

"They're moving here. They found a house in Tyndale Park, and he can see them and help them from here."

"Oh?"

Thurman leaned across the desk, caught me off guard, and kissed me.

In a reflex born of four years of dating, I kissed him back. But I didn't respond to his words. Instead I told him about Murphy. I told myself he would take me into his arms, and I'd find the familiar comfort with him, and then I could dismiss all my doubts and feelings of estrangement.

"Oh, I'm sorry. She was a sweet dog." He made a sad face. "Listen, I have a dinner tonight with the board," he said. "I'll call you when it's over and we'll make up for lost time. I hate when we're apart, all the confusion and . . ."

When he left the room, I sat down to better understand what had just happened. It was as if two conversations were going on at the same time: the words we said, and the words we didn't. He hadn't once asked how my time went in Seaboro, and he dismissed Murphy's death as a piece of news equivalent to the front-page story about downed trees in lower Cedar Valley.

If I had learned anything during this journey my dad had sent me on it was this: that over time, hidden truths morph in the dark soil of deceit into something much worse.

I pulled out the copy of the receipt I'd found in the files the night before. I could keep this to myself and help bury the lie under the celebration of Darius's signing. Or I could give this to the athletic director to pursue.

I started when the phone rang. I answered and Piper's voice came into my office through the speakerphone.

"Hey, girlfriend," she said.

I picked up the receiver. "Hey, Piper. What's up?"

"Same old stuff—carpool to church camp, Parker's on another business trip, laundry crawling down the hall, sick kid."

"Oh, the glamour," I said.

"You got it. Then I've got a fancy night out."

"You do?"

"Yep, taking Alice to dinner."

I laughed, leaned back in the chair, and closed my eyes. "Tell her hello for me."

"She twisted her ankle taking the hurricane shutters down—she didn't want to wait for Bobby, her handyman, to do it."

"Kiss her for me," I said over the lump in my throat that I knew was love for Alice.

Then Piper told me all the Seaboro gossip and about her boys' antics, which made me laugh again.

"Oh, the big Memorial Day picnic that got rescheduled is in two weeks. Any chance you'll come back for it?" she asked.

"No way. I have so much going on here." I watched new e-mails scroll in a list down the screen. There was the weekly notification of jobs at SU—one at the literary magazine flashed on my screen—and I dully wondered if Forrest had posted it. I deleted the message as Piper talked.

"Okay, I've gotta go. Zach is throwing up in various and sundry parts of the house."

"Lucky you," I said.

"Hey," she said. "Before I hang up. I was wondering, have you made up with your boyfriend, found out what happened?"

"We're working on it. I'm not really sure what's going on . . . I don't have real proof of anything."

I heard her long exhaled breath. "You don't always need proof to know something."

"I realize that. But look at you—you've stayed with one man, remained committed, and, as you told me, everyone has their struggles. It's been four years. I can't just throw it away." I was talking to myself as much as to my old friend.

"Cheating and lying aren't struggles, they're . . . reasons to break up," she said.

"I know, Piper. Listen, I have a ton of work. We'll talk later."

We hung up and I heard her last words as though they echoed in the room: *Cheating and lying . . .*

I stuffed the Darius house memo into an envelope and shoved it in my top drawer.

I left work and attempted to get back into the daily routine of life: called a few friends, grocery shopped, accidentally placed a bag of dog food in the cart and had to put it back, dropped off the dry cleaning, and went home to cook myself dinner.

I ate alone at the kitchen table and read the opening chapter of *To Kill a Mockingbird,* then watered the plants in Dad's office. I stood again in front of the bulletin board and read through the quotes, said them out loud. Then, as if a flat board suddenly became three-D, I saw it—the divisions, the quadrants. Buried underneath the scraps of paper were pieces of twine pinned to the cork, which divided the board into squares.

I placed my finger on the first quadrant, read a couple quotes—loss. Then the next square—love. Then the heart of writing, art . . . The seemingly random placement actually had order and meaning—a gestalt.

I wanted my emotions to do the same—divide into patterns that made sense. I wondered if it was time to tell Thurman, to share it all with him. Then a small shudder reached down my back, over my arms. He was at a business dinner at the steakhouse.

Doubt crawled over me like poison ivy, then inside me, where it itched in a desperate need to know the truth.

Smoke, boisterous talk, and the air of men making deals to the clink of Scotch-filled crystal glasses filled the dark-paneled restaurant. A square bar dominated the center of the room. I checked my appearance in the mirror over the bar: I wore a pale green dress that looked good against my tan and my Leary eyes.

I turned away and rubbed my bare arms, as I'd omitted the matching cardigan. I wanted to look confident and vaguely sexy if I was going to catch Thurman in some kind of affair. I wanted to appear more than the dutiful employee and girlfriend. I wore my hair down, a whisper against my bare shoulders.

I rubbed my lips together to even out the lip gloss, then strolled through the tightly packed tables with a drink in my hand. Maybe I would even throw it at Thurman when I found him with the woman. I squeezed behind chairs, said,

"Excuse me," scanned the room for him. My stomach began a slow roll that I hadn't felt when I'd confidently entered the restaurant. My hands shook; my feet felt too big for the heels I wore.

I didn't find him as I rounded back to the bar, which was sleek with God knew how many layers of polyurethane. It made me think of the scarred oak bar in the B & B, and then the varnish on Boyd's boat. Everything here was cleaner, more lustrous. I caught my reflection behind the bar and saw I looked scared, wide-eyed. I shouldn't have come on this foolish mission to a smoke-filled restaurant. How in the world did I think this would solve anything? Being embarrassed, humiliated in public would not answer all the questions I now had about what to do with the new chapters of my life.

Thurman's blond hair shimmered across the sparkling bar—there he was. His back was turned to me as he talked to a woman with long auburn hair. Imminent embarrassment did a stiletto-heeled tango in my gut. I waited, watched. Thurman moved from the bar and the woman followed. Their heads bobbed behind a nail-studded, high-backed leather booth, then disappeared.

I sidled up to the back of the booth, took a deep breath, and turned with a sudden twist of my heels to face a round table of five men, Scotch glasses at their elbows, cutting into huge steaks with oversize knives. Next to us was a brick wall with wine cellar insets behind wrought-iron gates. The men's speech was distorted as I stared, confused, at the table. The long-haired woman crouched down, writing on a tablet—the waitress. I took in the scene in jigsawed bits and pieces as I realized that, indeed, Thurman was in a business meeting with four other men.

His voice swelled above the noise. "Catherine, what are you doing here?"

My words shrank, faded; I covered my naked arms with my hands, wanted to throw a neatly folded napkin over my cleavage.

Thurman stood and grabbed me by the arm. "Are you okay?"

The waitress handed something across the table. "Here's the bar bill," she said to a man I recognized as Carl Lasinki—the chairman of the athletic board and once an all-American basketball player for Southern.

I was disconnected now, almost observing the scene as if it were a TV show and not my humiliating attempt to catch Thurman in an affair. Carl took the bar bill and scrawled his signature across the bottom.

Thurman shook me slightly. "Catherine," he said, "what is wrong?"

I glanced away from the table, still unable to absorb the fact that there was no woman sitting there. I forced a smile; I'm not sure where I found it, maybe the depths of well-practiced Southern womanhood. Dixie Appleton would have been proud.

"Yes, yes, I'm fine," I said. "I was just finishing some errands and thought I'd come by and say hello." I forced another smile.

Thurman excused himself, guided me away from the table and out the front door without saying a word. I focused on walking sure and straight.

We reached the parking lot and Thurman took a step away from me. "What the hell are you doing, Catherine?"

If I tried hard enough, I could see Boyd on a front porch; I recognized the controlled anger well enough.

"I just told you," I said, maintaining my shaking smile.

"Bullshit. What are you doing?"

"You don't believe me?"

"No, Catherine. I do not. This is the second time in a week you've thought I'm doing something besides working. I believe you're checking up on me, embarrassing yourself and making those men in there think I have a girlfriend who doesn't trust me." He shook his head like one would do at a misbehaving child. "You have been acting so weird since you got back from that asinine trip to the beach."

My resolve crumbled under his jackhammered words. I hated that I couldn't stop the tears, but they came anyway. How could I have thought this outing would solve anything between us? I attempted to hide the tears by walking away from him. I had wanted to prove I was right in my anger, in my suspicions, but all I'd done was look the fool.

"Catherine," he called after me, but I hurried to my

parked car, ignored him. I knew he wouldn't come after me, the same way he wouldn't turn the car around on my birthday morning. He'd just take care of it later.

At home I crawled between the sheets. Tonight I could not blame my restless sleep on a storm, but on my own internal turbulence. My mind wandered through a maze of images and choices in my life: saying yes to Ellie, a woman answering the hotel phone, Sam in his father's arms, Forrest diving to the bottom of the river.

I still lay awake when I heard the lock turn in my front door: Thurman had a key. I kept my eyes closed and yet I smelled the Scotch, the cigar smoke hovering over me.

"Catherine," he said, "we need to talk."

"I'm trying to sleep. I'm too, too tired," I mumbled into the sheets.

"Now," he said.

I rolled over and opened one eye. "What, Thurman?"

"We can't ignore this any longer. I can't have you not trusting me, checking up on me. I'm not doing anything wrong. I love you. I've loved you since the day you came into the Athletic Office and introduced yourself, tripping over the entryway carpet. I've loved you since the day you set your green eyes on me. Hell, I've never even thought about marrying anyone else."

I imagined Thurman practicing these words like he practiced a speech for a press conference. I saw him driving home saying this little sermonette over and over until it was polished and smooth and ready to hand to me like a gift. This image forced a smile from me, which he took for a positive response.

He ran his hand through my hair as he tilted my head to look up at him. I closed my eyes, unable to meet his eyes, another sign he misinterpreted as surrender or forgiveness, because he leaned down to kiss me with the same changeless kiss I'd known all these years.

I rolled over, pulled my pillow against my body. "Please let's talk tomorrow. I'm truly tired. Please . . . leave."

"Damn, " he said, and I heard the front door slam. And yet the exhaustion of both mind and spirit wouldn't let me rise to lock it.

# Fifteen

*"If you don't change your beliefs, your life will be like this forever. Is that good news?"*
—William Somerset Maugham

The morning after my humiliating episode at the restaurant, I arrived at the office to find that the NCAA investigators had announced Southern University was free of all recruitment violations. The boosters under investigation had been completely cleared.

I stood in my office and thought how Thurman had told the truth last night about being at the restaurant for a meeting. My humiliation ran deeper as I remembered looking like a pitiful girlfriend searching for something that wasn't there. Carl Lasinski had stared at me as he signed the bill.

The other men had withheld their laughter with furrowed brows and highballs in their hands.

*Carl Lasinki signing the bill with a large C and a squiggle with an S in the middle.*

Suddenly I stood with a faltering heartbeat to do something I had had no previous intention of doing: I walked into the office of the athletic director, Coach Fontaine, without knocking. I had walked in there at least once a day for the past five years since the athletic director held tight control over the media released from his department. His office was crowded with framed pictures of players and other coaches, championships won in various Southern University sports. I wondered how he could work in a space so crowded with past victories that it must be difficult to focus on today's challenges.

Coach Fontaine was a big man, white hair sprouting from his head in cotton puffs that shifted with every move of his head. His voice was a booming musical instrument that he utilized to get the absolute best from every athlete, to garner respect and mold teams.

I dropped the note from Thurman's file onto his desk. He glanced up at me. "What the hell is that? Who does the media want now?" he asked, and he drew out the word *hell* so long it could have been three words.

"It's not the media." I backed away from his desk, suddenly full of doubt about what I'd done. "But it seems important."

He glanced down at it. "Where'd you find this?"

"I do a lot of filing."

"Yes. But where'd you find this?"

"Do I have to say?"

He squinted at me. "What do you think this is?"

"I think it might be a receipt for a house on Tyndale Lane paid for by Carl Lasinski."

"That's a mighty big charge." He stood now and leaned across his desk.

I nodded. "I know that."

"I'll look into it," he said as his phone rang. He waved his hand toward the door, and I left with as much dignity as I could muster. I went back to my office to finish the day's work in a quiet, humming panic of the possible ramifications of what I'd just done.

I answered e-mails, sent a press release about Darius signing with Southern University, filed papers, and told Thurman, that yes, of course I'd meet him at the Pig 'n' Pull for our regular Friday-night dinner. He had his weekly poker game, but we could eat first. The extraordinary part of the day was merely that nothing extraordinary happened after I'd handed over the scrap of paper.

I drove down the pine- and cedar-lined street to meet Thurman for dinner, stopped at a red light, and saw a barricade—orange and yellow—with instructions to detour around

Indian Trail to Kerman Street, as there was huge pine tree down in the road. A crew of five men in bright orange vests surrounded the tree; one man held a chain saw, and the others seemed to be there to tell him what to do.

A blue-and-yellow truck with CEDAR VALLEY GAS AND POWER written on the sides was parked in front of me, so I had to maneuver a three-point turn to detour. It must have been a tree that fell during the storm—the one that tore down trees and crushed a car or two.

*A crushed car.*

*A totaled car.*

I came to a complete stop in the middle of the road. Tires squealed as the person behind me veered to miss me, and I made a sharp right onto my street.

I pulled my car into the driveway and pushed open on the garage door opener, parked, and ran for the recycling bin. The concrete inside the garage was slippery with something that must have dripped out of the car overnight; the Seaboro trip had been too much for my little car. My feet flew out from under me. I scrambled for a handhold, then fell while my bent wrists broke the fall. When I yanked my hands up and away from the shock and pain, my bottom landed with a resounding thump on the concrete.

I cried out and rolled onto my side, where whatever slick substance there was on the floor transferred itself to my silk shirt and linen suit skirt.

If anyone drove by, this is what they'd have seen: a thirtyycar-old woman lying on her side in an open garage in the middle of a slick puddle of oil.

I sat, scooted toward the recycling bin I had loaded only two days ago, and, with my good hand, grabbed the top newspaper off the pile. It was the one with the front page of the car squashed by a falling oak in a driveway. Now I knew why the picture had drawn my attention—it was a Lexus in the tract homes of lower Cedar Valley.

I stared into the grainy picture and attempted to decipher the license plate, but I had already seen what I needed—the small round basketball sticker on the rear window.

I took the newspaper, my throbbing right wrist cradled against my chest, and jumped back into the car.

Details I'd seen the past few days—the signature, the newspaper—were images I hadn't really noticed. They were now coming into focus, as if they'd been floating in developing fluid for a week. I always wanted proof, a guarantee that my heart was telling me the truth. But even without the proof—I'd been right all along.

The Pig 'n' Pull was overflowing, the air stifling with the smell of barbecue and butter. I walked to the back of the restaurant, where Thurman and I always sat. I found him in a booth with two plates already on the table. The pulled pork smothered in sauce had jelled on my plate while Thurman continued to pull meat off his ribs. He glanced up at me.

He wiped his mouth with a napkin, then stood, hugged me. "You get caught up at work?"

I stared at him without answering.

"I ordered for you," he said. "I hope that's okay. I knew we were in a rush tonight."

When I didn't answer again, he squinted. "What happened to you?" He pointed to my skirt, my hand held at an awkward angle against my chest. He touched my cheek. "You've got grease or something all over your face."

"I fell," I said. "Hard."

"Where? Are you okay?" He touched my elbow.

I couldn't stop staring at him, and a new thought blossomed: *I do not love this man. I have never loved this man.* And I was scared. Fear wrapped itself around my middle, squeezed me.

Thurman touched my neck. "We'll have to get you another necklace."

I tried to smile, but deep below I was searching for a feeling—the one I had when I was on the phone with Piper that morning, the one Dad felt for Ellie, and it was then that the fear crawled further. Maybe I just didn't know how to love. Because if I didn't love a man I'd been with for four years . . .

Then it came to me, released from someplace even deeper, someplace where the truth had been living all along. Of course I knew how to love: I loved Dad, I loved Ellie, I'd loved Mother, I loved Piper, I'd loved Murphy and the mountains and the sea and the very air of summer moving toward us that night.

I reached into my satchel, pulled out the ripped-out front page of the *Cedar Valley Herald* with the picture of the crushed car.

Thurman's face crumpled in on itself, as though someone had let go of the animating strings of his face. He opened his mouth to talk, but stuttering words came out. "That's not mine—well, it is, but I wasn't driving it. Bill borrowed my car. I wasn't there."

"Thurman." I held up my good hand. "You're making me nauseous. Stop. Of course a woman answered the phone in your hotel room. Of course there is recruiting fraud—I found the note about renting the house on Tyndale for Darius's family. Of course that's your car, and you were with someone and lied about still being in Alabama."

"You live in a fantasy world. I was not with a woman. I wasn't at that house, and there is no recruiting fraud. That rental is nothing more than Carl Lasinski offering to pay for *me* to have a better place to live—and, of course, I turned it down. It was not for a recruit."

"Here," I said, "is the amazing part—that you do not, in any way, even now, have enough respect for me to tell the truth."

"I am telling the truth." He pounded his fist on the table; sauce and sweet tea shook in their containers. "What about you? Huh? What about you? I heard through the grapevine that a certain old boyfriend went with you to freaking Seaboro. Is that true?"

I smiled. "That is true."

"Now who's the liar? Now who . . . is being deceitful?"

"I've wanted to believe in us, and I've ignored the truth for so long, but I can't anymore. What is true is true regardless of how long it is hidden. I haven't noticed, I mean *really* noticed things in a long time. But I'm starting to see them clearly now."

"You're acting crazy," he said.

There was a large smudge of barbecue sauce on the side of his mouth. I didn't reach to wipe it off; instead I walked out of the restaurant without a backward glance, not even a glance. I wasn't even tempted.

Outside, I lifted my face to the surrounding mountains that had cradled me all these years, hidden me from the wider places of the world and of my heart. I had never, not once, climbed any of the winding paths that would offer me a wide view of Cedar Valley, of the land around me.

But first, the emergency room.

# Sixteen

*"I cannot live without books."*
—Thomas Jefferson,
in a letter to John Adams

I stood at the filing cabinet in my office, a cast on my right wrist—bright pink. I'd spent the weekend reading, sleeping, and reading some more, allowing the long-gone ability to lose myself in story to wash over me once again. Browsing through Dad's books, I'd found quotes and stories I'd forgotten: Maugham, Chesterton, C. S. Lewis, Pascal. I hadn't called Forrest and he hadn't called me. Our voice mails about who had left the B & B first still lingered, unsorted and unsolved, like a puzzle we'd opened and left scattered on the table.

I waited for the regret of what I'd done to fill me: I'd walked out on Thurman, walked out on a four-year relationship. But all I found within me was a sense of such immense relief that I was smiling when, without knocking, Coach Fontaine entered my office on Monday morning.

"Catherine Leary," he said in that voice that would make even me run a four-mile sprint or jump over the defensive line to score a touchdown.

"Hello, sir," I said, and shut the cabinet with the hard edge of my cast.

"On Friday you dropped a piece of paper on my desk."

"Yes, I did," I said.

"Do you understand the ramifications of what you've started?"

"Yes, I do." I met him halfway across the room. "I most certainly do. Would you like to fire me now or later?"

"We don't fire people for telling the truth, Catherine." He reached into his pocket and removed a faxed form from the NCAA. "But there are consequences."

"Of course there are," I said, leaned against my desk. "There are always consequences to the truth."

"Correct, my dear. I just wanted to let you know that there will be a lot to deal with, investigations and probably some heads will roll, far and hard. But it won't be your head."

"Thank you, sir."

As he left the room, he tossed one last comment over his shoulder. "Catherine, you did the right thing."

I closed my eyes and said to myself, "I hope so," and

when I opened them I was gazing at Thurman. His mouth was pinched, his hands clenched into fists. "Do you have any idea what you have done?"

He didn't wait for an answer as he stepped closer to me. "I will probably lose my job, you will lose yours, the board will dissolve, the basketball program will go to hell, and Southern will be humiliated. All for one lousy scrap of paper." Spittle landed on his bottom lip and he punched the top of my desk, and I understood that he wished that were my face.

"Thurman," I whispered, "it isn't about that one scrap of paper. It's about all the things that came before it and all the things that would have come after it."

"You have no idea what you're talking about." He moved closer. "You can break up with me, act like you've lost your mind, and run to the beach with some geek writer-professor, but you don't have to take the basketball program with you."

I motioned toward the door. "Please leave now."

He turned on his heels and slammed my office door on his way out.

I took a long, deep breath and gathered my purse and briefcase. I was hurrying down the hall as fast as I could without running when Fontaine stopped me. "I heard all that," he said.

I clutched my satchel to my chest. "I'm not sure I can stay here, Coach."

"Take some time to think about it, okay?" He held up his hands.

"I will," I promised, then added, "Truth has a funny way of changing things, doesn't it?"

"You could say that," he said in an echoing, boisterous sound that followed me to the parking lot.

The Book and Browse was full to overflowing on a stifling afternoon punctuated by thunderstorms. People came through the front door shaking their umbrellas and wringing their hair, laughing as they brought the water in with them.

I wandered to the back of the store, inhaled the aromas of coffee and cinnamon rolls. During the weekend, I'd adored the old feeling of losing myself in a story, then returning to myself slightly altered. Now I was anxious for more.

I headed straight for the stationery and art section and grabbed a package of pastels and a sketchbook, then carried them to the fiction section. I ran my hands along the spines of the books, trying to decide where to start—classics or contemporary, love or mystery, Southern or Western. I smiled at the wide possibilities.

I found a book I knew Dad had read a month or so before he died: *The Pleasure Was Mine* by Tommy Hays, about a wife with Alzheimer's. I plucked it off the shelf.

"Hey, you," I heard and twisted around to see Forrest Anderson.

"Hey," I said, held the novel against my chest. "Fancy meeting you here." And I realized that I had come to this bookstore with several excuses, but the best reason was stand-ing right in front of me.

He touched the bookshelves. "Okay . . . I'm here almost every day. Haven't seen you cross these hallowed grounds in years." He touched my pink cast. "What happened to you?"

"I fell in the garage. . . ."

We stood there for a moment or longer, time and other things I couldn't yet name stretching between us.

"I'm sorry about Murphy." He touched my hand, then quickly withdrew as though it were scalding.

"How did you know?"

"I called the animal clinic . . . then went to say good-bye to her."

"Oh." I stared down at the tattered blue carpet. "So," I said, "what really happened at the inn? I got your message . . . but did you leave or was Mr. Hamilton confused? I don't get it."

"I tried to call. . . ."

"I know . . . but that morning in Seaboro I went to check on the osprey nest, make sure it didn't get knocked down by the storm, and when I came back, Mr. Hamilton said you'd paid the bill and left."

Forrest shook his head. "I paid the bill, stashed my duffel bag, then went for a run on the beach. When I came back, Mrs. Hamilton told me you were gone. I checked out with her when Mr. Hamilton was at the docks, and I guess you checked out with him when she was gone. . . ." He touched my chin, lifted my face to his.

"No," I said, "Mr. Hamilton told me you checked out, that you had a rental car delivered . . . so I packed and left. I am so, so sorry."

He nodded. "I rented a car when I thought you'd left." The space between us grew into sadness or regret. He released a long breath. "This is just great. I want to stay mad at you, and here you are with your green eyes and pouty face and I can't be mad at all."

"Really?" I smiled.

He glanced at his watch. "You playing hooky today? It's only three o'clock."

"I think I might have quit."

"You *what*?"

"Long, long story."

"I have a long, long time," he said. "The literary mag is looking to fill a PR position. I've got connections."

"I just might have to take you up on that."

He pointed to the café. "Want to get a coffee?"

"Sure."

I followed him to the coffee bar, where I ordered a green tea and he ordered a coffee, black. While he paid I stared at this man who had been there for me for so long that, like the mountains surrounding us, I hadn't taken the time to really look at or truly enjoy him. I'd been grateful for his presence, for his protection and comfort, but I'd never fully appreciated all that he'd given me. This new knowledge was fresh, crisp, and I couldn't—yet—find a way to express my gratitude.

We sat at a corner table and settled back in our chairs, stared at each other across the round marble surface.

"So," he said, "I finished the article."

"Can I read it?" My heart picked up to the panicky pace it had had when I'd walked out of the Athletic Office.

He reached down into his briefcase, yanked out a stack of papers. "Here it is. I don't need your permission to publish it, but I'd like it."

I glanced at the cover page: "The Lessons of Story."

"Go ahead," he said. "Since we're both here, go ahead and read it."

My shaky breath shimmered with so many possibilities. "Shouldn't I take it home to read?"

"No, I want to watch you . . . see your reaction; is that okay?"

I brushed a stray hair off my face and felt wobbly underneath his gaze. I took in a deep breath, checked my oxygen level. There was, I realized, a worse thing than drowning in the river, in the dark tidal waters—it was dying in everyday life, the slow leaching of oxygen from my soul until only an empty shell remained.

**Many of Professor Grayson Leary's students believed he could walk on water, and if they ever saw the Lowcountry where he once lived they would realize they weren't far off the mark.**

**Professor Leary was born at the base of the Cedar**

**Valley Mountains in a town of universities and colleges.
A child of a professor and an avid reader, he could read
by the time he was four years old.**

I looked up at Forrest. "Is that true? Did he read by four
years old?"

He nodded, then gestured for me to continue reading.
The article went on to describe Cedar Valley, and what Dad's
childhood had been like there, how he married a young
woman who was also from the area, and how they decided
they wanted to make a life by the sea.

**It was in Seaboro, South Carolina, in a land of more
water than earth, in a land of myth and mysticism, that
Grayson Leary came to believe all of life is a story, that the
themes and metaphors in great novels can help us to understand our world and ourselves. There in Seaboro, he came
to the firm conclusion that there was deep power in story.**

The article described Dad's theories, Seaboro, its history,
our home, Dad's office, and even its view of the cobblestone
streets outside. I held my breath as I reached the end of the
introduction—how would Forrest explain Dad's return to
Cedar Valley?

Then he described how much Dad loved my mother,
how they moved through life together from the moment
they met at seventeen until Mother's death seven years ago.

I closed my eyes, then opened them to Forrest. "You really think he loved Mother this much?"

"Of course."

"How could he have . . ."

Forrest shrugged. "Your dad never spoke of Ellie. Not once. He did talk about Alzheimer's and being lost, but not of a particular person." He took a long sip of coffee, leaned into the table. "He did talk of how much he loved your mother, how long they'd been together, and how there are trials and mistakes and even wars along the path of marriage. I know she appeared to be a cold person, Cappy. I know that—I was around her often enough. But your dad knew and loved the woman underneath all that. He truly did."

"I don't get it," I said.

"I don't either. But I do know that your dad never went to see Ellie when your mother was alive. He went—I think—when he found out Ellie was . . . sick."

"I don't want that life—you know? Where you live one way but love another?"

"He loved everything, every day of his life with an avid passion."

"I do know that," I said, glanced back down at the article.

**After thirteen years in the Lowcountry, Professor Grayson Leary did what Thomas Wolfe said you can never do: He returned home with his wife and twelve-**

**year-old daughter to bring to SU all he had learned, all
he had become in Seaboro.**

 **In Cedar Valley he began his mission in life: to assist
his students in finding the application of each novel that
touched them.**

The article spoke of how he taught his students to read
first for the literal meaning, then for the larger themes, and
then, if they were personally touched by the story, to seek
ways to apply the story's lesson to their lives. What followed
were descriptions of five students who had been changed by
a particular novel each had read in Dad's class. The students'
testimonies were indicated only by initials at the top of the
page, followed by the title of the novel.

I looked up at Forrest. "Well done," I said.

"You haven't finished."

"I'll read the lessons later." I placed my elbows on the
table. "Forrest, how'd you like to go hiking today?"

He ran his hands through his hair, leaned back in his
chair. "I don't think so. Not today. I have a lesson plan to
write for a new class I'm teaching in summer school."

"Okay," I said, my feelings bruised.

"Maybe next time," he said.

"Can I keep this?" I asked, held up the article.

"Sure thing."

He didn't rise as I walked away from him; I looked back
once and saw him leafing through the book I'd left on the

café table. I stopped at the front desk and bought the sketch-book and pastels with a sense of defiance and joy that made me want to laugh or cry, I wasn't sure which.

I rushed home to change into hiking clothes, and found my living room full to overflowing with roses, tulips, daffodils, peonies. Flowers were in vases, pots, some petals loose on the table. I took a deep breath of the overwhelming scents and looked for a note. Only two people had keys to my home: Forrest and Thurman.

I walked around the room, pushed aside flowers, picked up an arrangement of tulips, and found a card hidden beneath it. I pulled out a square of ivory stationery with the initials TDW on the upper right-hand corner in navy blue script. Then in Thurman's slanted writing I read:

> *Dearest Catherine,*
>     *As many flowers as there are here, that's how many years I will love you. I am a fool who has made the worst mistake of his life. I am nothing without you. I will wait for you. . . .*
>     *I love you,*
>     *Thurman*

I lifted a tulip to my nose, ran my finger along its silken interior. What woman did not want to hear those words?

I closed my eyes and reached deep for the place inside me where his promise and this outpouring should touch me. I came up with a single realization: It was not that I didn't know how to love. I had merely thought I didn't deserve it.

But I did.

I dropped the tulip and the note on the table and walked back to my bedroom to change.

The oaks and magnolias were lush with the deep hues of early summer green. Rhododendrons burst forth like firecrackers from the dark, leafy undergrowth. A woman came down off the hiking trail, her head back as she drank from a water bottle, which dimpled with her fingers on its sides.

A wooden sign heralded the start of the trail with carved red lines depicting the alternate routes for a day's hike. These lines reminded me of the small blips across the TV screen in a bar in Seaboro that announced the projected path of a hurricane.

It was, I reminded myself, only a projected path, one that could go in many different directions depending on the wind, the tide, the turn of the Earth. And how was this afternoon any different for me? There were many routes, alternate paths I had never considered. I walked up to the sign, ran my finger across the wood. All the trails led to the top of the mountain, to the wide panorama, but each separate path involved different degrees of difficulty and various numbers of miles.

I smiled, thinking that I'd like to have one of these signs for my life—*You can take this route or this one or even this one.* Standing at the bottom of the mountain, afraid to go right or left, wasn't getting me anywhere.

I followed the third trail, ran my hand over the pine tree trunks, the azaleas, the oaks. With pure joy I breathed in the fresh air and an abundance of nature until I reached the summit as the sun shimmied toward a horizon, far different from the one in Seaboro, where earth and sea melded in a soft haze.

This craggy-edged horizon was backlit as I stood on a rock and looked down to the valley below, to the town and the creeks, to the small houses, across sweeping mountain vistas. I needed to hike down before sunset, but it felt so good to sit up there after so many years living as if at the bottom of a river.

No matter how you explained Sam's death, I knew I was still partly responsible. But I was loved; I was forgiven. And knowing this opened a previously locked place inside me. Knowing that I hadn't compelled our move from Seaboro, our migration from the land my parents loved, allowed me to see everything in a new light, from a broader perspective, and let my heart out of its darkly veiled hiding place.

Maybe Shakespeare was right: "What's past is prologue."

This time I would allow the past to be a prologue to

a new life, a brighter, wilder life of taking chances, risking joy.

I traced my finger along the edge of the rock and watched a hiker come up the far trail—a different trail from the one I had taken. Forrest's SU baseball cap was pulled low over his face, but I saw the brown curls; he glanced up at me, smiled before stepping over a boulder.

Evening-rich sunlight fell on the landscape, and in the fault line between day and night there lay hope and possibility. This beautiful view had always been there for me: I had done nothing to deserve it and yet it had always been waiting.

Forrest sat next to me, handed me a water bottle with moist droplets on the plastic. "I know you don't do this very often—thought you might want this."

I took the bottle and held it to my forehead before taking a long drink. "Thought you didn't want to come."

"Changed my mind." He swung his legs around, faced me.

"It's beautiful. I can't believe I've never hiked up here."

"Never?"

I shook my head. "Not once." We sat with the sound of other hikers' shoes crunching leaves and gravel, a waterfall sighing in the distance, a low, shrill cry from a soaring bird. I glanced at Forrest's profile. "I read it," I said.

"The article?" he asked without looking at me.

"No, the book."

He stared at me now, squinted under his hat. "What book?"

"*The End of the Affair*. Have you read it?"

"Yes, your dad and I discussed it numerous times."

"Why did he love this terrible, sad story?" I kicked at a pebble, watched it float over the edge of the cliff, heard the sound of rock on rock and then the tumbling aftermath of small stones.

"It's not that sad—it has hope and . . ." He paused. "I'll shut up now. Tell me what it meant to you. Why did you think it was so sad?"

"It's about a man who loves a woman he can never have—and he isn't even sure why until it's too late. It's about a love that ruins a life . . . and a faith. About the agony of losing someone."

"What about the themes of hope of miracles?" Forrest said. "He ends up with hope . . . and with some belief, I think."

I shrugged. "That's not how I read it." Then I remembered something Dad had once said about letting the language and themes churn and settle inside the reader. "At least not yet," I added, then touched his knee, ran my finger around the bone. "And I decided something."

"What?" He stared at my hand as though he didn't know what it was.

I wanted to offer this man something in return for all he'd given me. I decided to answer the last question of the three he'd presented to me on my birthday a week ago. "I don't want a tombstone," I said.

His gaze wandered back to me. "The river?"

"No, I don't think so. I'm not sure . . . yet. But no final words about me engraved in stone." I touched the bill of his baseball cap. "You?"

"Something about having made a difference with my teaching or writing."

"Like what?"

He ran his hand across the top of the rock. "I don't know—exactly. Sometimes we know who we want to be and what we want to do long . . . long before we know how to get there." He stood and held out his hand. "Come on; we need to get down before dark."

"Okay," I said, followed him down the winding path to the foot of the mountain. At times he would reach back and help me over a rock or across a steep area on a path he knew and had traveled many times. We were silent all the way back.

We stood in the parking lot as the evening sky turned purple. "Want to come over for dinner?" I asked.

He stared at me for so long, with such sadness on his face, that I understood he'd say no. "Forget it." I took my car keys from my back pocket, turned away.

"Sure," he said. "What are we having?"

I looked over my shoulder. "I have the fixin's for a killer spaghetti."

"Okay." He paused as if he had more to say, and then climbed into his car, spoke out the window. "See you in a few minutes—let me run home and change, grab a bottle of wine."

His car moved across the parking lot, and I climbed into mine, picked up his article off the driver's-side seat, and then stared at it. I flipped to the part about the five students whose lives had been touched.

The last lesson: "Compassion: F.A."

A chill not of the warm evening air spread down my arms. I climbed onto the hood of my car, opened the article, and read in the dying light about a man who was once a student of Professor Leary's. This young man had written a paper on *To Kill a Mockingbird* and received the first C of his life. This student spent an evening discussing the story with Professor Leary only to discover that what the professor was looking for was not a summary of the story or a discussion of the obvious themes, but an exploration of how the novel spoke to the young man.

Through careful thought, analysis, and discussion, the young man discovered that the story spoke most strongly to him about compassion. This young man, F.A., had been walking through life believing in his own goodness and dividing others into good versus bad. *To Kill a Mockingbird* showed him how the flawed characters were influenced by their society and the beliefs of others around them.

This particular young man's life was changed as he began to

view other people as fully human, not just what they appeared to be on the outside, but what had shaped them on the inside. His judgmental attitude softened and his heart opened.

Professor Leary then gave this student a first book club edition of *To Kill a Mockingbird*.

My heart rose into my throat, and I sat on top of my old car and let silent tears fall for all I hadn't noticed in this precious life of mine, for the things lost because of neglect and fear. I wept for the chances I hadn't taken and the risks I had avoided, for the books I hadn't read, the words I hadn't said, the love I hadn't given or received.

Forrest's car was parked at the curb when I arrived home. I ran in through the garage door and found him standing in the midst of the flowers, Thurman's note in one hand, a bottle of wine on the table, a bunch of black-eyed daisies, clipped unevenly at the bottom and obviously taken from a field, in his other hand. His face was full of an emotion I couldn't read, and I went to him. "It was your book."

"What?"

"The copy of *To Kill a Mockingbird* you gave me for my birthday. It was yours from Dad, wasn't it?"

He dropped the note; it fluttered to the floor. "Yes. He told me it was your favorite and I thought—"

"Thank you so much. I know how much that book must have meant to you."

He spread his arms wide. "These flowers . . . an apology?"

I nodded, pushed aside a wilted tulip. "Yes, but it's past time for apologies. And"—I took another step toward him, touched the black center of a daisy—"these mean more to me."

Forrest placed the daisies next to the wine and gazed at me in silence. "I think I should go," he finally said.

I searched for an offering, one as meaningful as a sand dollar, a first-edition book, something to hold him there. I spoke in soft, slow words. "Answer one: I want to be watching twilight come over a horizon—sea or mountain, it doesn't matter—laughing and talking with someone . . . loving life hard and fast."

He closed his eyes. "Don't do this now. All the times I've wanted you to . . . Not now."

I took three steps toward him. "Answer two: I'd regret not loving . . . fully." I touched his arm. "Ever since that night in college at the poetry reading . . ."

"The night you told me it would never, ever work between us."

I nodded. "Ever since then I have taken this love we could have had and pushed it away, ignored it, shut it out. But I won't anymore. I can't now."

He touched the side of my face just as Boyd had all those years ago; the emotion Boyd had fractured open had closed with Sam's death, but if I let it, Forrest's touch could resurrect that joy and that expectation.

Then he spoke. "Don't," he said. "Please don't make this harder." He waved his hand toward the overflowing flowers. "You have some things you need to work out. There's no room for me here."

"Yes, there is," I said. "There's—"

He placed his finger over my lips. "No, there really never has been."

I exhaled and closed my eyes to search for the right words to say. Never had they seemed more important. He kissed the top of my head, and then his footsteps echoed across the wood floor. The front door creaked open, and then shut.

Warmth ran like a waterfall away from my heart as I stared at the empty room. I followed him out the door, watched him get in his truck and pull away from the curb. I ran down the driveway and into the middle of the road, standing under a streetlight, for once not caring if I looked like a fool in his rearview mirror, watching him leave. I took a few steps toward his retreating pickup.

"I'm sorry," I whispered under my breath. "I'm sorry I didn't see us clearly before. Please come back. Please come back."

He couldn't hear me, but his brake lights flashed. His truck slowed. The stop sign, I thought. Then my breath caught, became a smile because his truck reversed, turned around, and headed back down the road to my house.

I stood in the warm summer air. This story had just begun.

*P*atti Callahan Henry lives with her husband and three children near Atlanta, Georgia, along the Chattahoochee River. Visit her Web site at www.patticallahanhenry.com.

# THE TIDES

## Patti Callahan Henry

This Conversation Guide is intended to enrich the
individual reading experience, as well as encourage us
to explore these topics together—because books,
and life, are meant for sharing.

# A CONVERSATION WITH PATTI CALLAHAN HENRY

*Q.* Between the Tides *is your fourth published novel, but you've been working on some version of it since you first set fingers to the computer keys. Can you tell us a little about the inspiration for this novel and how it has evolved over the years?*

A. When I first set my mind and heart on writing a full-length novel, I wrote a manuscript that I called *Between the Tides,* but it was quite different from the book you are now holding. The original story took place during an entire summer in Seaboro, and Catherine was a married woman trying to decide whether to divorce her husband while she dealt with a daughter who was repeating some troubling patterns in Catherine's own life. Now, of course, Catherine is single and childless, and she spends only three days in Seaboro. It took me years to find the best way to convey my ideas, to figure out what shape my story should take.

During all my efforts, the ideas that originally inspired the novel remained unchanged—how someone can get stuck between a tragedy in the past and the uncertain future, and live a life of safe complacency without loving deeply or living fully. Since the beginning, this novel has been about how secrets affect lives, and about how tragedy reshapes personalities. Finally, this novel is about the redemptive power of unconditional love.

Because *Between the Tides* was my first novel, I ended up rewriting it many times. I've called it the novel that taught me how to write, and the novel that would never see the light of day. Now I also call it the novel that showed me the value of persistence. Four years after originally starting the manuscript, I pulled it out of storage and saw with new eyes the beauty that still lay hidden within its characters and themes. It has evolved in structure, voice, and plot through the years, but the heart and the title have remained unchanged.

The title works for me as a metaphor for living (even thriving) between the high and low times in life. For me, the shifting tide provides a perfect image of the ebb and flow of life.

*Q. Catherine's journey is prompted in part by three questions that are posed at the beginning of the novel and recur throughout it until the very end. What inspired these questions?*

A. Last summer, when I was halfway through completely rewriting this story, I was on a book tour in Florida for *When Light Breaks.* I went out to lunch with a few friends and they brought a friend, a nonfiction writer and a psychologist. She told us about these three questions. She believes that people's answers tell everything you need to know about them. My friend and I talked about these questions for the next two days, until I finally realized that I had received a key to the plot of the novel. I already had in place the tragedy in the past, and now I had three questions to represent the future, which Catherine has long refused to think about.

*Q. You have three children. Was it hard to write about losing a child?*

A. Yes, it was gut-wrenching to write about a lost child, but this heartbreaking emotion gave me great empathy for all the wounded characters in the novel. Each person is affected differently by Sam's death. Their behavior afterward is influenced not only by the pain they endure, but also by the secrets they carry. I wanted to look at the before and after of such a tragic event, add the burden of a great secret, and examine how both might influence the rest of the characters' lives.

*Q. Grayson Leary's favorite novel is* The End of the Affair. *What's yours?*

A. I'm not sure I could possibly name any one novel my favorite. Besides, my choice would change with the seasons of life. But, if forced, I'd narrow my choices down to: *The Lion, the Witch and the Wardrobe* by C. S. Lewis and *Beach Music* by Pat Conroy. Can I add *Gone With the Wind*? Now, how is that for eclectic?

I do believe novels influence our lives. I frequently give a speech on the power of story, and my premise is this: There is a human need for story; story is the language of the heart and of faith; powerful stories carry truth; stories can act as a mirror; and stories open our minds to new ideas. And, of course, novels filled many a lonely moment in my childhood. When asked why I write, I always say it is because I truly do believe in the power of story, not to mention that I feel a need to tell the stories running around in my head.

*Q. Do you have a bulletin board with quotes all over it, like Grayson does?*

A. In fiction, writers sometimes give our characters traits and quirks we wish were our own. I often find inspiration in quotes and wish I collected and organized them into categories. Right now, my bulletin board is covered with pictures of my kids, book ideas, and random notes to self. Maybe I'll start a new board. . . .

*Q. At the core of* Between the Tides *lies a secret that the adults keep from Catherine, which profoundly shapes her life. Do you think it was a mistake for them not to tell her the truth, or was it something she had to discover on her own?*

A. As the author, I am observing more than passing judgment. Whether and when Grayson should have told Catherine about Sam is not a question I ever asked myself. What I did ask was how such a secret might affect Catherine's life. I believe Grayson kept the truth from Catherine to protect her, yet it continued to influence her life in a profound way. I wanted to show that even an untold truth affects choices and patterns of living.

The way Catherine coped with her sense of loss and guilt was to push forward in life without ever talking about or thinking about Sam; to take control by keeping herself sequestered, safe and only halfway loving and living. She even gave up one of her favorite childhood activities—reading—to keep the past from impacting her life now. Her way of living is as much about the past as it is about fear, but it takes a trip to the place where she grew up, the full truth, and someone who truly loves her for her to understand that.

Then, of course, there is each character's life choices after Sam's death—Ellie living in love, even with a broken heart; Jim choosing death; Boyd allowing anger to consume him; and Grayson continuing to live and love the family he had next to him (although he did withhold the truth from his daughter). I feel great empathy for each person in this novel, as each is dramatically changed in a single instant.

*Q. Margaret Leary and Ellie Loughlin take very different approaches to child rearing and life. What influenced your choices in these women, and were they based on anyone you know?*

A. A magical moment in writing occurs when a theme emerges that the novelist doesn't see until she finishes the book. I had rewritten this book multiple times, and yet it was not until I completed this last version that I saw the echoes of the biblical Mary and Martha in Ellie's and Margaret's characters.

A story in the Gospel of Luke tells of two sisters, Mary and Martha, who are preparing to welcome Jesus into their home. Mary sits at Jesus' feet and listens. Martha, the ultimate homemaker, decides she must make the perfect feast; she is too busy to sit and talk, too distracted to appreciate the people in her home. Jesus says Mary has "chosen the better part."

Most women are a little of both Mary and Martha, sometimes able to enjoy life, and at other times so busy they can't take life in. As twelve-year-old Catherine observes, Ellie and Margaret are opposites in their approach to life, yet she needs both of them. So Ellie and Margaret are not based on any specific people I know, but on the ideas set forth in the story of Mary and Martha.

Q. *This is your fourth novel set in the Lowcountry. Will your next novel also be set there?*

A. When I begin to write something new, I have in mind a theme, a situation, and a character (or two), and they dictate the setting. All four of my previous novels have required that part of the story be set in the Lowcountry.

What I'm working on now is set in Atlanta, the perfect place for the characters and situations that are beginning to take shape for me.

*Q. You continue to travel throughout the South to promote your books. Can you share some of the best and worst experiences you've had on the road?*

A. Oh, the glamour of a book tour! I have come to one conclusion—the guy in the back row who asks the most questions about getting published is the guy least likely to buy a book. Okay, so it's not as glamorous as the media might lead you to believe, but there are wonderful surprises every day. I am constantly in awe of the booksellers who devote their time to talking about books, selling them, and hosting events. I am grateful to the readers who take the time and energy to come out to see me. The best part about being on the road—I get to meet fantastic people; hear new ideas; be reminded of the power of story and that what I write does touch readers; visit with friends I haven't seen in years; and, on top of all that, I get to talk about writing and books nonstop. The worst part? Being away from my family and eating food from airport vendors.

# QUESTIONS FOR DISCUSSION

1. Did you enjoy reading *Between the Tides*?

2. Patti Callahan Henry's four novels have all been set, at least in part, in South Carolina's Lowcountry. Is that a big part of this book's appeal for you, or could it be set elsewhere and be just as effective?

3. How did Patti Callahan Henry use sand dollars in the novel to convey Catherine's anguish and redemption? What images particularly stick in your mind?

4. As in many of Patti Callahan Henry's previous books, *Between the Tides* describes an idyllic childhood that is abruptly changed by tragedy. Does Catherine Leary's childhood in Seaboro remind you of your own childhood? Have you ever experienced an abrupt wrenching away from a place that you loved?

5. Discuss how the epigraph by William Shakespeare—"Whereof what's past is prologue"—applies to the novel, especially to Catherine. Is it true in your own life, and of those people closest to you?

6. Life is rarely neat and tidy, and like Catherine, many of us lose our parents before we've come to terms with the unanswered questions that linger from our childhoods, with the wounds we suffered and the love we failed to acknowledge. What do you find most striking about how Catherine comes to terms with Grayson's death? Does it remind you about anything in your own life?

7. How would you answer the three questions that Grayson meant to pose to Catherine: What do you want to be doing when you die? If you die today, what will you regret not having done? What do you want your tombstone to say?

8. Do you agree that "life is story"?

9. As a child, Catherine loved to read, but she stopped reading not long after Sam's death. Have you ever abandoned an activity you once enjoyed? If so, why? Why is Catherine able to return to reading, and what regret does she feel?

10. Grayson believed that novels could change people's lives. Do you agree? Is there a particular novel that had a profound impact on your life?

11. For years, Alice kept secret what she learned in the hospital room on the night Sam died. Was she right in doing so? Why does she tell Catherine now?

12. Children often interpret adult behavior in self-centered ways, and like the child Catherine, can blame themselves for events over which they had little or no control, carrying a burden of guilt and shame. How might the adults in the story have acted differently to spare her this anguish, or was her suffering inevitable?

13. Catherine believes that "Ellie and Mother were the antithesis of each other, and yet somehow together they made one complete mom for me." Discuss Ellie's and Margaret's strengths and weaknesses, as women and as mothers.

14. Discuss the roles of Boyd and Forrest in the novel. Do you think Boyd will ever find a new way to view the past, as Catherine does? Why does Forrest drive away at the end? Why does he return?